When Robins Appear

A NOVEL

DENSIE WEBB

When Robins Appear
Red Adept Publishing, LLC
104 Bugenfield Court
Garner, NC 27529
http://RedAdeptPublishing.com/

Cover Art by Streetlight Graphics[1]

1. http://StreetlightGraphics.com

"No trumpets sound when the important decisions of our life are made. Destiny is made known silently." –Agnes De Mille

Prologue

I hate sirens at night, slicing through the silence, sharp as a scalpel. Whenever I hear that mournful wail, I make the sign of the cross—something my mother taught me. "It's a silent prayer," she said, "just between you and God." But tonight, the siren drowns out any prayer I might offer up.

My heart jackhammers in my chest. My fingers are icy cold, my breathing shallow. Rivulets of blood pool on the floor of the ambulance, and I squeeze my eyes shut to insulate myself in the comfort of darkness. A chill runs through me, and I suck in air. My teeth chatter uncontrollably as a black mist seeps into my brain.

I want to barter with God on the off chance he's listening, but I have nothing to promise in return. The air is filled with the scent of alcohol—and terror. *A cruel preview of what's to come?*

"Tell me what you're doing." I've found my voice, but I don't recognize the phlegmy sound. The two EMTs exchange a look that makes my throat constrict and my silent tears turn into breathless sobs. "Please," I say.

One of them opens the Plexiglas partition and shouts to the driver, "ETA?"

"Five or less," she says, her voice hard and clear.

I feel faint.

This isn't happening. This isn't happening. The words hover over my brain before crash-landing on my heart.

This happens to other people, not me.

Never me.

Chapter 1

Deb

Eight Months Earlier

Pulling into the parking lot of Austin Java, I spotted Merritt sitting on a bench, her eyes closed, her face tilted up to the Texas sun. I ambled over and took in her blissful expression before announcing, "The sun causes wrinkles—and skin cancer."

Merritt cracked a smile before opening her eyes. "You really have to stop writing about all that health crap, Deb."

She looked up at me and squinted at the sun as she slipped on her knockoff Marc Jacob sunglasses. I hoped that in ten years I would look as good as Merritt. Her skin was still smooth, her smile youthful, and her hair subtly streaked with gray that looked like a style choice rather than the result of the passage of time. Our mother didn't fare nearly as well. Merritt was the oldest and I was the youngest of seven kids our mother had popped out in rapid succession. She'd spend the next three decades raising us, with precious little help from our father. We were Merritt and Ray—the twins—Isabelle, Nicholas, June, Janet, and me holding up the rear. By the time it was my turn, my parents were bereft of money, energy, and time. It wasn't until I married Richard and got an up-close look at his surfeit of attention as an only child that I fully understood what I'd missed. I decided that was what I wanted for my future child—a decision my mother repeatedly challenged until the day she died, holding Merritt up as an example of a fruitful life.

It was a decision I now questioned with aching regret. I'd called Merritt to meet me for lunch so we could talk it out, work through my doubts, and help me come to terms with my long-standing life choice. Or talk me out of my plans.

"What are you going to have?" Merritt asked as the waiter, a likely University of Texas student with more piercings than I could count and enough tattoos to fill a graphic novel, slouched his way to the table.

"The usual—veggie burger, sweet potato fries."

"Sounds good. I'll have the same."

"Since when do you eat veggie burgers?"

"Since today." Merritt flashed a grin at the waiter as he turned to head back inside. Her smile faded, and her expression shifted to sadness. She exhaled loudly. "Jessica's pregnant."

"Oh my God!" I sat up straighter and cocked my head. "But doesn't that take—a man?"

"Yeah." Merritt began chipping the cranberry-red polish from her thumbnail. "I guess I don't know my daughter as well as I thought."

"So, does she have a boyfriend? Is she keeping the baby? What about college?" I shook my head. "Sorry."

"That's okay. I bombarded her with the same questions."

"Who's the father? Where's the father?"

"She's not sure who the father is." Merritt forced an uneasy laugh before her voice cracked. "I just can't believe it. She got in yesterday—went to Planned Parenthood this morning."

Merritt looked out at the traffic as if she desperately wished she were a part of it. "The 'procedure' is tomorrow morning, and then she's going back to school."

"Wow... Merritt, I'm so sorry." I reached out, placing my hand over my sister's clenched fist on the table. "How's Jessica dealing with it?"

"You know Jess—tough as nails."

"Just like you."

She shrugged. "She could've done it in California, but at least she's coming home and not being so bullheaded as to do this completely on her own."

Jessica was Merritt's middle child and more like Merritt than her other four—stubborn, opinionated, and willing to do anything for the people she loved. Around the time Jess turned thirteen, Merritt had shared with me her thoughts on what she presumed was her daughter's sexual orientation. There had been no giggling with her girlfriends about the latest boy band, no gossiping about who had kissed whom at the movies. Jess had shown no interest in the opposite sex and went everywhere with her passel of jock girlfriends.

Merritt had strived to be astute and accepting. She had no intention of being one of *those* parents—the ones who were blindsided or unwelcoming when their son or daughter walked in the door with a same-sex partner. Instead, here she was, handwringing and pale with worry upon learning that her daughter was, it appeared, straight—a late bloomer, perhaps, but straight just the same.

"Is she absolutely sure this is what she wants to do?"

"Yes." Her voice cracked, and her eyes filled with tears.

"I even told her I would help out, you know, with the baby, while she finished college, but she refused to even discuss it." She shifted uncomfortably in her chair. Merritt was hurting. I wanted to make her feel better, but I wasn't in the mindset to do that.

She sighed, and her shoulders slumped. "Wes wanted me to have an abortion when I was pregnant with Josh."

I hesitated, mentally replaying her words to be certain I'd heard her right. I fell back against the wooden bench and crossed my arms. "I can't believe you never told me." Josh was Merritt's youngest, the artist of the family, living the bohemian life in the Williamsburg section of Brooklyn. He was unpredictable—some would say flighty—but Merritt loved him fiercely and had said more than once that she couldn't imagine life without him. I took a breath. "But wait. Are you saying you think Jess might be making a mistake?"

"Yes... maybe... no, not really. I don't know what I'm saying. I know she'll have lots of other chances for kids when the time is right—whatever the hell that means. But maybe this would be her Josh. She'll never have another chance to have *this* baby. I know it's really screwed up. I know she's only twenty, but that's not much younger than you were when you had Amanda. I can't help but worry that she'll end up regretting her decision, despite what she thinks right now. She's so young."

That was when it hit Merritt. I saw it in her face. "Oh shit, Deb. I'm sorry. I shouldn't have... I wasn't thinking... God dammit."

I took Merritt's hand. "Jess is making the right decision. She'll be able to get on with her life."

"I know. You're right. *You're right.*" She avoided my gaze and continued peeling polish from her thumbnail. "Maybe it's just me lamenting the fact that my baby-making days are over," Merritt said, sounding wistful.

Her words didn't register right away. "Merritt... don't tell me you wish you'd had more kids."

Merritt's face was draped in shame, her secret laid out on the table. "I know it's crazy, but if money were no object and Wes had been on board, yeah, I would have had more," she said, staring at the few remaining spots of polish.

"Even after we watched Mom struggle? And you always complained about how out of control your life was—how you never had any time to yourself."

She locked eyes with me. "But did I ever seem seriously unhappy to you?"

Rethinking our bitch sessions over the years, which started as soon as Merritt stopped thinking of me as her baby sister, I realized her griping had always been lighthearted and self-deprecating, not the my-life-is-over lament I often heard from harried moms that made me want to stick my head—and theirs—in the toilet.

It was a revelation.

"I had five kids for a reason, Deb. You were always fine with just Amanda, and while I never understood it, I actually envied your ability to say 'enough.' I complicated life for me and Wes way more than I needed to."

The waiter returned with our order. "Two veggie burgers with everything and sweet potato fries." He set the plates in front of us. "Anything else I can get for you ladies?"

"No. We're good. Thanks."

"Enjoy!"

He turned to head back inside, and I leaned in to whisper, grinning, changing the subject. "What do you think his mother has to say about all those piercings and tattoos?"

"What do you think his mother would say if he was irresponsible enough to get a girl pregnant? If he were mine, I'd opt for the holes and body art." Merritt was staring at her food, not making a move to grab the ketchup, a mandatory condiment at every meal. Now was clearly not the time for me to whine to her about my muddled midlife regret.

"It'll be okay, Merritt. Jess will be okay."

"I know. I've just been thinking... about Ray."

Ray had been Merritt's twin. She couldn't know I had a permanent space in my mind and my heart dedicated to torturous thoughts of him.

Merritt hesitated before looking at me again. "Can I ask you a weird question?"

"Sure, what is it?"

"If you were pregnant but somehow knew the child was going to die young, like Ray, would you still have the baby?"

I didn't hesitate. "No. Not after seeing what Mom went through after Ray died—the depression, the drinking, the bottomless pit of grief. No, I wouldn't. I couldn't do that to myself or to the rest of my family."

"I kind of figured that's what you'd say."

"What about you?"

"I would have all five all over again and just savor every second I had with them. I can't imagine giving up the opportunity to spend time with my kids," she said. I was still trying to process her words, decipher if they were aimed at me, when Merritt flashed an ironic grin. "So, I'm not sure who's more selfish in this scenario—me or you."

Chapter 2
Amanda

I'd waited a year and a half for Ingenious Imposter to come to town, and I'd poured a lot of half-caff double lattes with almond milk and served a lot of gluten-free muffins to a lot of assholes at Monkey Hut to finally get the money for a ticket. That night, on stage, colored strobe lights flashed on a screen, a pixelated slide show of an imagined dystopian future. The scent of Hadley's musky perfume and Karin's apple-scented shampoo cut through the sweaty hordes, while the pounding bass rhythm burrowed deep into my chest, reverberating in my collarbone. Hadley and Karin pumped their fists in the air, mouths wide open, their screams drowned out by the din of the crowd and the beat of the music.

The mosh pit forming to my left was terrifying, exciting. A girl was lifted and passed over the top of a pulsating swarm of drunk, stoned, frenzied fans. Her back was arched, her red thong and tiny heart tattoo exposed, her right boob about to pop out of her top. She didn't look like she would notice or care. Red-Thong Girl clearly wasn't worried about college applications.

Whether I was ready or not, my senior year was around the corner, but Ingenious Imposter let me forget about my "future," this fuzzy concept my mom kept bugging me about. She wanted to know what I was going to do with my life when I wasn't even sure what I'd be doing later that night. All I wanted was to enjoy one more awesome summer night with my best friends.

I glanced over at Hadley. Her eyes were shut tight, and she was whipping her hair around, dancing as if the world were ending. I pulled out my phone and snapped a picture. The mosh pit shifted, and the next surfer passed over my head just as the band segued into our favorite song, the one we always listened to in my room with the volume maxed out, which would prompt my mom to scream from downstairs, "Turn that thing down!"

Hadley and I looked at each other and mouthed, "Oh my God!"

I closed my eyes. The air was stifling, and the smell of stale beer, cigarettes, weed, and sweat suddenly overwhelmed me. I lifted my massive curls on top of my head, fanning myself, trying to catch a pocket of cool air.

As I opened my eyes, I spotted a guy to my left rising above the crowd—a head, a chest, an entire body precariously perched on someone's shoulders. He was pointing in my direction and gesturing like crazy. I looked around. No one else seemed to have noticed his plea for attention. As I turned toward him again, he cupped his hands over his mouth, yelling in a futile attempt to be heard.

I hesitated, pointed at myself, and mouthed, "Me?"

He nodded enthusiastically and waved me over. Trying to maintain balance, he gave a ride-'em-cowboy swing of his arm, laughing. Then he was gone, dropped back into the crowd.

I knew him... sort of. He was that guy who'd stood next to me at last year's Downtown Beat. I'd run into him at two concerts after that. Totally random. But we'd talked and laughed for a few minutes before the music started up. Though we went to rival high schools, we clearly shared the same weird taste in music. At first, I'd been sure he was making a move, but I soon decided he was just being friendly. Was he gay? Not likely, if the way he kept eyeing my boobs was any indication.

What is his name? Greg? No. Gary? No. Gil? No. It was a *G* name, though.

I turned back to the stage and leaned over to hear Karin, who was yelling something in my ear. She was having a blast. After a lengthy "pre-clearance" from her parents, she'd been given the green light to spend the night with a friend from her Christian youth group, who felt as imprisoned as Karin and had offered an airtight cover story.

I felt a tap on my shoulder and whipped around. *Graham! That's his name. Cuter than I remember. Shorter. Cool hair—a headful of blond dreads. Wears a Deathwish T-shirt. Must be a skateboarder.*

What color were his eyes? It was too dark to see—like the other times we'd been thrown together. I gave him a four-fingered wave and tilted my head toward my shrugged shoulder, a pose I reflexively struck when nervous.

He pulled his phone from his jeans pocket, typed a message, and turned it toward me. The backlit screen said, *Remember me? Graham, like the cracker.*

I pointed to my head to let him know I remembered, nodded, took his phone, and typed, *Amanda*. I smiled and handed it back to him.

His eyes smiled back as he mouthed, "I know." Yeah, he was cute all right. As in, seriously cute. The blasting sounds faded into the background.

He waved at Karin and Hadley, and their faces morphed into a single question mark. Graham stayed close for the rest of the concert, and we danced our asses off, side by side. As the band left the stage for the last time, he grabbed my hand and pulled me through the crowd and out of the building. When we finally made it into the smoke-free night air, we each took a deep breath and turned to face one another. I guessed he was about five foot six to my five foot three. I'd always wished I were taller—at least as tall as my mom—but not that night.

He shoved his hands into his pockets and rocked back on his heels. "Graham Scott."

"Huh?

"My name. It's Graham Scott."

"Oh, yeah." I laughed, nervous.

He leaned forward. "And yours?"

"My what?"

"Your name?" He smiled.

Stupid, stupid, stupid. "Um, Amanda Earle."

"I like it. Sounds British."

"My mom calls me Mandy."

"Less British." He chuckled as he took a step closer. "You hungry? Wanna go get a burger or something?"

I looked at my phone. *No way I'll make my midnight curfew.* "Can you take me home after?"

"No problem."

"I need to text my friends first."

Karin and Hadley had watched, wide-eyed with a dash of envy and a touch of concern, as I took Graham's hand and left. They'd probably be calling every five minutes, beginning at midnight, to squeeze all the juicy details out of me.

I sent a group text: *His name is Graham Scott. Going to Kirby Lane Cafe. Fill you in later.*

Graham led me through the parking lot, weaving in and out of the post-concert traffic until we stopped in front of a vintage Triumph motorcycle.

I let go of his hand. "I've never ridden a motorcycle."

"Is that a problem?"

"No, it's cool." I shrugged. But my gut was sending a very different message.

"Here, you take the helmet."

I put it on and looked at myself in the rearview mirror. "Not liking this look," I said, laughing.

"Seriously? You look totally hot!"

His comment pulled the hair trigger on my blush response, and heat covered my face like a mask. I desperately hoped he couldn't see it in the dim lighting of the parking lot. He pulled the keys and a hair tie from his pocket and climbed on, his feet barely touching the ground. In a single move, he pulled his hair back and wrapped the tie around his dreadlocked ponytail as expertly as any girl.

I climbed on the back. It felt awkward, like riding a horse, though I'd never actually done that either. I secured my purse and gripped the bar at the rear of the seat.

"Hold on to me. Don't want you falling as soon as I take off."

I let my hands gently rest on either side of his waist.

He laughed. "Wrap your arms all the way around."

Unlike Jack, my ex-boyfriend, who was lean, almost concave, Graham was solid. Holding onto him was like hugging a tree.

"You good?"

My breasts were pressed up against his back, my palms against his abs, and I felt the rumbling of his raspy voice in my chest as he spoke. Yeah, I was "good," and the Grand Canyon was a hole in the ground.

"I'm ready," I said.

"Oh, and lean into the curve, not against it."

I frowned. "I'm not sure what that means."

He turned to me and smiled. "Just lean with me whenever I take a turn."

Strands of my hair peeked out from the helmet, dancing frantically in the wind, and the engine growled each time he shifted gears. I felt like a freaking daredevil as I leaned with him at each turn. The night air surfing over my arms was electrically charged. I wanted to let go of Graham, raise my arms high in the air, and scream at the top of my lungs. This was what I wanted my future to be.

Too soon, we pulled into the parking lot. Inside, the diner hummed with the raised voices of the after-concert crowd. Graham pointed at an empty booth in the back, and we settled in. As we stared at each other across the table, I couldn't think of a single smart thing to say. But Graham was a talker, and I was ready to be a good listener.

In the bright lights of the all-night eatery, his eyes were a hard-to-ignore shade of blue-gray—like the Texas sky just before a tornado whipped through and flattened a town. Trying not to stare, I had to fight off the urge to tug on that soul patch that moved up and down with his very full, very red lips as he spoke. I wanted to grab one of his dreadlocks and rub it between my fingers.

He reached out and gently took my hand. I swallowed hard. My face flushed. Again. His hand was warm, softer than expected, his grip firm but gentle. He turned my palm up. I looked at him, trying to read his expression. Was he going to say something romantic to melt my heart?

"Cool tat."

"Huh?"

"Your wrist."

I stared at my wrist as if it belonged to someone else. "Oh, that. No, it's temporary. My folks would freak if I got a real tattoo. This was just for the concert tonight."

"Why a butterfly?"

"I don't know. I just find butterflies really hopeful. You know, the ugly caterpillar morphing into something beautiful and flying away?" I looked up as I made a flying motion with my fingers, watching an imaginary butterfly lift its wings and fly. I realized I had a stupid grin on my face. I pulled both hands back, tucked them under my thighs, and stared at the pocked silverware on the table. "Dumb, huh?"

"No. Actually, it's very—"

The waitress set the food in front of him before he could finish.

"Looks good," he said before digging in.

I was dying to find out what he wanted to say, but he was focused on his cheeseburger. I grabbed the ketchup and squirted a glob on my fries. I was working on a mouthful of burger when he said, "I'm going to a skating exhibition this weekend. Not signed up. Just gonna watch. A good friend of mine is competing. Wanna come with? If you've never been, it's pretty intense—in a good way." He chuckled.

That was when I noticed the scar on his chin, the only spot free of blond stubble, probably the result of an ill-timed move on his board. He was not the kind of guy I would generally consider potential boyfriend material, and his look was definitely not one my parents would embrace. His tiny gold hoop earrings might be the proverbial straw.

Pointing at my mouth full of burger, I gave a thumbs-up.

"Cool." He nodded to himself. And just like that, I had a date with *Graham, like the cracker.*

By the time we left, it was almost two o'clock in the morning. I hadn't expected to so completely lose track of time.

Chapter 3
Deb

The incessant yapping of the Jack Russell next door pulled me from an unsteady sleep. I rubbed my eyes, looked over at my husband, and listened to his muffled snores before I grabbed my phone and glanced at the time—two o'clock in the morning. The creak of the hardwood floors was always the comforting signal that Amanda had made it home safely as she tried, in vain, to stealthily slip up the stairs and into her room. Only after I heard that sound could I fall into a deep, satisfying sleep. That night, there had been no telltale creak.

I sat up, snatched the powder-blue L.L. Bean robe Richard had given me five Christmases ago, and headed toward Amanda's bedroom. I opened her door, pushed aside the silver-beaded curtain, and squinted into the dark. I frantically flipped on the light to confirm that the moonlit shadows weren't playing nasty tricks on me.

Her bed was empty. I placed my hand on the permanent impression her body had left on the mattress. Cold.

I tiptoed back to our bedroom, retrieved my phone from the nightstand, and rushed downstairs, out of earshot of Richard, to call Amanda. No answer. Her voicemail picked up. "Not the real me. You know what that means... leave a message."

"Where are you, Amanda? You were supposed to be home two hours ago. Call me!"

I texted her. Once. Twice. Three times.

I sank into our newly upholstered sofa—graphite linen. Amanda had insisted it was "classy" and made a gagging motion when I'd pointed at a watercolor chintz pattern. I ran my fingers over the coarse fabric as I stared at the ticking clock on the wall. I clasped my cell phone, my unanswered text messages staring back at me, as the fingernails of my other hand dug painfully into my palm. I slowly stood, headed to the kitchen, and set about making a cup of tea. Coffee was my morning wake-up call, but tea was my middle-of-the-night comfort. Every few minutes, I checked the time.

2:10 a.m. *Who's driving? Please, please, don't let it be Hadley. Sweet girl, but scatterbrained and reckless, just like Ray was at that age. Ray.* A painful sense of regret crept into my chest, lugging incessant second-guessing and self-blame along with it.

2:15 a.m. *Why did I have that argument with Amanda right before she left for the concert? She was dragging her feet with college applications and accused me of being a nag. She actually called me a nag.* A delay in her college applications had seemed monumental just a few hours before, but it hit me how truly inconsequential it was. Amanda would be leaving for college in a year, and our relationship, which had always felt airtight, was slowly deflating. Our faltering mother-daughter connection created an emotional undertow that pulled me even deeper into my ocean of worry.

2:18 a.m. I jumped up at the sound of a passing car, ran over to the window, pulled back the curtain, and panned the barely lit street. *How many times have I contacted the city about those streetlights?* Returning to my post on the sofa, I tried to erase the mental image of Amanda, broken and bleeding on the side of the road, her phone just out of reach. I desperately hoped they weren't drinking and driving. Or smoking. Where had Amanda gotten the naive notion that marijuana didn't impair driving skills? I'd overheard that—hopefully theoretical—conversation the week before as I discreetly loitered outside her door.

2:25 a.m. A half-empty mug of lukewarm tea sat on the coffee table in front of me. *Is Amanda blatantly ignoring her midnight curfew—sidestepping my calls and texts?* This wasn't like her. She always let me know when she would be late or if she was sleeping over at a friend's. I could wake Richard and have him worry with me, but I preferred to do my worrying solo.

2:30 a.m. *That's it. I'll wake Richard then call Hadley's and Karin's parents. And the police. Oh God.*

As I took a deep breath to fortify my resolve, I thought I heard a motorcycle in the street, quickly followed by a key rattling in the lock. I exhaled in blessed relief. But almost as quickly, my anger gathered momentum. Amanda was attempting a covert entrance, her boots in one hand, a Coke in the other, tiptoeing in and slowly sliding the lock back in place. She was so focused on entering silently that she didn't spot me sitting on the sofa in the dark.

"Amanda Earle, do you have any idea what time it is?" I stood up and flipped on the light.

Amanda squealed and dropped her boots and the Coke can, splattering the sugary contents over the tile entryway. "God, Mom, you scared the crap out of me!"

"I scared *you*? Where the hell have you been? It's almost three o'clock in the morning!"

"We were just talking, and I must have lost track of time. "

"Who's 'we'?"

"You know... me, Karin, and Hadley."

"You don't talk to them enough during the day?" I asked.

In this light, with that startled expression, Amanda looked eight years old.

"Were you on a motorcycle?" My question came out sounding more interrogational than I had intended.

"Me? No way!"

Her denial amplified my anger, but I had more pressing questions. "Why were you ignoring my calls and texts?"

"I wasn't ignoring you," she said with a sigh that spoke volumes. "My phone died."

I decided to set aside Amanda's denial and her favorite little white lie and focus on the fact that she was home, in one piece—no blood, no broken bones, no police knocking on the door to deliver devastating news. My world would keep rotating on its axis.

It had all been so much easier when Amanda's little body was ensconced in a swaddling blanket or confined to a playpen. If her little fingers reached for that bottle of pills on the kitchen table or the razor Richard had left on the bathroom counter, I was there to scoop her up and take her out of harm's way.

But looking at Amanda now, I could see clearly that my daughter was practically a woman. I had no idea what Amanda did once she walked out the door. *Sex? Drugs? Alcohol?* I'd experimented with all three by that age and suffered the consequences. And then there was Ray. He'd been about Amanda's age when he died. Of course I worried—some might say obsessed—about her. More than once, I'd been accused of being a helicopter mom, but I just didn't want my precious daughter to go through what I'd experienced and have to live with the emotional scars.

"I swear, Amanda, you almost gave me a heart attack. Don't ever do this again. Midnight means midnight. And if you know you're not going to make it home in time, find a working phone, and call me."

"I figured you wouldn't want me to wake you and Dad."

"Next time, wake me! And lucky for you, I didn't wake your father—two minutes later would've been another story!"

Contrite, Amanda looked down at her bare feet, and her auburn curls fell in her face.

"Don't you have anything else to say?" I stood, stiff and silent, angry that she'd made me suffer so with worry.

"I'm sorry, Mom," Amanda whispered.

Her softly mumbled words soothed the deepest part of my soul—the part where all my fears, love, and regrets resided. The remnants of my anger gave way to drop-to-my-knees gratitude. My child was safe. That was what mattered—the *only* thing that mattered.

I spread my arms open wide. The feel of Amanda's delicate frame in my arms made me want to sob in relief. She was a bit musty, sweaty. Her clothes reeked of cigarette smoke, but her eyes were clear, no hint of alcohol. I'd let my own careless adolescence, painful memories of Ray, and maternal paranoia overtake me. Risk-taking was no longer my forte, but this parenting business provided all the adrenaline rush of a bungee jump, with me not knowing if the cord would bounce back, yanking me to safety, or snap, plunging me to an agonizing end.

"You can't do this to me, Amanda."

"I know," she said with a half shrug.

"Okay. I'll clean up this mess, and you go to bed." I sighed. "You're going to be exhausted in the morning. What time do you want me to wake you?"

She rolled her eyes. "Mom, I can get myself up. And anyway, I have to make sure Hadley is up. We're going to the SAT prep class together."

I placed my palms on Amanda's flushed cheeks and looked into her hazel eyes, clear and bright. "You know I love you, Mandy." I kissed the top of her head and brushed loose strands of hair from her face. "Never again. You hear me?"

"Loud and clear, Cap'n Jack." She smiled, as she pulled away. Amanda had dubbed me Cap'n Jack after watching *Pirates of the Caribbean* when she was nine. Each time she uttered the endearment, it lessened the tension between us.

I chuckled and shook my head. "Good night, sweetie." I watched Amanda climb the stairs and listened for the telltale creak.

Then I wiped up the sticky brown puddle from the tile, threw away the empty can, tossed the dishtowel into the laundry room, and dragged myself up the stairs and back into bed. With my state of vigilance dissipated and my energy reserves depleted, I quietly slipped under the covers, warm from Richard's sleeping body.

He rolled over and mumbled, "Everything okay?"

"It's fine. Go back to sleep," I said, patting his arm.

He rolled back on his side and resumed his muffled snoring. Richard was a caring father and a loving husband, but like most husbands I knew, he wasn't tuned in to the daily minutiae of family life. He'd wake up in the morning, kiss me goodbye, and spend his day at the store, blissfully ignorant of the minidrama that had played out in the living room the night before. It was an unspoken contract between Amanda and me, gradually developed over seventeen years, that blips like this were not to appear on his radar. Life was easier that way, more manageable. Richard's "missing" dress shirt that Amanda had used as a kite tail, the failing grade she'd gotten in geometry in middle school, and the dent in the bumper that I'd taken the blame for were all secrets we kept from him. It was my job to shield Amanda from unpleasantries whenever I could. This was no different. Amanda would be on her own soon enough, and she would have to deal with life without my preemptive actions. I closed my eyes, cocooned by the warmth of Amanda's presence in the next room and the knowledge that my life wouldn't be destroyed the way I'd decimated my own mother's.

Twice.

Chapter 4
Amanda

I had dodged a major confrontation, a boring lecture, a laying down of the law. I plopped down on the bed, closed my eyes, and squeezed my purple princess pillow to my chest. I'd long outgrown my middle-school pink-and-purple phase, but I couldn't bring myself to toss out that pillow like so much garbage. It was proof that I'd powered through puberty and come out the other end pretty much in one piece.

I rolled onto my stomach, grabbed my laptop, and scrolled through Graham's Instagram photos. His last girlfriend was ridiculously gorgeous, athletic. Dominique Dujardin. Probably spoke French fluently. My four years of French had left me with the ability to say "*Oú sont les toilettes*?" and not much else.

There they were together at the beach, at a game, at a party, at a skateboarding event. In every shot, she was gazing lovingly down at his face. Her Rapunzel-like blond hair was a perfect contrast to that little black dress she was apparently fond of. I imagined her twirling in slow motion, her glossy tresses floating through the air like something in a L'Oréal commercial. She probably smelled like Aveda shampoo or amber oil.

Shit. My hair was a genetic blend of my mom's flaming red and my dad's nondescript brown. I'd grown fond of my expanse of auburn curls, but they didn't exactly drive guys crazy—not the way her blond mane probably did. *Looks like she goes to Greystone High with Graham. Once school starts, he'll see her every day.* That thought triggered an uncomfortable clenching in my gut that felt an awful lot like... jealousy. *Geez. Relax, Amanda.*

My phone dinged with a text from Graham: *Make it inside okay? No drama?*

Me: *Mom pounced but she's cool now. You?*

Graham: *Mine are pretty laid-back. No prob.*

Me: *SAT prep tomorrow. Need to crash.*

Graham*: Ok see you sat. Pick u up at 11?*

Me: *Sounds good.*

Graham: *Have a Graham cracker before bed. You'll sleep better* ☺

Me: *Ha ha. Nite.*

I closed my laptop and rolled onto my back. I glanced at the poster of Ingenious Imposter on the wall and smiled. It had been a good night—a really good night.

Chapter 5
Deb

Richard stumbled into the kitchen, dressed for work, but sleep still covered him like a warm blanket he was reluctant to throw off. He gave me a good-morning kiss on the cheek and neatly folded his suit jacket across the back of the chair. A few strands of his dark hair fell onto his forehead, and he brushed them back into place, a familiar gesture. I caught a whiff of the woody-scented cologne I'd bought him the previous year when we'd been in Paris—the trip we had talked about since we started dating. We'd put the trip on hold as we got married, started new jobs, and signed off on a mortgage, and then Amanda came along—sooner than planned. In other words, real life got in the way of our Air France fantasies. The scent of his cologne conjured up the biting taste of dark chocolate melting on my tongue, the air filled with the essence of warm baguettes, and postcard images of freshly washed Parisian streets. We'd made love more in our week in Paris than we had in a month at home.

"Coffee?"

He glanced at his watch as he sat down. "Meeting a supplier in about an hour, but I have time," he said, his voice hoarse.

"What's the matter? Didn't sleep well last night?" I handed him his favorite Texas Longhorn mug. His supplements were neatly lined up on the kitchen counter, as always, so I handed him those as well.

"Well, I did until you crawled into bed at... what time was it?"

"Two thirty or so."

"Insomnia again?" He took a sip. He always checked to see if it was sweet enough. It always was.

"No. Amanda was late coming in." I tensed. To Richard, curfews were etched in stone. "The girls had some car problems."

He set his mug down on the table a little harder than necessary. "What kind of car problems?"

"Amanda wasn't driving, so I'm not sure. We didn't talk that long. Anyway, I waited up for her."

He hesitated, frowning, as he took another sip to wash down his supplements. "I don't like the idea of her being out until all hours of the morning, Deb. Her curfew is midnight."

"Rules or no rules, it couldn't be helped."

"I still don't like it."

"Okay, Papa Bear. Just take a deep breath."

His voice softened, signaling that the worst was over. "Where is she, anyway? Doesn't she have that SAT-prep thing today? I hope she realizes how important that is for her to get into NYU."

"She'll be up soon."

"You want me to talk to her?"

His well-intentioned offer was a nonstarter. They would both end up in foul moods, and I would catch the fallout. "That's okay. I'll talk to her later today."

I poured myself a second cup and took a sip. Still facing the coffee maker on the counter, I said, "Richard, have you really thought about what it's going to be like around here when she leaves for college?"

"We've gone over this, Deb. I'll miss her. You'll miss her. She'll miss us, but she's ready."

"I'm not."

"I know." He sighed. "Neither am I." He stood up, gulped the rest of his coffee, and put the mug in the sink. Then he turned to face me, stood at attention, and raised his chin, waiting as I adjusted the knot in his mauve silk tie.

"All done." I patted his chest.

"It'll be okay, hon. We'll adjust."

He made it sound so simple, but the thought of her absence made me feel like I was on a sinking ship with no lifeboat. In choppy seas. With no land in sight.

He kissed my forehead. "Busy day today?"

"One deadline but mostly errands."

"Ah, the life of a freelancer." He grinned. "I'm hoping to be home for dinner. I'll let you know." He leaned over to kiss me goodbye—on the lips this time—picked up his jacket, and slipped his arms into the sleeves and over his broad shoulders.

I took secret pleasure in watching Richard dress for work. His body movements were reassuring, calming. He walked out the kitchen door, got into our new-to-us Volkswagen Passat, held the steering wheel, and opened his mouth to sing along with the radio. He sang in the car the way he sang in the shower. His unselfconscious belting out of the latest pop tunes was one of the things I would include in the Top Ten Things I Love About Richard list. I was hit with a pang of desire as strong as the night we'd first met, a reassuring reminder that Richard and I were solid.

An overcrowded frat party in an iffy part of town had brought us together. I was with Kevin. He was loud and full of himself, but he was really cute, and I was really bored. He left me standing alone against the wall, the chaos swirling around me, while he weaved his way back to the keg in the kitchen to refill his cup, though he'd clearly had enough. That was when the tall guy, looking like he just came in from an Ultimate Frisbee tournament in the park, caught my eye.

Dressed in a dive-bar T-shirt and frayed cutoff jeans, he glanced both ways as if checking for oncoming traffic before he crossed the room. Standing in front of me, he shoved his hands in his pockets. "Who put that look on your face?"

I looked up. Way up.

"Let me guess. You and your boyfriend had a terrible fight, and the douchebag left you here to fend for yourself." He paused.

"Is that right?" I crossed my arms tightly across my chest. I'd made a snap judgment that he was an entitled jerk invading my personal space.

He leaned in closer. "Girls like you don't come to parties like this alone."

I was reluctantly flattered, unsure whether he was just a decent guy trying to get his game on or a well-practiced player. I was still frowning when he took a step back.

"Sorry. That was my lame attempt to start a conversation with the hot girl in charge of holding up the wall." He grinned.

I looked into his eyes—eyes the color of key limes and warm as melted butter.

"You want a drink?" Before I could answer, he said, "I'm Richard," never breaking eye contact. He was clearly comfortable in his own deliciously tanned skin. He reached up to push his dark hair from his face, and his bicep flexed. I couldn't help but wonder if it was a peacock display. If so, it was working.

"Deborah, but my friends call me Deb."

"Okay, Deb it is." He flashed his I've-got-a-secret smile, a look that I would come to know and love as well as I knew the peaks and valleys of his body. He sidled up next to me, and I felt the first flutter.

After Kevin passed out on the couch, Richard and I stood outside, away from the clamor and pounding music, and talked until the early morning hours. He told me that he was majoring in recreational administration. I told him I was studying journalism. He said he was an only child. His eyes widened when I said I was the youngest of seven. He lived off campus. I lived in the dorm. He offered me a ride. I accepted.

As we turned into the parking lot of my dorm, the *Will he or won't he?* question was a flashing neon sign in my head. First kisses were always tentative and awkward—head tilted left or right, mouth open or closed, tongue or no tongue, quick or lingering? And I'd just met this guy. But when it happened, it wasn't like a first kiss at all—it was natural, like we'd just made love and were sealing it with a kiss. Richard still kissed me like that.

The creaking of the stairs pulled me from my thoughts. Amanda was shuffling into the kitchen, dressed in SpongeBob boxers, bunny slippers, and an Ingenious Imposter T-shirt she must have bought at the concert the night before.

"Well, look what the cat dragged in," I teased. The truth was, she looked gorgeous no matter what.

Amanda grunted good morning, her auburn mane bigger than usual, her voice smaller.

"You want some coffee? Toast? Cereal? Bagel?"

"Mom, please. I'm not even awake yet. But yeah, coffee would be excellent."

Amanda was surely the only adolescent on the planet who took her coffee black. I reached for her favorite mug from the cabinet—the one that said Got Milk?—poured a cup, and set it on the table in front of her.

She took a single sip and looked up at me, her forehead crinkled in concern, and whispered, "Has Daddy left yet?"

"You just missed him."

"What did you tell him?" she asked, her perfectly plucked eyebrows arched.

"I told him that you girls had car trouble and that's why you were late."

"Thank you," she said, her voice dripping relief.

"Listen, Mandy, I'm not doing this for you. I'm doing this for him... and for me. If he knew you had wandered in at almost three o'clock in the morning for no good reason, he would worry himself into an apoplectic state every time you walked out that door. And then I'd have to talk him down."

"I know, I know," Amanda mumbled.

"Okay. Just so we're clear, this *will not* happen again."

"Never again," Amanda said as she raised three fingers on her right hand in a pledge.

"Okay. You'd better hurry. I'll throw on some clothes, and if we get going, maybe you can make it on time."

"Hadley's going to pick me up."

I hesitated. "Okay. Just make sure she drives safely."

Amanda rolled her eyes. This had become her regular means of unspoken communication. Translation: *I don't need you anymore, Mom, so butt out!* She ran up the stairs.

I never understood how Hadley had gotten a driver's license. The school where the prep classes were being held was less than a mile away, but I worried as if she were about to take a perilous journey navigating narrow mountain roads.

I reached for the refrigerator handle. A bright-orange sticky note from Richard popped against the stainless steel: *Remind Amanda about college applications.*

When did he put that there? When we were first dating, I'd found the barrage of sticky notes odd. He had a Post-it Note on the coffee pot with instructions for brewing coffee, one on the bathroom wall, reminding his roommate—Stan—to flush and turn off the light, and one by his nightstand, prompting him to set his alarm.

"What's with all the sticky notes?" I asked.

"Just want to make sure I don't forget anything."

"What about the note in the bathroom?"

"Stan's a pig."

I had long ago accepted the brightly colored notes as part of the Richard Earle package deal. Richard's orderliness was one of the things that had drawn me to him in the first place. But Amanda sometimes liked to write *No!* on them in bright-red marker just to get under his skin.

I was nursing my second cup of coffee when Amanda yelled from upstairs. "Mom! Where is my black jacket you got from the cleaners?"

"It's on the right side of your closet. It's still in the cleaner's bag!" I yelled back, exasperated. I always said that my headstone was destined to read Mom, the Finder of Things.

At the ping of a text message, I reached into my robe pocket, but it was Amanda's phone next to her half-empty coffee cup. The screen brightened with a message from Karin. A glance was all it took to read the message: *I want to know everything about last night with Graham!* My heart sped up, and my chest seized. I swallowed hard.

Hadley pulled in the driveway, honking some sort of Morse code from her sun-faded black Volvo—at least the car was safe—and Amanda bounded down the stairs dressed, her hair still wet from her shower, smelling of honey and almonds. She grabbed her phone from the table, heaved her backpack over her shoulder, and took the granola bar I passed to her like a baton in a relay as she hurried out the door. "Later, Mom!"

"Bye, sweetie. Have a good—"

But Amanda was already slamming the door, greeting Hadley with a rapturous grin, and sharing secrets I would never be privy to.

I turned to gaze out the kitchen window at the bird feeder—the one four-year-old Amanda had insisted we hang. She loved watching the "robbers," as she'd called the robins that frequented the feeder. I would pick Amanda up so she could see out the window, and I'd kiss her soft cheek. "Yes, sweetie girl, it's a robber." When I was a kid, my mother had hung a plaque in our kitchen that said, "Robins appear when lost loved ones are near." I'd never asked her who she thought might be near.

After a while, the robins stopped coming to our feeder as the squirrels took advantage of the free food, pilfering birdseed by way of impressive gymnastic moves from a tree branch. As I stared at the faded wooden feeder, melancholy consumed me. Amanda would be gone soon, and Richard and I would be writing a new chapter in our lives. I regretted not using the brief time alone with him to talk about my dream for the future. But he looked tired. Maybe he was coming down with a cold. Whenever he was sick, he morphed into a 175-pound toddler, and I always took care of him, bringing him tea and toast and decongestants. And the remote.

Anyway, it was better that I hadn't brought it up. I was crazy to even consider it. We were just getting to a point in our lives where we could afford to do more things—just the two of us—like that trip to Paris. We'd talked about Rome next, or maybe Barcelona, Croatia, Budapest, or Prague. It was exciting to fantasize about the possibilities. Maybe I could do some travel writing, start a blog, take photographs from all our trips. We would Skype with Amanda—hardly like being apart at all—and start a new, adventurous chapter in our lives.

But then there was this tug, this desire, this need. And it was a real need, not an I'm-getting-older impulse that would eventually fade into the background when I finally came to my senses. Despite my long-standing ban on the subject, I wanted to talk with Richard the first chance I got. I had to let him know what I was feeling. We hadn't talked about it in years, but with Amanda about to leave for college, I had a different idea of what our new chapter could be, and it didn't involve flitting around the globe to foreign countries, all the while battling jet lag. I wanted to stay right here with Richard.

And a new baby.

Chapter 6
Amanda

"So?" Hadley demanded before I'd even shut the car door. "Were you blowing me off last night? Why didn't you answer my texts?"

I half shrugged. "It was late, and I was going over some stuff for the SAT."

"Okay, whatever. Tell me about the skater."

"Wait. How did you know he was a skater?"

"The Deathwish T-shirt."

"Oh yeah. Anyway, we went to Kerbey Lane Café, and I totally lost track of time. I was like two and half hours late coming in. Mom was pissed." I took a breath. "He's really cute, don't you think?"

"Too short for me. I'd be looking at the top of his head all the time, but yeah, if he was five or six inches taller, I'd do him."

"Oh, shut up, Hadley." I laughed. "You're such a liar."

She was all talk. While Hadley had gotten close a couple of times, she was just as virginal as I was but clearly more disappointed in her status.

"He was totally into you," she said.

"You really think so?"

"Come on. Seriously. Didn't you see the way he was looking at you?"

I let out a giggle as Hadley backed out of the driveway.

"Jack *never* looked at you like that," she said over her shoulder.

Jack. My first serious boyfriend. It wasn't love or anything like that. It was more like an opportunity that presented itself, and I didn't want to graduate from high school boyfriendless. So when he asked me out, I said yes. He asked me not to see anyone else. I said okay. But then he asked me to lie down and spread my legs. Again and again.

I considered saying yes just to shut him the hell up, but he wasn't the one. When I told him we were over, he began a campaign to win me back with flowers delivered every day, stuffed animals with love notes, texts filled with heart emojis. Then he started "coincidentally" showing up wherever I happened to be—HEB Supermarket, Torchy's Tacos, Starbucks. His stalkerish behavior was beginning to scare me, but he hadn't actually done anything I could report to the school or the police, so I kept it to myself.

"So, does that beard thingie tickle?"

It took a second for me to refocus. I sighed. "It's a soul patch, Hadley, and I don't know. He didn't kiss me."

"Well, fuck me!"

"Maybe next time."

Hadley's face lit up as she turned to flash a conspiratorial grin at me. "So, there's gonna be a next time?"

"Had! Fuck! Watch out!"

Hadley had a death grip on the wheel as she swerved, just missing a black lab galloping across the street.

"Look where you're going. Jesus! That's the third near disaster this week!"

"Okay, eyes on the road. So?"

I took a shaky breath as I watched the dog, oblivious to his near miss, make his way between two houses. "He invited me to a skateboarding competition on Saturday."

"Sweet," Hadley said.

We pulled into the school parking lot and maneuvered into the first empty space. It was more crowded than I'd expected. I guessed I wasn't the only one who had procrastinated and then panicked over senior year, SATs, and college applications.

"Oh fuuuck! Don't look now, but Jack Off's lurking." Hadley nodded toward the school entrance.

Jack was standing on the steps to the front entrance with his buddies. They looked like a pack of wild dogs, hackles up, ready to pounce on their prey. His sights were trained on me.

"Shit!" I ducked and slunk farther down in the seat. "Let's just sit here until they go in."

"We can't be late. They won't let us in once the practice test starts." Hadley gathered her backpack and her phone.

"What about the side entrance?"

"They started locking it ever since that guy with the gun, remember?"

"Oh yeah." *How could I forget?* We'd been on lockdown for a whole morning. Then we'd been sent home, badly shaken but safe.

"What's his problem, anyway?" I was angry with Jack but not angry enough to confront him. I picked up the pumpkin-orange backpack I'd had since middle school and looked at Hadley. "Stay with me, and let's walk fast."

"Ignore him, Amanda. He's a dick. A teeny-weeny little dick."

I laughed against my will.

"He's just pissed because you wouldn't give it up. Anyway, you can do a lot better than Jack *Off*erhaus. Who the hell names their kid that, anyway? Why not just name him Dick Wad and get it over with?"

I chuckled as I shoved Hadley's arm.

"Okay. On the count of three... one, two, three." We opened the car doors and closed them in synchronized-swim-team rhythm, coming together at the front bumper of the car. Hadley twisted her torso with a grunt and few audible cracks. "Whoa, I think I just knocked my ovaries out of whack."

I gripped my backpack close to my chest. My pulse pounded in my temples as we approached the front entrance. Halfway up the steps, I caught a glimpse of Jack from the corner of my eye. His ink-black hair was trimmed just above his ears, his white button-down Oxford shirt fresh from the cleaners, and his khaki pants newly pressed by Elise, their live-in help. There was nothing but disdain in his eyes. His tall, lanky frame leaned bonelessly against the brick wall.

Hadley and I had reached the top step unscathed when I heard his distinctive Canadian clip. "Hey, Earle, heard you're really scraping the bottom of the barrel now."

I clenched my fists. His testosterone-fueled pack snickered on cue. I stopped short, staring at the hastily tied laces on my purple high-tops.

"He's not worth it. He's just trying to salvage his rep. But check out those social rejects he's trying to impress." Hadley shook her head.

I hesitated, nodded, and kept walking. The door slammed shut behind us, and I exhaled. "What the fuck? I can't believe him."

My phone pinged. Sure that it was Mom, I almost ignored it, but guilt got the better of me, and I looked at the screen. I turned to Hadley, unable to suppress a grin. "It's Graham. He wants to pick me up after."

"See? He couldn't wait till Saturday. Screw Jack!" Hadley shouted and raised her fist in the air, her blond curls flying, her giant hoop earrings bouncing as she ran down the hall ahead of me.

Chapter 7
Deb

I sat at the kitchen table, sipping the last of my now-cold coffee, mentally crunching the numbers. I was thirty-eight. Okay, almost thirty-nine. If I got pregnant right away—an iffy proposition at my age—I'd be nearly forty by the time the baby was born, sixty by the time the child graduated from college. Amanda would be close to forty. I gasped, dizzy with the realization of how time could tiptoe by unnoticed.

I took the last sip of coffee and wandered over to the kitchen sink. I now found it impossible to recall the sureness of my decision not to have more kids. Each month, the opportunity presented itself to create another unique human being from randomly selected strands of DNA. And each month I said, "No, thank you."

But I couldn't help contemplating the unrealized possibilities. Another child could have been an artist like my nephew Josh or a tall, athletic dark-haired boy like Richard or a girl so much like Amanda that people would have confused the two. I could see them clearly, these children who didn't exist and never would, marching off into the distance and fading away.

I'd devoted all my parenting efforts to Amanda, willingly losing myself in her, reveling in the videotaping of her first taste of solid food, her first steps, her first word. I read *Goodnight Moon*, Dr. Seuss, and Shel Silverstein to her until I no longer needed to turn the pages, watched all the Disney movies until I could mouth the dialogue, and took her to piano lessons, ballet class, and soccer practice. I soaked up every delicious minute of her childhood. But I discovered Richard had a paternal instinct as strong as any woman's maternal tug. It was no secret that he wanted another child—maybe another two or three. I'd tried to explain to him that a house full of kids tugging at my pants leg all day would have fractured my time and diluted my energy. I'd watched my mother trying to care for her brood, and I didn't want that life for myself or for my child. Richard hadn't understood it.

Now, eighteen years later, I found myself wishing Richard had fought harder for what he wanted. No, that wasn't right. He had fought... we had fought. And I'd won. But what did I have to show for it other than bracing myself for an empty nest at the age of thirty-eight?

Still, having another child now would mean we'd both have to work several years longer than planned. Would he be on board for that? What would Amanda think of having a brother or sister almost twenty years younger than her? What about her future?

She'd always wanted a little sister, but with another mouth to feed and another college fund to fill, we wouldn't be able to help Amanda as much as we'd planned. She deserved our help in paying for college. *And what about our future?*

The ringing of my cell phone upstairs rattled my concentration, and the mug slipped from my fingers into the stainless steel sink, breaking the handle. I loved that mug. I could glue it back together, but it would never be the same. Surprised by my sense of loss, I turned and ran up the stairs and into my office, high-stepping over piles of books, files, and binders.

I picked up the phone and answered without looking. "Merritt?"

"Who the hell else would it be?" Merritt laughed loudly.

I took a calming breath and glanced at the clock. Ten o'clock in the morning. Right on time. Merritt hardly ever missed a day. She craved company—specifically, my company, especially now that her kids—all five of them—were out of the house, scattered across the country and around the world. I collapsed in my well-worn office chair, the leather crackling under my weight.

"Has Mr. Fancy Pants left yet?" she asked.

"Don't you ever get tired of making fun of the way Richard dresses?"

"No, not really."

"I know you're kidding, but..."

"Okay, I won't say another word. Not today anyway," she said.

Silence.

"So, how is Jess?" I asked.

"She's fine. Mostly resting." Merritt sighed.

"How are you?"

"I'm just glad it's over."

"And...?" I asked.

"There is no 'and.' It's done, and Jess can move forward, like you said."

She didn't want me to dig any deeper, so I traded in my shovel for a garden trowel. "I know you weren't one hundred percent sure that Jess was doing the right thing. But I truly believe she made the right decision."

She hesitated. "I know that."

"If you feel like you want to talk, you know I'm always here to listen."

"Yeah, I know that too."

I heard Jess yelling in the background. "Mom!"

"Oops, gotta go. We'll talk later," she said breathlessly, and she was gone.

Immediately, my phone vibrated with a text from Amanda: *Be home late. Library study group.*

Me: *Should I save dinner?*

Amanda: *Going out after. I'll get something there. Your awesome daughter Amanda.*

My awesome daughter was forging a life of her own. Without me. Oh, I understood that she would always need me on some level, but if I were to diagram her emotional needs as a pie chart, the portion designated for me would be an ever-shrinking slice. The cruel irony was that my need for her was taking up an ever-increasing portion of my own emotional pie. Was I trying to make up for that shifting distribution of affection by having another baby? Or was I still trying to prove myself a better parent than my mother ever was? *Does the reason even matter?* I didn't have answers. All I knew was that I desperately wanted another baby. And with Amanda away at college, I would be able to provide the same attention and affection to my next child that she had enjoyed as an only child for almost eighteen years.

I opened my laptop to focus on the assignment of the day—an article titled "The Increasing Incidence of Noncommunicable Diseases." I positioned my fingers on the keyboard, but my concentration was as scattered as the books and papers spread around my bare feet. The wheels of my chair squeaked as I pushed back from my desk and rolled over to the file cabinet in the corner. I unlocked the bottom drawer, reached into the back to retrieve the pack and lighter from their hiding place, and began the ritual of sliding a cigarette out and placing it between my eager lips. I spun over to the window, opened it, rested my elbows on the wooden sash, and tilted my head to light the cigarette.

Smoking was a habit I'd kicked the day I found out I was pregnant with Amanda, but it had become a security blanket I occasionally cuddled up next to. My pregnancy, followed by almost twenty years of writing about the devastation of smoking-related diseases, had cured me of the habit. But then one day, after Amanda had taken the car, I found a familiar gold-and-white pack of my old brand stuck under the car seat. I had sternly laid out the awful statistics to Amanda—cancer, stroke, blindness. And wrinkles. That last one had struck a chord. But acting as the health hypocrite I revealed myself to be, I pilfered the pack and occasionally lit up. After years as a nonsmoker, there was the added bonus of a dizzying head rush that accompanied each drag, and I was once again an unfettered college student, getting high. For a few precious moments, the concerns of a thirty-eight-year-old wife and mother of one drifted away and dissipated in a puff of smoke.

Chapter 8
Amanda

The algebra portion of the SAT practice test sapped the entire morning, but instead of variables, constants, and exponents, the only thought taking up space in my mind was *I'm going to see Graham.*

When it was finally done and Mr. Roi said, "See you all tomorrow, bright and early," I sprang from my seat and shot for the door. "Oh, and everyone, there's a tutoring session this afternoon in room 232 at four thirty." Mr. Roi, who was monitoring the practice test, also happened to be my calculus teacher from the previous year and the year before that.

"I suggest that you all be there." He paused for effect and adjusted his hipster glasses.

I glanced at the clock on the wall.

"Those of you who need it the most know who you are."

It felt like Roi was wagging a judgmental finger in my direction. How unfortunate that Roi knew my mom, though I couldn't remember from where. *Book club, writers' group, health club?* Gripping my backpack with both hands, I actually considered—for a millisecond—going to the tutoring session.

He arched his thick eyebrows and slipped his hands into the pockets of his jet-black chinos. Hadley actually thought he was kind of cute for a guy my mom's age. Personally, I couldn't see it.

I pushed my way through the crowd, hoping to be first out of the classroom and the front door and on to the fun stuff. The real stuff. Graham might have already been out front, waiting for me.

"Also, guys..." He raised his voice to be heard above the mass exodus. "When school starts up again, it'll be time for parent-teacher conferences. I think it's really important that your parents know what's going on with your grades!"

Rockin' Roi, as we all called him, was sending a message as clear as the four-o'clock bell: *Study. Don't socialize.* He hadn't been in high school in at least twenty years. He'd forgotten what it was like. Or maybe he wanted to forget.

The worst part was, I knew he was right. I wouldn't have admitted it to him on a bet, but I had to get serious if I was going to get into NYU. *Shit!* But the pull of Graham waiting for me just a few steps away was too strong.

I hurried through the hallway to the main doors leading to the parking lot. I pushed the handle, and the hydraulic door squealed open, exposing the blazing Texas sun. Shielding my eyes with the back of my hand, I scanned the area. My heart sank. Not a motorcycle in sight.

As I consoled myself, the door to a car opened, and a guy stepped out. "Hey, Amanda! Over here!"

My impression of Graham quickly shifted as I walked in his direction and smiled, nervously sweeping my hair behind my ears.

"I was beginning to think you stood me up," he said, not acting like he thought anything of the sort.

I pointed at the car. "What happened to the motorcycle?"

"Oh, that was my dad's. My car wasn't charged, so he let me use it for the concert."

"And this is yours?" The tiny vehicle looked like it had been squeezed out of a metal crusher.

"It was a present from my very environmentally conscious parents for my nineteenth birthday. It's not a muscle car, but it gets me where I want to go on the cheap." He looked at the car then at me. "It rides smoother than it looks."

I shifted the weight of my backpack on my hip. "You're already nineteen?"

"Actually, I'll be twenty before the end of the year."

I added the almost three-year difference in our ages to the growing list of reasons my parents would not be happy with me dating Graham. *But we were just hanging out, right?*

"My mom homeschooled me in the beginning, but she was doing her own thing, and the school board wasn't happy," he said. "Anyway, I started school about a year and a half later than I should have."

"Homeschooling? How was *that*?"

"I was just a kid." He shrugged. "I don't think I even realized that's what we were doing. I thought she was just spending quality time with me." He smiled and walked around to the passenger side.

I was still standing by the open driver's-side door. Was he offering to let me drive?

"What's the matter? You afraid it won't hold the two of us?" He laughed as he held the passenger door ajar for me.

I walked around and sat in the passenger seat of the super compact. He smiled as he shut the door, went to the driver's side, and slid in. From the corner of my eye, I caught him looking at me. It made my skin tingle. Maybe he was checking in the light of day to see if his initial assessment had been accurate.

"So, you in summer school?" he asked.

"No, thank God. I'm taking an SAT prep course."

"Ah, an overachiever."

I shook my head. "No, the opposite, actually."

"I like overachievers."

I opened my mouth to argue the point but thought, *He just complimented you, Amanda. Shut the hell up*. My seat belt snugly fastened, I asked, "Where are we going?"

"It's a surprise." He pushed the start button.

As we headed south, I turned to him. "So, what's downtown?"

"Not downtown. Zilker Park." He swerved suddenly and pulled into a parking lot.

"What's going on in the park?"

"I told you, Amanda, it's a surprise," he whispered as if someone might overhear. Hearing him say my name like that gave me goose bumps, despite the heat.

He parked the car, came around to open my door, and said, "Okay. Now, close your eyes."

"Seriously? How far is it? I can't walk through the park with my eyes closed. I'll look weird, and I'll feel even weirder. People will stare."

"Who cares? Anyway, you won't see them staring." He laughed. "And I'll make sure you don't trip. It's not far. Come on, don't screw up my surprise."

I closed the door, sighed, and closed my eyes.

"Put your hand over your eyes so I know you're not peeking, or I'll have to get that bandana I have stuck in the glove compartment and blindfold you. And I can't really tell you the last time that thing saw the inside of a washing machine." He was so enjoying this.

"Okay," I said, trying to act as if I hated playing his little game. I put my left hand over my eyes.

After a few minutes and more than a few stumbles, he said, "Okay. You can look."

The sun blinded me for a second, but when I was able to focus, a giant butterfly was in my line of sight. No, it was a huge chair shaped like a butterfly—a brightly painted orange-and-black monarch.

"That's so cool! How come I didn't know this was here?" That night at the diner, I'd rambled on about butterflies being hopeful. I didn't think he was paying much attention, but he'd remembered. I ran up to the chair, sat down, threw my head back, and dramatically draped my arms across the wings. "I love this! Take my picture!"

"Hey, let's get someone to take a shot of us together," Graham said. "A selfie won't get the chair in the shot."

A jogger passed, arms and legs glistening with sweat. She wiped her brow with her forearm.

"What about her?" I asked.

"Doubt she'd appreciate us messing with her cardio. Anyway, too sweaty. Nothing to dry her hands with."

I spotted a twentysomething guy being walked by two border collies straining against their leashes. Graham let them go by.

"What was wrong with him?"

"The dogs. No way he could snap a shot."

An older couple holding hands strolled by.

"Excuse me," Graham said. "Would you mind taking our picture?"

"Sure," the man said.

Graham handed the man his phone, showed him which button to push, and ran over to where I was sitting. The seat of the chair was too small to comfortably hold us both. He looked at me. "Get up."

I stood and shrugged at the couple patiently waiting. Graham sat down in the chair and patted his lap. I hesitated for a fraction of a second before I sat on his legs and leaned into him for the shot. The scent of sandalwood surrounded him. My mom had told me about research showing that sandalwood had healing properties. Did it also have aphrodisiac properties? I wasn't going to ask her about that one.

The man smiled and winked at Graham as he handed the phone back to him. The man and his wife held hands again as they walked away. I wanted to be like that with my husband when I was old and gray—still holding hands.

"Let me see," I said. He had encircled me with his arms and was holding the phone in front of me. We were elevator-stomach-drop close. I was staring at the picture, trying not to look at him, when the screen went black. "Bring it back up. I'm not finished looking."

"Amanda," he said, his voice deepening.

He was going to kiss me. I could feel it in my bones. I slowly turned my head to look at him. Could he feel me trembling?

He slid his fingers through my hair. "I want to kiss you. Can I kiss you?" he whispered.

I nodded. And he was kissing me. And he tasted like warm chocolate. And I let myself melt into him.

He pulled away, and it was as if someone had pulled the plug on my energy source. Without thinking, I pulled him back to me and pressed my mouth against his. *I* was kissing *him*—not like I used to kiss Jack. When Jack's tongue invaded my mouth, I would think about how I needed to clean my room before Mom got pissed off and wonder where that navy camisole was. No, this was like nothing I'd ever experienced before. When we pulled away at the same time, my face was hot, and I was breathing as if I'd just run a six-minute mile.

"Well," he said, chuckling, "that was a surprise."

Chapter 9
Deb

My thoughts were gridlocked as I crawled the car into the narrow garage, the space shrunken by Richard's piles of boxes of sporting goods from his store. I'd been so sure that my lunch with Merritt a few days before would help me work through my baby decision—that she would help me determine if I was out of my ever-loving mind to even consider it. Instead, Merritt had more important things on her mind, prompting her to ask me some odd existential question about killing off yet-to-be-conceived children.

The automatic garage door slammed down, and as the last bit of the midafternoon sun was squeezed out, I turned off the key and sat in the dark, replaying bits and pieces of my conversation with Merritt. Jess had been drafted into motherhood against her will and was just as anxious to go AWOL as I was to re-up. It added a twisted, in-your-face irony to an already confusing situation.

Jessica was young, but was she crazy to so readily give up the opportunity to be a mother? Or was I the one who was truly off her bird, considering having another kid at this stage of my life? Was I having my own existential crisis, somehow trying to fill a vacant space in my heart?

I gripped the steering wheel and pressed my forehead into the leather. Having drifted away into the land of "what-ifs," I was startled by the ringing of my phone.

"Merritt? Is everything okay?"

"Listen, have you told Richard about Jess?"

"No, not yet. Why?"

"I'd rather we just keep this between us for now."

"Merritt, I don't think..."

"Deb, please? I'd feel better if you kept this to yourself."

I sighed. "Okay. Promise."

I hung up. A sudden tapping on the window sent me whiplashing to the headrest. "Richard! Shit!" As he motioned for me to open the door, I reached for the handle and began speaking before I'd set foot on the concrete floor. "What are you doing home?"

"I think I'm running a fever. Not much going on today in the store, so I figured I'd come home, take some ibuprofen, and rest up."

I brought his head down to place my cheek on his forehead, convinced it was more accurate than any thermometer. He was warm. I took a perverse pride in my ability to detect even the slightest shift in the well-being of either Richard or Amanda.

"Want some tea?"

"Is there any mint?"

"In the garden. I'll get it."

"CAN I GET YOU ANYTHING else?" I sat on the edge of the bed, watching him curl himself into a tight ball and pull the covers up to his neck. I'd brought him green tea with mint, some toast, the newspaper, and a book, none of which he had touched. Usually, at this stage, he'd have been flipping through the channels at warp speed and reading the sports section. But he hadn't even asked for his laptop.

"Don't forget to take your ibuprofen. It'll lower the fever."

"I'm just really tired. I think if I take a nap, I'll feel better."

Richard tired? Despite his being acutely aware of every ache and pain, he always ran circles around me and exhausted everyone who worked for him.

I smoothed the blankets and tucked him in. "Maybe I should call the clinic and see if they can squeeze you in today."

"No, it's fine," he mumbled. "I just want to rest. I'll take a nap, and then I'll be..." His voice fell away as he drifted off to sleep mid-sentence.

I tiptoed out of the room and back into my office. My day so far had not been conducive to working, but I had to get a few words down on paper or I'd never meet my deadline. I started reading through the stacks of research the client had sent me—noncommunicable diseases included cardiovascular disease, diabetes, and liver disease.

Where to start? I was diving headfirst into an information rabbit hole. *Might as well go alphabetical. So, cardiovascular disease it is.* I started skimming through the statistics. Cardiovascular disease was the number-one cause of death in the US—787,000 people died of cardiovascular disease each year. It killed more people than all types of cancer combined. Someone in the US had a stroke every forty seconds.

I shook my head at the grim numbers but found myself smiling at the thought of sharing the information with Richard. He was the healthiest, most fit man I knew, but he had a touch of hypochondria. He always avoided going to the doctor because he was sure they were going to find something seriously wrong with him. I had learned not to terrify him with the graphic details of what I learned while researching diseases. If he asked what I was working on, I'd answer "Heart health" rather than "Heart disease" and "Blood sugar" rather than "Diabetes." I never quoted scary disease statistics or went into detail about any of the bizarre medical cases I'd read.

Merritt teased Richard relentlessly about his preoccupation with his health. "So, what's the disease of the week, Richard?"

But it had never bothered me. He was strong in every other way. Hypochondria was his Achilles' heel. Richard was just more vocal about his than most people.

At four o'clock, I heard Richard stir and head to the bathroom. I saved what I'd written, stood up, and stretched before going back to the bedroom. I tapped on the bathroom door. "Richard, how are you feeling?"

He didn't answer. "Richard, are you okay?"

Silence.

"Richard?"

"Sorry. Yeah, yeah, I'm fine." He opened the door. "Is my skin a weird color?" he asked, leaning down to give me a better vantage point.

"I think it's just those new energy-saver light bulbs over the sink. You look fine to me."

He did look a little "green around the gills," as my mother used to say, but I didn't want to encourage his tendency to self-diagnose.

Chapter 10
Amanda

Saturday morning, I waited anxiously for Graham to pick me up. I couldn't stop daydreaming about the bonus afternoon we'd spent together earlier in the week. It wasn't supposed to be a big deal—a walk through Zilker Park's butterfly garden, some frozen yogurt as we talked about our favorite bands, our schools' ridiculous rivalry, and the jocks, cheerleaders, nerds, and headbangers who populated our lives during the week. But when he kissed me and I kissed him back, it raised our time together to a whole other level. It was the perfect afternoon with the perfect guy, the one I'd always fantasized about. He would be talking, and he'd just stop and look at me with those blue-gray eyes, and it felt like he was looking into me, seeing me—the real Amanda. I'd taken a mental snapshot of his smile and recorded his infectious laugh. Just thinking about it made me happy.

He was different from Jack in every way that mattered. Whenever Jack had looked at me, he had only one thing on his mind. When I turned him down, the look disappeared and had been replaced with... a look I wanted to forget.

My bedroom door flew open, the doorknob banging against the wallpaper I'd meticulously designed, made up of vintage photographs from estate sales. My cousin Josh said the idea was brilliant, and he'd spent time helping me put it all together when he was home for Christmas. I was afraid to check if the doorknob had ripped a hole in our masterpiece.

"Amanda, seriously?" Hadley asked as she barged in.

I looked at myself in the mirror. I'd changed clothes half a dozen times already. The rejects hung off the edge of my bed like dust ruffles. Desperate for help, I'd recruited Hadley and Karin for input from opposite ends of the fashion spectrum.

"What's wrong with it?"

Hadley laughed. "Was the plan to come off looking like a librarian? You need to kick it up a notch... or two. What about that low-cut blue top you bought last time we went shopping? It really shows off your C cups."

Hadley saw cleavage as bait. In a moment of weakness, she'd talked me into buying that thing, now earmarked for Goodwill. I already regretted asking for help. Hadley's fashion sense lent itself to tight, barely there skirts and clingy blouses or embarrassingly short cutoffs with strategically placed rips down her impossibly long legs, paired with skimpy tank tops. *Me*? I tended to shop at vintage stores and secondhand shops and had a sixth sense for picking up cool items at bargain-basement prices. I wasn't ready to be so out there. All I could think of were the pictures of Graham's perfectly proportioned ex in that sleek size-two black dress.

"Hadley, I'm freaked out here. Can you just help me?"

After an hour of doing her cellphone-zombie routine, providing useless fashion advice that resulted in enough discarded clothes on the bed for me to start my own secondhand store, Hadley gave a dismissive laugh. "Okay, go ahead, play it safe. I'm out." She left in a huff.

She'd get over it. She always did. I heard the front door slam shut just as Karin walked into my room, a textbook in hand.

"How'd you manage to get out?" I asked.

"Just so you know, we're studying for the SAT exam."

Karin's parents didn't exactly like me. I guessed they hated me less and trusted me slightly more than any of Karin's other potential friends, but I was sure the day would eventually come when they would lock her in her room and throw away the key to protect her from bad influences like me.

"So, when's he supposed to be here?" Karin asked.

"Soon. So, what do you think?" I was wearing white shorts frayed at the bottom and a powder-blue camisole with spaghetti straps.

"You don't need help. That's perfect!" Karin jumped up, her single braid bouncing, and began digging through my jewelry box. "Where are those earrings you got on South Congress? You know, the silver-and-blue dangly ones. Ah, here they are."

I glanced at myself in the mirror. "They're not too matchy-matchy?"

"Nope. Perfect."

I slipped on my sandals and put the final touches on my freshly indigo-painted toenails. "What are you doing today?"

"The usual. Nothing. Promise you'll text me and let me know how it's going," Karin said, rubbing her hands together in anticipation.

I always wished someone nice would ask Karin out, instead of her always having to live vicariously. She'd gone solo to homecoming and to the junior prom. It would soon be senior year, and while she hadn't said anything, I knew she'd be devastated if she had to go to the senior dance alone—if her parents would even allow it. Why didn't the guys see what I saw? Karin was beautiful inside and out and an awesome friend, but she usually had her head in a book and was too timid to start up a conversation with a guy, much less flirt. And even if she met someone, it couldn't go anywhere. Her uber-conservative, scary-religious parents always had her under house arrest.

"Amanda, someone is here to see you!" Mom shouted from downstairs.

Shit! I hadn't heard a knock on the door. I'd told her that Graham would be coming to get me, but I hadn't prepped her for the dreadlocks, the soul patch, the earrings. And the skateboarding.

Too late now. I grabbed my purse. "Wish me luck!"

"You won't need it."

Karin peered over the railing from above as I ran down the stairs and took in the totally unnatural scene—my mother and Graham standing next to one another in the entryway. Fire and ice. Rock and a hard place.

Graham was dressed for the day in board shorts and flip-flops, sunglasses hanging from the neck of his T-shirt. He looked up at me and smiled, and concern about my mother's reaction slipped away.

"Amanda, you didn't tell me you were going to watch *skateboarding*," she said with a shaky smile. "Graham tells me he's a skateboarder." It came out more like an accusation than a conversation starter.

"Oh, I thought I mentioned that." I scrambled down the last few steps and squeezed in between the two of them. An awkward silence expanded then shrank back as I said, "Well, we're going to be late if we don't leave now. I'll text you later, Mom."

"Nice to meet you, Ms. Earle."

"You too, Graham," my mom mumbled, not sounding the least bit pleased to have made his acquaintance. As we walked to the car, she shouted, "I'll expect that text, Amanda!"

"Your mom didn't know I was picking you up?" Graham backed out of the driveway.

"She knew. Why?"

"She just seemed, sort of... I don't know, shocked I was there."

"I think maybe it was just that you're not exactly what my parents would have expected."

"What is it? The hair?" He laughed and shook his head. "Wouldn't be the first time."

"Well, that and the earrings. My mom wants every guy I go out with to look like my dad."

"And what's that like?"

"Super clean-cut, corporate dresser, no jewelry above the neck, and no tats."

"No tats. That's one point in my favor. So, if your dad answers the door next time, should I duck in the bushes?" He laughed.

"They're really not that bad."

"Good to know." He snorted a laugh and shook his head. "My dad's an aging hippie. So's my mom. But they're cool."

"I can't imagine ever describing my parents as 'cool,' but they're okay." I knew I was lucky as far as parental units went. It sounded like maybe Graham was too.

Karin came bounding down the driveway and waved at us as she headed in the direction of her house a couple of blocks away. I waved back before turning to Graham. "That's my friend Karin. She has really scary-weird parents. They're so formal, I feel like I need to curtsy when I walk in the door and quote a Bible verse before I leave. All her conversations with them are about Christian life lessons." I stopped to take a breath. "They weren't always like that. They used to be okay, but two years ago, Karin's little brother, Sam, died of leukemia. It was sudden and awful. Really awful. They sort of went off the deep end—thought that they'd done something bad to cause it, decided it was God's punishment. They joined this culty church for support. Now they actually believe the devil is all around and is trying to take Karin like it took her brother. They think they can pray it out of her. She can never let her guard down, and they've cracked down on her time away from home. They tried to get her into this uber-religious school, but it was too expensive. I really don't know how she's kept it together—how she's turned out so normal... TMI?"

"No. But man, that sucks." He curled his upper lip in disgust.

We drove in silence for a few minutes before he turned up the music, vintage Bob Marley—good sounds for such a small car. We drove for the next several blocks with Marley's voice filling up the silent space and entertaining anyone else within earshot. Despite the building heat, Graham had the windows down, and I was trying really hard not to sweat.

"Where are we going?"

"House Park. It's close to downtown. We don't have to stay long. I thought we could get something to eat after." He braked for the traffic light and turned and looked at me, his chin resting in the crook of his arm.

My stomach clenched as I looked straight ahead. "Sounds good."

From the corner of my eye, I saw him still staring. The car behind us honked, and with a sheepish grin, he pressed on the gas and focused on the road ahead.

As we pulled into the parking lot, a group of sweaty, sunburned guys approached, skateboards in hand, all smiles. Graham parked, opened the door, grabbed a small cooler, and stepped outside. I was gathering my purse from under the seat when I heard them greet him enthusiastically.

"Hey, dude, what's up? Where the hell you been? You disappeared after the concert."

Graham shifted the cooler under his arm. The guys gave high fives and fist bumps all around. "Just been busy."

"Where's your board?"

"Not today. Just hanging." He nodded toward the car.

All eyes were on me, and I could feel the heat blossom from my neck to my face. I opened the car door and was stepping outside when one of them muttered, "Nice, dude."

"Amanda"—he motioned me over—"this is Corey, Brandon, and Rocket."

Rocket? He looked like a redheaded hobbit.

"Nothing to do with skateboarding," Rocket volunteered. "My mom says I shot out like a rocket. She has a warped sense of humor."

I wasn't sure how to respond. And how could I possibly have relaxed when they were all staring at me like I was lunch?

"Hey, G, you give her your 'graham cracker' line yet?" Corey said, elbowing Graham.

"Jesus, Corey. You're a fucking idiot. Come on, Amanda. Let's go find a place in the shade." He took me by the hand, like he had the night of the concert, and led me away from the three sets of eyes boring holes into my skin. I couldn't resist looking back. They were laughing and nudging each other, going on like a gaggle of middle-school girls. "Douchebags," Graham grumbled.

"So, the *graham cracker* comment is one of your standard lines?" I asked, stopping to look at him so I could gauge the truthfulness of his answer. I wanted to ask if he'd used it on his ex, but I didn't dare go there.

"Um... no... yeah... sometimes." I'd managed to fluster him, but he regrouped. "But it made you laugh, right?"

I looked around at the dozens of guys in the skate park—not a single girl in sight—defying gravity over and over again, taking crazy chances with their bodies as they flew unnaturally through the air. It was more than one hundred degrees. Heat vapors rose off the cooking concrete. The cloudless blue sky offered no relief.

Graham and I found the shadiest spot we could amid the concrete and asphalt. He opened the cooler and handed me a bottle of ice-cold water. The rickety sounds of wheels against concrete ramps created an energetic musical rhythm. Graham was absorbed in the action as each skateboarder swooped and swayed, up and down, arms out, in a sort of boy ballet that separated them from their boards and brought them back to earth in split-second timing.

He edged closer to me and reached for my hand. If simply holding his hand felt this good, I was in serious trouble. But when his friends ambled over to where we were hiding from the sun, he suddenly let go. A wave of disappointment washed over me. Was he part of a pack like Jack? If he didn't get what he wanted, would he eventually turn on me in an effort to impress them?

"So," Rocket said, his carrot-top curls escaping from the knot on top of his head. "How do you guys know each other?"

"From the concert, dude. I told you."

"Oh yeah, the concert," he said, nodding thoughtfully.

My camisole strap slipped off my shoulder, and Corey's eyes zoomed in. He wanted to know if Graham had already gotten lucky. I could feel it in his gaze.

Graham pulled me up off the ground and took a step forward. "Core, knock it off." He took my hand and pulled me closer.

"What? What'd I do?" he said, the picture of unfairly accused innocence.

Graham ignored him. "So, you guys going back out? I wanted Amanda to see what we can do."

"Sure," Rocket said, "but then I gotta go. My mom's expecting me." He shrugged one shoulder. "You know how it is."

He snatched his board and hit the ramp. Each time he bottomed out and came flying up the other side, I held my breath. But then he would nail it, and I'd exhale.

"Can you do that?" I asked Graham, impressed and concerned at the same time.

"Not exactly like that. Rocket's way better. He may be getting sponsors soon."

"You mean, like, getting paid to use stuff?" I asked.

"Yeah, he's about to go pro. And he'll get a much better board. Pretty cool, huh?"

Rocket completed one last gravity-defying double flip, grabbed his board, and sauntered over. "So, what'd you think?" he asked, smiling as if he'd just won Olympic gold.

"*Sweeet*," I said, "but scary. You couldn't get me out there on a bet."

"That's not even my best move. Right, Graham?" he said, rearranging his wild hair. Rocket vibrated with pressurized energy. Maybe skateboarding was his release valve.

Graham turned to me. "You wanna come to the contest next week?"

"Definitely."

Rocket pulled his phone from his pocket and glanced at it. "Oh shit!" he said under his breath. "Sorry, guys. Gotta book it." He raced to his car, his skateboard tucked under his arm, the knot on top of his head bouncing each time his feet hit the pavement.

Graham sighed. "Rocket's a really good guy, but he's got some serious shit going down at home."

When he didn't offer an explanation, I didn't ask. I barely knew Graham. I didn't know Rocket at all.

Chapter 11
Deb

Three Weeks Later

I came down the stairs, and before my foot landed on the last step, I stopped short. Amanda was already sipping coffee at the kitchen table. An unexpected cool front had swooped in overnight, and she'd opened the kitchen windows to let in fresh air that would inevitably turn into blazing heat later in the day.

"What in the world are you doing up at..." I looked at the wall clock. "Nine fifteen on a Sunday morning?"

"Graham's picking me up."

"But we'd planned to go over your college applications today and get started on your essays." Conscious of the whiny tone creeping into my voice, I checked myself. "Remember?"

"It'll still be there when I get back. It's not like I'm running away to join the circus. We're just going to Barton Springs."

I remembered lots of lazy summer days Richard and I spent there as college students, wading into the brisk sixty-eight-degree water before spreading out a towel on the grass to soak up the sun. Despite the warm memories, I was wrangling with the same queasy feeling I had each time I waved goodbye to Amanda and watched her and Graham rush, side by side, to his car. Their body movements were a little too in sync. He couldn't take his eyes off her. Who could blame him? She was beautiful—so fresh and full of life. And frightfully happy. Still, as I had watched this boy, this stranger with the knotted hair and the earrings—three by my count—casually slip his arm around my daughter's waist and walk away, the hair on the back of my neck stood up.

I wasn't oblivious to the irony tapping me on the shoulder. I could still see my mother's twisted expression each time my long-haired, guitar-playing, tattooed high-school boyfriend would drive up in his beat-up Ford truck. While her worst fears about what would happen were justified, I could only hope mine were unfounded.

"Mom, can I have some more coffee, *please*," she croaked. "It's way too early for the college conversation."

"Well, since you're seeing him again today, it's safe to assume you like him?"

Amanda shrugged. "Yeah, he's okay."

The shutdown. I calmly stirred my coffee as if my maternal antenna hadn't gone up and my emotions weren't running amok.

"Just okay?"

Amanda shot me *the look*. "If we decide to get married, I'll send you an invitation. Okay?" She stood up, took the coffee from my extended hand, and paused before leaning over and giving me a peck on the cheek. Translation: *I love you, but butt out.*

"When are you leaving?" I asked.

"Graham said he would be here around ten thirty." The inflection in her voice shifted upward when she said his name. It was almost imperceptible, but like a mother bat recognizing her offspring's squeal among millions, I heard it.

"When do you think you'll be back?"

"I'll text you." And with that, she turned and went up the stairs, taking all the fresh air with her.

I didn't want to make this Graham boy seem like a bigger deal than he really was. Amanda couldn't afford the distraction. Not with college around the corner. She'd have all the time in the world to fall in and out of love—if that was what this was.

At exactly ten thirty, Amanda came bounding down the stairs in shorts and a bikini top.

"Amanda, don't you think you should be wearing a cover-up? Better yet, maybe you should change. I think you've outgrown that top."

"I told you, we're going to Barton Springs. You know, to swim? So I have to, you know, wear a swimsuit? Anyway, no time. Graham's outside."

I glanced out at the driveway. He had stealthily arrived in his almost-a-car car.

So—what? He just texts her, and she comes running?

"Bye, Mom. Later."

She and all her girly parts bounced out to meet him. He leaned over and opened the car door for her from the inside. He was shirtless—chest hair, muscular arms, blond stubble—he was way past the little-boy stage. I remembered how when Amanda was three, she'd begged me relentlessly for a two-piece swimsuit, and I had given in, but when she stood looking at herself in the mirror, her little face scrunched up, on the verge of tears. "But, Mommy, there's nothing there."

"Nothing where, sweetie?"

She placed her little hands on her chest. I had to bite my lip to keep from laughing as it dawned on me—she had expected the top to endow her with breasts like the ones she'd seen on the mannequins. As I watched my little girl—correction, young woman—drive away with that young man, I ached for the sweet innocence of my long-ago toddler.

"Morning, Deb."

Startled by Richard's voice, I took my eyes away from the driveway just long enough to miss their departure. "Good morning, sleepyhead. How're you feeling?"

He'd been complaining about feeling tired over the last several weeks but dismissed out of hand my suggestion of going to the doctor, even when I offered to make the appointment. His distrust and disdain for doctors and the healthcare system in general was always a hurdle I had to push him over.

"Better."

Dressed in his Under Armour running gear, new Nikes, and Patagonia cap and wearing a Fitbit on his wrist, he looked ready for the cover of *Runner's World.*

He eyed Amanda's half-empty Got Milk? mug on the breakfast table. "What's Amanda doing up so early on a Sunday?"

"You just missed her. She's with that Graham boy. She ran out the door like the house was on fire."

Richard scowled and bit his lip, the subsequent pout neutralizing his edgy expression. "So, how long have they been going out now?"

"Several weeks, if you count the concert."

"The concert? The night she came in so late?"

Oops. "Yeah, I guess it was."

"I'm not even going to ask." He shook his head. "Okay, so you've met him. Does he seem like a good kid?"

This was it. I could either share my concerns and then deal with his angst, on top of my own, or hope Amanda was in the throes of a teenage crush that would very soon be a thing of the past. "Well, he's very different from Jack, but Amanda seems to really like him, and I think we should trust her judgment."

Mollified, he retrieved his coffee from my hand and took a sip to check that it was sweet enough. He took another sip and grabbed his supplements from the counter. He never missed a day, convinced they would keep him young and fit forever, or at least for a long time. He had recently begun stocking them in his sporting goods store and sold them to customers, fueled by his earnest belief in their benefits. He popped a couple of capsules in his mouth and took a sip of coffee to wash them down.

"You know, I can't stop thinking about Jess's situation." Despite my promise to Merritt not to tell Richard, I had to share it with someone.

"Me too. But Merritt says she's fine. I think it's hit Merritt hard, though. She's still trying to accept Jess's decision." Richard shook his head. He hesitated before looking up at me. "When was the last time you gave Amanda the condom lecture?"

"Richard, I think you're jumping the gun. It's only been a few weeks, and I'm pretty sure she's still safely in virgin territory. She and Jack never—"

He held his hand up to stop me. "Okay, okay. Just checking."

The days of Amanda being Daddy's little girl had passed. He missed having her run to the front door to greet him the second she heard his key in the lock. "Daddy's home!" She would latch on to his legs before he even had a chance to close the door.

"How's my baby girl?" he would ask.

She would giggle, and he would walk in, dragging her on one foot as she hitched a ride. Amanda had worshipped him. It shamed me to admit it, but I'd actually been jealous.

But at seventeen, Amanda was pulling away from us both. It wasn't like she would ever come right out and tell me if she was sleeping with Graham—she always blushed and squirmed each time I uttered the "s-e-x" word. She just walked away if I brought it up. But when Amanda and Jack were together, they'd never given off a vibe that suggested that kind of intimacy. I'd liked Jack. I thought he was good for Amanda. His dad was CEO of Blue Sails, a thriving tech company in Austin, and his mom was the head of a nonprofit. He'd always been polite and considerate. And unlike Graham, he always brought Amanda home before curfew. I hadn't worried about him the way I was already fretting over Graham.

"Change of subject. What do you want to do for your birthday? Last chance to misspend the years of your youth—the big thirty-nine," Richard teased.

"Thanks for reminding me, but you're in the same boat, you know. Two months from now, you can join me in my decrepitude."

He got up from the table, came over to me, and slid his arms around my waist. "You're anything but." He kissed my neck and nibbled on my ear. "Amanda's gone for the day," he whispered. "Wanna go upstairs?"

"You *must* be feeling better. I thought you were going running." I turned around to face him and planted a soft kiss on his lips.

"This'll get my heart racing just the same."

Making love with my husband on a Sunday morning felt deliciously decadent, even if it was with the man I'd made love to approximately five thousand times, an estimate he'd come up with. He whispered, "Let's make it five thousand and one," as he slid his hand between my thighs. We knew each other's moves—there were few surprises—but knowing everything I could possibly know about Richard was my aphrodisiac. I still craved his touch, his warm breath on my skin, the scratch of his stubble on my neck. Each time we made love was an affirmation of our life together.

Afterward, we lay spooning in bed, naked at noon, the ceiling fan circling slowly overhead, scattering the scent of sex, of love, of commitment. It was now or never.

"Richard, I wanted to talk to you about something."

"Uh-oh. Not sure I like the sound of that."

I forced a laugh. "Don't you think we're a little young to be going through the empty-nest syndrome?"

"Ummm, yeah, I suppose."

"I've been thinking that maybe, if you wanted to, and if we could afford it, and if you didn't think it was a ridiculous idea..." I swallowed and cleared my throat.

"What is it?"

"What would you think about having another baby?" I asked.

I felt his arms stiffen around me.

"You know what? Now that I've said it out loud, I realize just how ridiculous it is. Forget it. I don't know what I was thinking."

He propped himself up on his elbow and focused on my face. "But all these years, you made it pretty damn clear you didn't want any more kids."

"I know, but I've been thinking maybe it was a mistake. I've been mulling this over for a while, and I can't remember ever wanting anything so badly... not since I was pregnant with Amanda."

"I mean, I was kidding with the decrepitude comment," he said, "but it has been eighteen years. It might not be so easy for you now."

I'd done an assignment about advanced maternal age pregnancies. When it came to having babies, a woman was considered over the hill at thirty-five. Funny, I didn't feel over the hill, especially at that moment, lying naked in bed with my husband.

When I didn't say anything, he continued. "You're really up for the heartburn, the nausea, the sleepless nights, running to the bathroom every fifteen minutes, followed by another eighteen-plus years of parenting?"

I rolled over to face him. "I am. But don't forget the other thing," I said as I ran my finger down the line of dark hair on his abdomen. After the morning sickness passed, I couldn't get enough of him, enough of us, right up until the day before I went into labor with Amanda.

He gave a quarter smile, but then it was gone. "We said we were going to travel." He let out an exasperated breath. "And what about early retirement—our plan to sell the store when the time came? Shit, Deb. Why didn't you want this ten or fifteen years ago?"

"I know I forced my decision on you. And now maybe it's too late—in more ways than one."

He lay back down, put his hand behind his head, and stared at the ceiling for a few seconds before turning to me again. "Can I at least think about it?"

I scanned his face for any sign of what he might be thinking. He hadn't said no. I felt hope taking hold. I wanted to yank it out by the roots before it dug in too deep. "You know," I said, "maybe we'll both decide it's a bad idea to start over with all that at this point in our lives."

"Yeah, maybe."

Chapter 12
Amanda

"You ready?" Graham whispered in my ear.

I shook my head. Given the choice, I preferred to take it slow. Just jumping in without thinking about the consequences was not my usual MO.

"Come on, Amanda."

"I'm not ready."

But Graham was insistent, a firm grip on my hand. He wanted me with him.

Contemplating the jump into the ice-cold spring, I spotted a group of supersized women in brightly colored one-piece swimsuits, lying on the grass, sunning themselves—a school of beached manatees. I looked back at the spring. The sun's rays were dancing on the crystal-clear water. It looked inviting but was deceptively cold.

"Don't chicken out on me," he said.

"Why can't we just get in a little at a time?"

"Nope. It's all or nothin'. You with me?"

"Yeah," I said, resigned to my fate. "I'm with you."

"One... two... three... Geronimo!" We took a running start and cannonballed into the frigid water. He never let go of my hand.

Gasping for air as I resurfaced, I croaked, "Oh God, I can't breathe! I seriously hate you right now!"

The red-faced lifeguard blew his whistle, pointing at us. "No cannonballing!" he yelled from the stand.

Graham was laughing when I yanked my hand away from his death grip and swam toward shore. "Amanda, wait! Where are you going? The worst is over."

Ignoring him, my heart pounding from the shock of the icy water, I reached the concrete stairs and took the first step to climb out, but Graham grabbed my ankle with the same insistent hold he'd had on my hand. I reached around and rearranged my bikini bottoms. Maybe Mom had been right about the suit being too small.

"What? You really mad?" His little-boy expression made it tough for me to stay irritated.

I shook my leg to wriggle free of him. "Let go!"

Instead of releasing his grip, he pulled himself closer and slid his hand farther up my leg. "Come on, Amanda. I'll be good. Scout's honor." And he held up the fingers of his other hand in a pledge.

I imagined him in Boy Scout khaki shorts, knee socks, and a sash of badges across the patches of blond hair on his chest, which made it impossible to stifle a chuckle. "I knew it was going to be cold. I just didn't realize how cold." I glanced at my arms and legs sheathed in goose bumps. Despite the sun beating down, rapidly evaporating the water droplets on my skin, my teeth chattered.

"Come back in. I'll keep you warm."

I relented. How could I not? He was just so freaking cute. "Okay, but if I go into cardiac arrest, it'll be your fault."

Smiling at me, he shook his head and held out his hand. Again, the arctic-like waters reached my waistline, and I took in short, shallow breaths. He, on the other hand, looked relaxed and at ease, like he was paddling in warm ocean waters.

"Come here," he said, pulling me close.

Skin to skin with him, I felt his body heat. "How come you're so warm?"

He leaned in to kiss me, and I wrapped my arms around his neck, kissed him back, and rested my head on his shoulder as we bobbed up and down in the water. In the beginning, I'd kept count. *This is the first time Graham kissed me. This is the third time... the tenth time.* After that, I figured, *Who cares?* As long as he kept it up, I was good. At least he wasn't pressuring me for sex—yet. Jack had begun his campaign to claim my virginity on day one. I couldn't help but wonder if Graham would eventually become like Jack, insisting he was going to explode—that his balls were turning a nasty shade of blue and he was going to die if I didn't let him.

Mom had given me *the talk* more than once. She'd mainly told me about the down-and-dirty logistics of it all and how to not get pregnant, which I already knew by that point. Well, most of it, anyway. And I certainly didn't want to be hearing that stuff from my mom. But the words from her last sex talk still rang in my ears. "Remember, Amanda, girls want to have sex to get close, but guys just want to get close to have sex." I hadn't fully understood just how desperate a guy could get, to the point of shamelessly begging. Sometimes, saying no to Jack felt like swatting a puppy on the nose for chewing up your favorite shoes—when it was just doing what came naturally—but then other times, it felt like being pinned down by a rabid dog.

But the thing was I was pretty sure I wouldn't be able to say no to Graham. In fact, I didn't want to say no to him. Not that he'd asked. But it was nerve-racking to think about... me naked, him naked, our bodies touching... *Like now...*

"Amanda, your heart's pounding. Maybe we should get out and sit in the sun for a while."

"Uh, sure."

We climbed out of the water and settled in side by side on our towels. I slipped on my sunglasses and propped myself up on my elbows. Turning my face skyward, I said, "The sun feels a hundred times better after a dip in that ice bucket."

"Told you." He took a breath. "You're not a big risk taker, are you?"

"I'm with you, aren't I?" I lifted my sunglasses and smiled at him. "I like to think I'm being smart. I mean, why put myself in situations I know I can't or don't want to deal with? Just because I don't fly around on a skateboard or bungee jump doesn't make me boring." *God,* I was channeling my mom.

"Whoa, I never said you were boring. And how did you know about the bungee jumping?"

"Just figures."

He shrugged. "So, you admit it was fun?"

I pursed my lips and frowned. "Well, yeah, but it was..." I stopped.

"It was what?"

"Nothing." *But it's because I was with you—that's what made it fun.*

"Listen," he said, "my folks want to have a thing for my twentieth birthday next week, and they want you to come."

"Whoa, you're already going to be twenty?"

"Well, yeah, twenty does come after nineteen." He laughed. "I know. I'm the world's oldest senior. Like I said, blame my mom."

I felt my eyes widen. "Wait, you've talked about me with your parents?"

"You sound shocked. Are we a secret?"

Well, yeah, kind of. The fact that he was twenty and I wasn't eighteen yet was definitely best kept a secret—from my parents, anyway.

"No, it's just... okay, so when is it exactly?"

"I think they have a barbecue planned for next Saturday—a vegan barbecue."

"A *vegan* barbecue? Isn't that like an oxymoron?"

He laughed. "You'll see. It's actually pretty good. They're hardcore vegans."

"And you are *so* not," I said, thinking back to the double bacon cheeseburger he'd scarfed down at lunch.

"Not a chance. But they're okay with it... sort of."

"So, I'm dating an older man. You better be careful. I'm jailbait, you know."

"Actually, in Texas it's only if you're under the age of seventeen," he recited.

I sat up straight and looked at him. "I know I'm going to be sorry I asked, but why the hell do you know that?"

"My dad's a lawyer—retired, but he was always full of legal trivia. Used to quiz me on legal shit at dinner. Still does sometimes." He laughed. "Plus, he drilled it into me with my last girlfriend. I was eighteen, and she wasn't seventeen yet."

"Oh."

He cocked an eyebrow, grinning. "Jealous?" He was enjoying the idea a little too much.

I shrugged.

His smile faded. "You wouldn't be if you met her."

What the hell was he talking about? Danielle was gorgeous. But I would be branded an online stalker if I admitted I'd looked her up that first night.

"Your dad's retired already?" Changing the subject was always a good tactic. "What, is he, like, super rich or something?"

"I wish. No, my folks are probably old enough to be your parents' parents. He retired, but then he opened a coffee shop downtown. Maybe you've heard of it? Urgent Café. Serves only sustainable coffee and organic stuff—vegan, of course."

"Your dad owns that place? Sweet."

"I'll take you there sometime." He took my hand, skimming his thumb across my knuckles, and he leaned over, and gave me a quick kiss before he lay back down and settled in for some sun time.

I looked over at him, thinking back to the night before, when his kisses had been fevered, almost frantic, his tongue tracing my neck, his hands exploring my body. My insides liquefied just thinking about it. He was so not the type of guy I ever pictured myself with. But each time he came close, held my hand, or barely brushed my lips with his, I quivered. At home, alone in my room, it was easy to convince myself that the two of us, as a couple, was a terrible idea.

Then he would call, and we'd talk until well after midnight about everything. And I knew. I just knew.

Chapter 13
Deb

The tension I had constructed, brick by brick, during the day fell away when Amanda finally wandered in just before five o'clock, sun-kissed and tired but happy. She bestowed a cursory greeting, grabbed some chips and a water bottle, and vanished into her room, where she stayed locked away for the next several hours. When I asked if she wanted to join Richard and me for homemade tacos, "No, I'm good" was her curt reply from behind a closed door. I returned to the dinner table and Richard's expectant expression. I shrugged.

"And you want to have another one?" He snorted.

Richard turned in early that night, Amanda never left her room, and after a few quiet hours of reading and watching Netflix, I checked the doors, turned out the lights, and headed upstairs to bed. As I passed Amanda's door, I heard the unmistakable lilt in her voice—she was talking to Graham.

THE NEXT EVENING, RICHARD had to work late, and I was nestled in the comfortably soft blue leather sofa—we'd owned it fifteen years and counting—in his ersatz office. I was opening up a new book when I felt Amanda's presence. She was leaning against the doorframe, regarding me with mock disdain.

"Why do you always do that?" she asked.

"Do what?"

"Turn to the end before you've read the book."

"You know I don't like surprises." I pushed my reading glasses to the top of my head. "Why does it bother you so much?"

"I just don't get it. That takes away all the fun."

I closed the book and held it against my chest. "I'll read my way, and you read yours."

"Whatever." Amanda clicked her tongue as she walked over to Richard's desk, a forced casual cadence to her step, and sat down in the chair.

"Looks like your redness from yesterday is turning into a tan," I said, trying to ease into a conversation Amanda clearly wanted to have.

"It would have been worse, but I put sunscreen on after a couple of hours." She started tracing the grain of the wood on the desk with her finger. "Graham doesn't burn. He just tans. It's so annoying."

She was talking about him with such familiarity, like I might say, "Richard likes his coffee sweet."

"Mom," she said, interrupting my musings.

"Yes?"

"Why didn't you tell me about Jess?"

I flinched, my mind scrambling to figure out whether Amanda was mad at me for not telling her or hurt that Jess hadn't confided in her beforehand. Maybe both were true. "I figured that was Jess's decision to tell you, not mine. How did you find out?"

"Jess called. I can't believe you didn't tell me. She said it was over a month ago."

"Is she okay?"

"She's fine. You know how Jess is." She shook her head and looked away.

"What did she say?"

Amanda sighed and stared down at her clasped hands in her lap. "She told me everything. Sounded really gross, but I think she wanted to talk to someone besides Aunt Merritt. Did you know she had to have an ultrasound, listen to a description of the fetus's development or something, then go home to 'think about it' and come back in twenty-four hours before she could get it done?"

"Merritt told me that was going to happen. It's required."

"They force you to do that? God, that sucks. I can't even imagine what that must be like. I mean, if you never see it, it's not so real." She shook her head again as if to clear her thoughts. "And there were protestors yelling at her when she walked by, shoving pictures of dead, bloody babies in her face." She stopped talking, her brows furrowed in thought. "Mom?"

"Yeah?"

She looked straight at me, daring me to tell the truth. "Did you ever get an abortion?"

Taken aback by my daughter's sudden frankness on a subject she had long since declared off-limits, I set the book down in my lap and took a deep breath.

"Mom, I'm almost eighteen. I can deal with it if you did."

I hesitated. "No, Amanda, I never had an abortion." The truth monitor in my brain zigzagged off the charts.

She stopped, clearly thinking things through before speaking. "How come you and Dad never had more kids?"

Ah, the question I was asking myself. I sighed. "Well, I was just so happy when you got here..."

Amanda rolled her eyes.

"... that I decided I wanted to devote all my time and attention to you. You know how my huge, crazy family is—scattered, unfocused. I wanted to give you my undivided attention."

"Well, you did that." She snorted. "But sometimes, I wish I had a sister, like you've got Aunt Merritt."

I felt my heart contract. There were some decisions you could never reverse. This was as good a time as any—probably better than most—to broach the subject.

"Well, since you've brought it up, I was wondering... um... what would you think if... I mean, would you think it was weird if... well, I know you're going to think it's weird, but I wanted to gauge your reaction to..."

"Jeez, Mom, spit it out." She laughed.

"Okay. What would you think if we had another baby?"

She looked confused. "Who?"

Now it was my turn to roll my eyes. "Me and Dad."

"Seriously? Aren't you, like, too old?"

"Amanda, I'm only thirty-nine, and everything still works."

"Ewww, Mom!" She stood silent for a few seconds before turning on her heel and heading for the door.

So much for being frank. I had no intention of doubling down and asking the question again. After all, I hadn't even gotten an answer from Richard yet. I slumped back into the sofa and opened my book again.

"G'night," she said.

"Good night, sweetie."

Well, that was a train wreck and a half. Amanda's reaction made me realize that just because I could get pregnant didn't mean I should. And truth be told, I was almost as relieved as I was disappointed by her lack of a response. *Anyway, should my seventeen-year-old daughter have veto power over my life?* Then I thought of Richard. He might have already decided it was a go, and if I knew my husband, his head would be filled with sticky-note plans. I wiped my eyes on the sleeve of my robe, took a deep breath, and stared at page one of my book.

"Mom?"

Startled, I jerked my head up. "You scared me. I thought you went to bed."

"Look, I'm sorry. I don't know, maybe it would be kind of cool to have a baby brother or sister. Weird but kinda cool."

"Nothing's been decided yet, but I appreciate it."

Amanda nodded and left. I listened to the creak of the stairs and then her footsteps overhead in her bedroom. I returned to the last few pages of my book to read the happily-ever-after ending.

Chapter 14
Amanda

S*enior year. Not quite living up to the hype.* My mind wasn't on whatever Rockin' Roi was droning on about in class. Instead, I replayed the conversation with my mom until two in the morning, when I finally crawled into bed and turned out the lights. Even then, I couldn't get the thought out of my head. *A baby? Okay, she isn't that old. Stephanie's mom had twins last year, and she was forty-three.*

The idea of having a baby in the family didn't seem too strange. In fact, it was kind of cool. Maybe Graham and I would take her to the park, to the petting zoo, to get ice cream or a snow cone. My daydream drifted to Graham and me getting married, having kids of our own. Okay, so I was really jumping the gun, but the image of the two of us together for always was completely in focus, the colors sharp and defined.

I was smiling to myself when Mr. Roi jarred me from my thoughts. "So, Ms. Earle, how would you work this equation?" His words swirled around the fluorescent lights in the ceiling before raining down on my head.

"I'm sorry, what was the question?" I felt my face redden as all eyes turned to me.

"Pay attention," he said before turning to Claire, who was frantically waving her hand in the air.

I nodded, more aware than ever that I had to snap out of it.

At lunch, I swam upstream through the throngs to the common area outside, where I sat on the last empty bench, enjoying the warmth of the sun—a fabulous sensation after sitting in air-conditioned classrooms that always overcompensated for the Texas heat. While I waited for Hadley, I caught scraps of conversations.

"Can you believe she said that?"

"I hate that fucking bitch."

"He finally asked me out!"

"You should have kicked him in the balls."

"I got so wasted last night."

My stomach growled. I scanned the area for Hadley, but my eyes landed on Jack ducking through the door. He let it slam behind him as he reached into his pocket for his sunglasses. I opened my book as a shield, faking intense concentration. His size 13 Nikes on the brown patchy grass entered my field of vision.

"Amanda."

I looked up. His expression had softened considerably since our last encounter on the front steps of the school, but the air suddenly felt like a furnace set on Hades high.

"I thought maybe, uh, you know, we could talk or something?"

I sighed. "Seriously? Just go away, Jack."

"So, you're seeing someone else now?" he asked through clenched teeth.

"Not that it's any of your business, but yeah."

He sat down beside me, our thighs touching. I scooted away. His incredible sense of entitlement was something I hadn't picked up on when we first got together.

"Hadley's going to be here soon, and I'd like to eat my lunch in peace."

"Come on. Shit, don't be like that. I still don't understand what I did for you to fucking dump me like that." He was whispering, glancing around for eavesdroppers.

"What do you want me to say? We're done. Now, please, go away."

He frowned, the anger and frustration spreading on his face. "Are you fucking him?" he growled.

"Jack! God, you're disgusting."

"You are, aren't you?" He stiffened and tightly crossed his arms. He had that expression—the one I hadn't told anyone about, not even Hadley. The one that had made me end it.

"Well, if it isn't my good friend, Jack Off," Hadley snarked as she settled in next to me.

Hadley knew precisely where all of Jack's buttons were located, and she frantically pushed them like a kid in an elevator, excited to see what would happen.

"Fuck off. This is none of your business."

"You're such a charmer, Jack. I have a great idea. Why don't you go to the little boys' room and—you know, live up to your name. It'll calm you down. Whaddaya say?"

He stood up and took one long step to where Hadley was calmly spreading her lunch on the table. "I'm warning you, bitch."

I could see this easily turning into a brawl. Campus security would come running, there would be suspensions, parents would be called, and Jack would be pulled from the basketball team, his precious MVP trophy removed from the display case. I wanted him to leave me alone, but I didn't want to ruin his life.

Hadley pushed her lunch farther back on the table and stood up to face him. Her five-eleven frame could be intimidating, but Jack was six-three, one of the tallest boys in the senior class.

"Or you'll do what?" she said, inching closer. "Hit me? I dare you, bitch boy."

Jack was seething, and Hadley wasn't backing down. Not that she ever did. He balled his fists. *Did Jack ever hit a girl?* The thought made me sick with anxiety. I spotted the police officer who routinely patrolled the campus.

Jack followed my gaze. Unclenching his fists, he was backing down, refusing to look at Hadley, accept her challenge, or erase the scowl on his face. He glanced at me instead and, barely moving his lips, growled, "We're not done yet."

He stomped off, and Hadley turned to me and shrugged. "What a wuss." She was reveling in her victory, but my insides were churning.

WHEN THE DAY FINALLY ended, Hadley gave me a ride home, and as we pulled into my driveway, the last person I wanted to see was parked at the curb, leaning against his shiny black Lexus. Jack.

"What's his fucking problem?" Hadley shouted, the veins in her forehead popping out. "That's it. I'm going to straighten him out once and for all." She reached for the door handle.

I grabbed her arm. "Don't. It'll just make it worse. He's not going to take it seriously unless I'm the one to convince him to leave me alone."

'You sure? This is fucking stalkerish behavior."

"I'm sure."

"You want me to stay... just in case?" she asked.

"No, I'll be fine. Anyway, Graham should be here soon. Pick me up tomorrow?"

"Yeah, but call me after Jack Off leaves, and let me know what happened."

"Will do." Still weak-kneed from my earlier confrontation with Jack and filled with a dark sense of dread, I stepped out of the car and strode over to him.

He cocked his head. "Mandy," he crooned.

What the hell is going on in that head of his? Is he expecting me to fall into his arms, sob, and say all is forgiven?

He picked up where he had left off earlier in the day. "Look, to-day didn't go the way I planned. And your bitchy friend, Hadley, wasn't helping matters." He nodded in Hadley's direction as she backed out of the driveway, shoved her arm out the window, and shot him the finger.

"Well, you're not winning any points by calling my best friend a bitch."

"I know." He sighed. "I keep screwing up and apologizing, and you keep knocking me down. But this time, it's just you and me, and I'm telling you I'm sorry for the way I acted today. For everything."

If someone were just walking in on this conversation for the first time, they'd think, *Aw, give the guy a break. He seems so sorry.* Yeah, he was sorry all right—a sorry excuse for a boyfriend.

"Okay, you're sorry. Fine. Now, can we *please* be done?"

"I thought we were good together, you know? I mean, what the hell could you have in common with that fucking dreadlocked dude from Greystone?"

"Jack, I don't know how many more ways I can say it. There's no more 'we.' I'm with Graham now." I looked him in the eye, daring him to react, to retaliate while standing in my front yard. I gritted my teeth and hissed, "Just leave me the hell alone. I don't want you."

I stepped back, creating a safe space between us, and, as I did, he stepped forward, grabbed my wrist with a hand that could span half the circumference of a basketball, and yanked me in. My body slammed against his, and my backpack slipped from my hand. "Jack! Let go of me!"

I was trying to break free from his viselike grip when Graham's car silently glided into the driveway. He jumped out, sprinted toward us, and pulled me away. Jack looked too surprised to react.

"Hey, asswipe, what the fuck do you think you're doing?" Graham turned to me. "You okay?"

My wrist was on fire, and my heart was about to leap out of my chest. I trembled, willing myself not to hyperventilate. "I'm fine."

Graham protectively put his arm around my shoulders. "What the hell is going on?" he demanded, looking back and forth between Jack and me.

"Nothing," Jack said. "Amanda and I were just talking."

"You know this guy?" Graham asked, nodding in Jack's direction but looking at me.

I felt sick, embarrassed. "This is Jack."

"Well, Jack," he said, "I think you're done here."

It was like watching a standoff between a pit bull and a greyhound. The greyhound might have had the height advantage, but unless he made a run for it, my money was on the pit bull.

My mother stepped out onto the porch to get the mail.

"Hi, Ms. Earle," Jack yelled, waving enthusiastically in her direction, his face taking on an all-American-boy look. "How are you? And Mr. Earle?"

"We're fine, Jack. And you?"

"Great. Everything's great. I just came by to say hi to Amanda, but I can see she's busy, so I'll just take off. Good to see you again." He turned his back to my mother and shot Graham a caustic look before folding himself into his car and driving away.

Mom frowned in Graham's direction before going back inside.

"What the fuck was that? Did he hurt you?" Graham asked, looking at me with a combination of concern, curiosity and... a healthy dose of jealousy.

"Jack's just being... Jack. Don't worry about it."

"He grabbed you, and I saw the look on his face."

I met his gaze. "He wants to get back together."

He stepped back, and his eyebrows shot up in surprise. "Is that what you want?"

"Seriously? No and hell no. He's an asshole, but he puts on this good-guy act. You saw how he was with my mom. She thinks he's awesome," I said, shaking my head.

"I know the type. Just steer clear of him."

"It's not so easy. I see him every day at school. He was waiting here when Hadley and I pulled up."

"Okay, then, let me take you home after class from now on. Won't take me but maybe twenty minutes to get there from my place. You can wait in the office."

"Graham, really, you're making too big of a deal out of this."

He turned his head in the direction Jack had driven. "No," he stated flatly. "No, I'm not."

The next day, Jack started rumors that I was a nymphomaniac, a lesbian, a cruel tease, an ice queen. Clearly, he couldn't make up his mind which one put him in the best light.

Chapter 15
Deb

It was ten thirty, and Merritt hadn't called. I picked up my cell and dialed her number. "Merritt?"

"Hey," she said, her voice flat.

"You okay?"

"Fine."

I waited for more, but all I heard was Merritt's breathing on the other end of the line.

"Is Jess okay? Amanda said she talked to her a while ago, and she seemed to be doing well."

"Uh-huh."

Merritt wasn't a crier. Not at graduations, not at weddings, not when any of her kids left for college, not even at Ryan's or our mother's funeral. She always held it in and helped everyone else wade through their sadness, throwing them a life preserver so they didn't drown in their own grief. So when she burst into pitiful sobs, I felt as if a moving sidewalk had suddenly stopped, pitching me forward to land flat on my face.

"Oh, hon, what is it? What's wrong?"

"I just couldn't bring myself to tell you before now, but she had to look at the sonogram." She blew her nose. "I was with her the whole time."

"I know. It's just so awful. Amanda was just telling me about how—"

"Deb... it was twins."

I NUMBLY STARED AT the computer screen for over an hour, my hands hovering over the keyboard, the cursor taunting me. *Twins?* Was fate flicking Merritt in the face? Or was it taunting me? I couldn't forget the well of depression that Merritt had fallen into when Ray died. As close as Merritt and I were, I couldn't possibly put myself in my sister's place and know what it felt like to lose a twin. Merritt and Ray had been best friends, but he'd lied to her—a grisly lie of omission.

I rolled the chair back to the file cabinet and grabbed the lighter and the last cigarette in the soft pack. After crumpling the empty and tossing it in the trash, I pushed myself over to the window, opened it wide, and took a breath of the hot, humid air thick with the sweet scent of freshly mown grass. I glanced up and down the street. Miss Gibson from three houses down was pulling her two basset hounds, Rocky and Bullwinkle. She never missed a day of walking her dogs—in the rain, sleet, cold, or blazing heat. But whatever the weather, she always looked so sad, a dark cloud hovering over her. Then there were the Kennedys next door. The family of five pulling into their garage heralded a hurricane of activity. Were they happy or just staying busy to stave off sadness? And then there was Mr. Krantz, the widower across the street. He'd lived there for the same fifteen years that Richard and I had lived in our house. Before his wife died, I used to watch them work in the yard together, turning over the soil, planting pansies, zinnias, and hydrangeas. Sometimes, when the wind shifted just right, I would catch a whiff of gardenia. But the garden now reeked of neglect. Watching them go about their lives as if everything were fine always made me wonder how they compartmentalized their emotions to minimize the impact. I had a black belt in compartmentalization, but every once in a while a door would unexpectedly burst open, leaving me defenseless.

I lit the cigarette, took a long drag, and listened for the distinctive crackle. I held it out the window, watching the embers brighten and the smoke drift away. I rested my chin in the palm of my other hand as my mind darted darkly from one thought to the next. Jess's situation created a stinging, in-your-face irony for Merritt. And for me. If Richard and I were going to move forward with baby plans, time was in short supply. And then my mind jumped to Amanda. My spidey sense told me something was seriously wrong with the scene I had witnessed of Amanda, Jack, and Graham standing at the curb. Amanda looked upset. No, she looked scared. Jack had seemed fine, but Graham was pissed off. Really pissed off. Was Amanda afraid of Graham?

"Deb?"

I flung the cigarette out the window and swung around to face Richard. "What are you doing home?"

"I feel like crap. I'm going to lie down," he said. I rose from the chair, but he shook his head and held his palm out to stop me before I could speak. "I know what you're going to say. No doctors. I'm fine. I just need to rest." He shuffled toward the bedroom but then came back and leaned into the room. "You know that your 'secret' smoking is not really a secret, right?"

Chapter 16

Amanda

"Amanda, I'm so glad you could make it for Graham's birthday," his mom said, the scent of sandalwood wafting from the open door.

She was exactly like Graham had described—her silver hair cropped close to her head, slim, dressed in distressed jeans and a peasant blouse embroidered with red and yellow roses. *And she's, um, braless.* She looked every bit her age, but her fluid movements made her seem a lot younger.

"I'm Navy."

If Graham hadn't already mentioned his mother's name, I would have been stumped.

Navy's softly lined hands enveloped mine. "Graham's out back with Cade. Come, he's anxious to meet you."

The decor was nothing like my house, where everything was uniform, coordinated, purposeful. Graham's house was eclectic with a garage-sale vibe. The house was undeniably warm and inviting. Like Graham. In the corner stood a three-foot-tall black-and-brown urn that looked like something from an archeological dig. A cross-sectioned tree trunk served as a coffee table. On top sat a crystal ball nestled in a black wooden stand and a small African sculpture of a man holding a woman, and they were...

I quickly looked away. I picked up my pace and followed Navy to the glass sliding door that led to the backyard dotted with batches of wildflowers and a barrier of barely contained bamboo plants. The mouthwatering smells of the grill replaced the scent of sandalwood.

"Amanda!" Graham rushed to me and cradled my face in his hands, greeting me with a lingering kiss. Mortified, I glanced in the direction of his parents, waiting for shock and reprisal, but they simply smiled.

Graham slipped his arm around my shoulders. "You met my mom. This is my dad, Cade. Cade, this is Amanda."

Did he just call his dad Cade? "Nice to meet you, Mr. Scott."

"Mr. Scott?" He dismissed my words with a wave of his spatula-wielding hand. "It's Cade and Navy," he said, nodding in his wife's direction.

Standing guard over the grill, his dad was dressed in khaki shorts, a T-shirt that read Planet Over Profit, and flip-flops, his hair pulled back in a ponytail that emphasized his receding hair line. Graham's parents were a matched set except for their height. Navy was almost as tall as Hadley, but Cade was an inch shorter than Graham. Instead of reaching out to give me a crushing handshake, as Daddy would surely have done with Graham, he came over and gave me a crushing hug.

"Graham's been talking about you nonstop," Cade said.

I shot a glance at Graham, and he pulled me closer. I would never have been comfortable with PDA around my parents, but Graham clearly felt like he could act the way he did when it was just the two of us. Well, almost the same.

"Amanda, how would you like to see pictures of Graham as a kid?"

"Navy, seriously?" Graham rolled his eyes. "Already dragging out the photo album?"

"No... just the ones in the hall."

"Oh man... okay, Amanda. If you decide to slip out the front door, I get it."

"No way," I mouthed over my shoulder as Navy led me back into the house.

Standing at the bottom of the stairs, I glanced up at the walls zigzagged with framed family photos. There were snapshots of Navy and Cade with lots more hair and a lot fewer wrinkles, probably not much older than Graham was now. A row of photos had them standing underneath the Eiffel Tower, in front of the Taj Mahal, on a beach in Thailand, in Dubai, Morocco, Tunisia.

Navy pointed at another row of photos. "These are from when we were in the Peace Corps."

I leaned in to get a better look and glanced at Navy as she placed her hand over her heart. "You were in the Peace Corps? Wow, that's amazing."

"I found out I was pregnant with Graham while we were in Niger. It was unexpected, to say the least."

"I'm not even sure where Niger is."

"You're not the only one—believe me. It's in West Africa. So much turmoil, violence, and starvation." She ran her fingers over the photo and sighed. "Anyway, when we found out I was pregnant, we returned to Iowa, and a couple of years later, we moved to Austin." She hesitated. "Peace Corps activities in Niger were suspended in 2011. That's when they would have needed our help the most." She never took her eyes off the photo. "I always felt like I abandoned the children of Niger, putting my own child's safety first. But we just couldn't subject Graham to such conditions. It was a choice we made." She shook her head and hugged herself as if to ward off a chill. "Privileged selfishness, I know."

I couldn't look away from the photo of a skeletal child with big brown eyes, sitting on Navy's lap, resting his head on her shoulder.

Navy moved up a step, and her voice lightened. "And here is Graham as a baby," she said, full of the kind of pride that mortified me when it came from my own mother. "He was just learning to walk in this one. Oh, and this is my favorite." It was a picture of Graham as a toddler, sitting on a plastic potty chair, his pants down around his ankles, giving the thumbs-up, smiling the same slanted, joyful smile I knew well. "Once those days are gone, you can never get them back, you know?"

The little blond boy perched proudly on his throne was a Graham I could never know. Only these photos and embellished tales from his parents could introduce that boy to me. The images brought into focus for the first time the reality of Jessica's decision. I would never get to know Jessica's baby—no one would.

When we reached the last photo, Navy bowed. "And that ends our tour of the Graham Scott Gallery."

"Oh man, I am so going to torture him over that potty chair picture." I chuckled.

"I'd be disappointed if you didn't."

"Navy!" It was Cade's booming voice. "Can you bring the plates and silverware?"

We returned to the kitchen, where Navy opened a drawer and handed me four square plates.

"These are really cool, and they're so light," I said.

"They're constructed from palm leaves that fall to the ground," she explained. "They're disposable, biodegradable, and compostable. Plus," she said as she leaned in to whisper, "I don't have to wash dishes."

I glanced around the kitchen. "No dishwasher?"

"Bad for the environment. Uses way too much water. And there aren't any really good dishwasher detergents that will clean and not pollute. Anyway, it's just the two of us most of the time, and Cade helps."

I figured my mother would sink into a deep depression if the dishwasher broke. And I couldn't see Daddy washing dishes.

Once the table was set, Cade turned off the grill, and the four of us sat down at the picnic table—made from recycled tires in New Jersey, he explained.

I examined the food on my plate before taking a taste. I wasn't too sure about the stuff that smelled like licorice, but the grilled tofu with homemade BBQ sauce, the squash, the eggplant, and the potatoes with rosemary were great.

"So, have you always lived in Austin?" Cade asked.

"Yeah, I was born here."

"Where are your parents from?"

I laughed. "Austin. They went to UT. That's where they met."

"Unicorns!" Navy said. "Native Austinites."

So, this was the getting-to-know-you portion of the meal. I'd gone to Jack's for dinner a couple of times. The table was set like they were expecting a head of state, and his parents' questions made me feel like I was being interrogated by the CIA. I barely touched the elaborate meal they served. But Graham's parents weren't demanding answers—they were handing me a handwritten invitation to a conversation. They asked what I was going to study.

"Photography and journalism."

"Ah, maybe you'll get to travel," Cade said, spreading his arms as if offering the world to me.

"I hope so. I've never been out of the country. Don't even have a passport."

"Well, if you get the chance, it changes the way you see the world. It'll change your life. Your future." Navy smiled warmly at Graham.

I set down my fork and looked at him. "So, you've traveled out of the country?"

Graham shrugged. "Yeah, a few times."

"Don't listen to him. He's a world traveler, since he was a baby. We took him with us all over Europe, Asia, the Middle East."

Graham wore his experiences like a comfortable T-shirt, one that I was dying to try on and hoping would fit.

"Graham says he's been introducing you to skateboarding." Cade dug into the same thing on his plate that I couldn't identify on mine. He reached across the table for the sea-salt shaker, revealing the edges of a faded tattoo on his forearm.

"Yeah, it's pretty wild," I said.

"Did you get to meet Rocket? Gets crazy on that board." Cade shook his head and laughed, his ponytail swishing from side to side. "But it sure looks like skateboarding may be the answer to his situation."

"Um... his situation?"

Graham and Cade exchanged a look.

"Oh, sorry. I thought... never mind."

As the meal wound down, Graham cleared the table, and Navy and Cade retreated to the kitchen to wash the silverware and glasses. Graham pointed at my plate. "You don't like fennel?"

"Oh, is that what that was?" I shuddered.

"That bad, huh? I guess it's kind of an acquired taste. You'll get used to it."

We gathered the plates, and I followed him to the compost bin on the side of the house. When he opened the lid, I recoiled. "What do you do with this stuff?"

"Once the weather cools, we'll plant a garden in the back"—he nodded toward the bamboo border—"and use this shit for fertilizer." He took my hand and placed it on the side of the bin. "Feel how hot it is?"

I jerked my hand back. "Wow, that's so weird."

"It can get up to one hundred thirty degrees. But if you don't tend to it, it can cool down, and it'll just be a bin of shitty-smelling garbage."

"We got a composting bin from the city, but my dad refuses to use it. Too messy, and he thinks it would attract flies and rats."

"Really? We've never had a problem, but you never know."

When we came back in the house, Navy and Cade were standing at the sink, talking softly. Graham took me by the hand. "We're going up to my room."

"Okay, hon. We're going for a walk." Navy dried her hands and neatly folded the dish towel on the counter.

I stood, stunned. My parents would have freaked out if I'd asked to bring a guy up to my room, and they would never, ever have left us alone in the house. Peace Corps volunteering, composting, all-natural vegan, permissive parents—Navy and Cade existed in some kind of alternate universe from my parents. I couldn't imagine any scenario that had them all sitting down over free-trade coffee and getting to know one another.

I held back as Graham opened the door to his bedroom. Jack and I had a few make-out sessions in his bedroom, but the door was always open, his parents were always downstairs, and they were always unusually quiet. I was sure they were listening, prepared to barge in if it sounded like things had gone too far. I lacked the pedigree they expected for Jack, and the very last thing they would have wanted was the product of careless breeding. They didn't have to worry, since I wasn't going to hook up with Jack, no matter how much he begged.

Graham closed the door behind me, sat on the bed, and patted the spot next to him.

I scanned the area. "So, this is your room," I said, immediately aware of how stupid that sounded. The walls were dark chocolate, almost black. Posters of skateboarders poised as if they might crash to earth any second lined one, and his well-scuffed skateboard rested on the floor beneath them. A beat-up Deer Crossing sign sat in the corner. A few magazines and textbooks lay on a desk with his open laptop. There was none of the boy mess I had expected. Or the sweaty boy smell. Instead, the room carried the scent of floral air freshener. He had set the stage.

"Amanda." He patted the bed again.

I ambled over and sat down, taking in the warmth of his bare arm, the thatch of blond hair tickling my skin. I glanced down as he slowly interlaced his fingers with mine. His touch triggered a muscle memory of other nights—of breathing him in and never wanting to stop. I wanted that again. I leaned in and pressed my lips against his.

He pulled me to the center of the bed. "I'm glad you're here," he said, as he peppered my neck with kisses, and his hand gradually slid under my sundress. He stopped midthigh and whispered, "Is this okay?"

I nodded, and my breath hitched as his fingers slowly made their way up. A sudden knock on the door made my heart beat even harder. I pushed Graham off and sat straight up.

"Wait! Wait a minute," Graham yelled.

I straightened my hair and clothes and scrambled to the edge of the bed while Graham stood up, rearranged himself, and sat back down.

"It's just me, dude," Rocket said as he walked in.

He took in the scene. "Oh, wow, dude. Sorry. Shit. No one was here, so I just used my key."

Graham cleared his throat. "Rocket, you remember Amanda?"

I couldn't help but laugh when the blush on his freckled face looked every bit as crimson as mine felt.

He raised one hand. "Hey, Amanda." Then he shoved both hands into his pockets.

"You staying here tonight?" Graham asked.

"Yeah. I'll put my stuff away and just go downstairs to get something to eat. So... I guess I'll catch you later." Rocket skittered out of the room and closed the door.

I turned to Graham. "He just walks into your house like that?"

He sighed. "Whenever it gets really bad at his house, which is a lot, he sleeps here. Been doing it since, like, third grade. He has his own key."

"So that's what your dad meant about 'his situation'?"

"Yeah. Man, he deserves a fucking break," he said, staring at the closed door. He pulled me in for a kiss before leading me back downstairs. Clearly, that was all he was going to say on the subject.

Chapter 17
Deb

"HOW WAS DINNER AT GRAHAM'S last night?" I asked, knowing I might be venturing into treacherous mother-daughter territory.

Amanda stopped, the toasted bagel hanging midair between the plate and her mouth. "It was a barbecue." She flashed a bland smile, giving nothing away, and slathered on more cream cheese before taking a bite.

"Well, what are his parents like? Are they nice?"

It was quite a trick, the way Amanda managed to let out an exasperated sigh while chewing and swallowing. "Yeah, they're super nice, actually."

I wasn't going to let my daughter so easily slip into the someone-I-used-to-know category. I pulled up a chair and sat across the table from her. "Sweetie, I'm just interested. I would be asking the same questions of... well, anyone who was telling me about someone they just met."

Amanda finally looked up, cream cheese smeared across her upper lip. "Yeah, I know."

"So?" I asked.

Amanda set her bagel down, sat up straighter, wiped her mouth with a napkin, and smiled—really smiled. "Well, they're very cool, like, aging-hippies cool. They're a lot older than you and Daddy, and they served in the Peace Corps in Africa before Graham was born. They've traveled all over the world. They have pictures from Europe, Asia, India." Amanda stopped and took a breath. "And their house is… I don't know, it's hard to describe. It's full of awesome souvenirs from all the places they've been. Oh, and they're vegan."

"A vegan barbecue?"

"Yeah, it's a lot better than it sounds." She paused. "Except for the fennel." Amanda curled her lip.

I chuckled. "Not my favorite vegetable either."

"I didn't even know it was a vegetable," she said. We both laughed, and I appreciated the moment for what it was.

"Navy showed me pictures of Graham when he was a baby."

"Navy? Is that a nickname?"

"That's his mom's real name. Kind of awesome, don't you think? And guess what? Graham calls his parents Navy and Cade."

"So, what do *Navy and Cade* do?" My question came out tinged with unintended attitude.

If Amanda picked up on it, she gave no indication. "I think they're kind of retired. His dad was an environmental lawyer. Now they own a vegan coffee shop downtown—Urgent Café."

I opened my mouth to ask another question, but Amanda shook her head. "Can I eat my cold bagel now?"

I was itching to ask more, but the bagel wasn't the only thing that had gone cold. Amanda finished her breakfast in a chilly silence then jumped up, leaving her plate and half-empty coffee mug on the table. I started to call her back to clean off her place, but then I thought, *Pick your battles, Deb*. I stood up, collected the dishes, rinsed them and put them in the dishwasher, and stuck the cream cheese back in the refrigerator.

"Morning." Richard was standing in the kitchen doorway.

"How are you feeling? You look better."

"Yeah, I slept like the dead last night." He glanced at the coffee maker.

"Sit, I'll pour you a cup."

"And can you get me my supplements?"

I always felt empathy for Richard's efforts to stay on top of his health. He'd watched his father slowly weaken, gradually robbed of his sight, his ability to walk, and eventually even to speak coherently until he died from complications of multiple sclerosis. Richard was only sixteen, younger than Amanda. Ever since, he'd been running as fast as he could to escape the clutches of the disease, uncertain if or when it would eventually catch up and destroy him. It wasn't as if I never worried about him, but I always put his complaints in the context of his mild hypochondria. If I pressed the panic button each time he had an ache or a pain, I would have gone crazy. He worried enough for both of us.

I handed him his supplements along with a cup of coffee and watched him check for the level of sweetness.

"Mmm. I needed that."

I leaned back against the kitchen counter and took a sip of my own coffee along with a prenatal vitamin that I'd started taking on the sly. *Just in case.* "Amanda had dinner over at Graham's house last night. Correction, she had a vegan barbecue over at Graham's house."

He stopped midsip. "A what?"

I laughed. "A vegan barbecue. Evidently, his parents are vegans."

"I tried the vegan thing when I was in college, but it was way too hard." He shook his head.

"Really? I don't remember that."

"It was a short-lived effort." He chuckled.

Amanda rushed in, already dressed. "Morning, Daddy." She kissed his cheek.

"There's my beautiful girl." He took another sip of coffee along with a couple of capsules. "I hear you were treated to a vegan barbecue last night."

His comment lacked the incredulous tone of his inquiry just seconds before. Richard and Amanda always put their best versions of themselves forward for one another. Their relationship was pure, unadulterated by a collection of messy truths.

"We seem to be passing ships," he said. "How about we have a Daddy's Day sometime this week?"

"Yesss!" Amanda pumped her fist in the air. Her unbridled enthusiasm came from the knowledge that, during their time together, Richard would spoil her rotten and say yes to every request.

When Amanda was in grade school, Richard had been hunkered down at the sporting-goods store from dawn to well past her bedtime as he worked to get it off the ground. He felt like he was missing out on her childhood, so he would set aside time for just the two of them to go out. It was always the restaurant of her choice, which had evolved from Chuck E. Cheese's to Hopdoddy's, a hip burger spot downtown. She'd dubbed their time together Daddy's Day.

Amanda wandered over to the sink and craned her neck toward the window. "Look at that!" she said, pointing at the backyard. "It's an albino squirrel! Looks like a stuffed toy—or a ghost."

The three of us gathered at the window and watched the mutated squirrel doing the things that squirrels do. "Wow, I wonder how unusual that is," Richard said.

I didn't know, but I was acutely aware of how unusual it had become for the three of us to be so close, sharing. Times like this would soon be coming to an end.

The Volvo horn blasted, and Amanda wrapped her arms around Richard's neck before coming to me and brushing my cheek with a kiss. "Going with Graham after school," she yelled as she rushed out the door. It seemed like she was always rushing to get away. My eyes lingered on the invisible trail she left behind.

"So," Richard said, pulling my attention away from Amanda's departure. "I've been thinking."

I sat down at the table with him, my hands caressing the coffee cup. "About what?"

"You know. The baby thing."

My heartbeat quickened. In the most together voice I could muster, I said, "And?"

"You know I always wanted more kids..."

The sun shone a little brighter through the kitchen window, the coffee tasted richer, and a surge of excitement filled my heart. I already felt a spark of maternal love for this child that had yet to be conceived.

"But, Deb, I have to tell you, I feel like it's too late."

I was stunned. I didn't have to check a mirror to know my face had fallen. I felt foolish.

He looked at me from across the table. "I'm sorry, babe."

"You're sorry?" I dropped another spoonful of sugar into my coffee, sugar I didn't need or want. "That's it? End of discussion?"

"Deb, have you actually done the math—how old we'd be when a kid would graduate, how long we'd have to work? I don't think that's something either of us wants to do."

"You mean it's not what *you* want."

"Deb, you're not looking at this logically. You've let your emotions take over."

I slapped my palm on the table and leaned into him. "Oh, so I'm just being an emotional woman?" I leaned back in my chair and tightly crossed my arms. "Seriously, Richard? Seriously?" It felt like I'd just proven his point.

"Deb, if this was fifteen—even ten—years ago, you know I would have been on board one hundred percent." He stood up, took two long strides to the sink, and plopped his coffee mug in. "Anyway, what happened to your nonnegotiable rule all these years, insisting that Amanda be an 'only'? A rule that you reminded me of on more than one occasion, I might add."

"Amanda will be away at college. She's going to start living her life. I'll have the time and the energy for another child. It would be like having another 'only.'"

He leaned his hip on the edge of the sink and ran his hand through his hair. I spotted a strand of gray lit by the sun, as if to emphasize his argument. Looking at the floor, instead of me, he said, "It's a hard no for me."

"But..." My voice cracked. "Richard, this is something I really want." I almost said it was something I needed, but that would have sounded even more irrational and desperate.

"I get that." His tone had shifted to one of irritation as he looked up at me. "But when will it be *our* time? Deb, this is as much my decision as it is yours. You made the decision a long time ago not to have any more children. Now it's my turn to say no."

"But I'm the one who'll be at home with a baby!" I'd matched his tone and raised the volume a turn or two.

"And you'll need to take some time off, just like you did with Amanda. And where's that money going to come from?"

"We've got savings," I said.

"For Amanda's college and for our retirement, which is at least twenty years away as it is. If we had another one, I'll be selling basketballs until I'm seventy-five years old. I'm sorry, Deb. I'm just not up for that. "

"But—"

"I'm not going to change my mind."

"What if—"

He pushed off from the sink, took two long steps to the door, and hesitated but didn't turn around. Then he was gone, and I was left bereft, desperately wanting something that he'd made crystal clear I would never have.

Chapter 18
Amanda

While I was waiting for Graham to pick me up, my butt had become numb from sitting in the hard plastic chair in the school office. I glanced at the pale-green walls that really needed painting and the school calendar announcing that it was, in fact, still August, and listened to the shuffle of papers. I crossed and uncrossed my legs and shifted in my seat, trying to get comfortable. I looked at my phone again, compulsively checking the time as if it were a Magic 8-Ball that would eventually say, *All signs point to yes.* I chided myself to stop. But then I pressed the button again, and the screen lit up—only three minutes had passed. The stampede of students in the hallway, vying for position to get the hell out of there, sounded like a cackle of hyenas busting loose from a circus train run off the rails. Jack was likely leading the stampede.

The double doors to the school office suddenly swung open and banged hard against the trophy case, rattling the awards inside. I jerked my head around too fast, and a burst of heat flashed through my neck. It wasn't Jack, thank God, but it was the next worst thing—his little sister, Janette. She adored her brother and had developed a serious girl crush on me when Jack and I were together. I was flattered, but when I dumped Jack, Janette dumped me. She breezed past me to the front desk, flipping her waist-length chestnut hair and running her gel-manicured nails through the length of it. I was dead to her. She ignored me, and I was ignoring her ignoring me.

I prayed that Jack wouldn't be dropping by to get her. If he did, that would eliminate the school office as my safe haven. I strained to listen to the conversation Janette was having with the student worker behind the desk, trying to hear Jack's name, certain it would stand out like an off-key note.

My prayers were answered when Janette simply turned and exited the same way she'd entered, her chin lifted a fraction higher as she passed me, her frown a fraction deeper. The thought began to gnaw away at me. Would she snitch, tell him where I was? Would he show up and drag me out of the office like some Neanderthal when Ms. Hathaway wasn't looking? I wouldn't have put it past him.

The sounds in the hallway waned, and the chairs next to me that had been occupied emptied one by one. Twenty minutes had passed since the bell signaled the end of another school day, and the unnaturally upbeat school secretary was smiling at me expectantly. She slipped her rhinestone readers onto her head. "You been here a while, hon. You sure I can't help you with somethin'?" she asked in her West Texas–born-and-bred twang.

"No, thanks. I'm just waiting for someone."

"Well, you've got about fifteen more minutes before we lock up." She smiled wider, pushed her glasses back in place, and returned her attention to her computer screen.

I texted Graham again. No answer. *Did he forget?*

I reluctantly considered calling my mom to pick me up. Waiting in the school office sucked for more than just the obvious reasons. It triggered a memory of my sixth-grade fiasco when I'd thrown up in the middle of math class, and the boys had cracked up while the girls had shrieked and run for the door. I was forced to wait for my mom in the main office, wearing a way-too-big faded Mickey Mouse T-shirt the school nurse had on hand, the scent of puke drifting from my clothes stuffed in the plastic bag at my feet. But the peak of humiliation came when my mom burst through the doors in baggy sweatpants and dirty Converse, wild-eyed and short of breath, her hair twisted in a lopsided ponytail. She whooshed right past me to the secretary's desk. "Where is she?"

"I'm right here, Mom."

She whipped around and exhaled loudly. Even at that age, I'd understood all too well that I was solely responsible for her panic.

Ten more minutes crept by before my phone buzzed with a text message. *In the south parking lot*. I slung my backpack over my shoulder and shot out of the office, fueled by a high-octane blend of irritation and relief. There was Graham, waving, happy to see me but not as happy as I was to see him. I rushed to him, and he slid his arm around my waist, kissed me, and pulled me closer, his lateness immediately forgiven, my anxiety already relegated to a distant memory.

"So, you ready to see Rocket strut his stuff?"

"Most definitely."

We drove off, the windows down, and I watched his dreads flouncing in the hot breeze, wondering what he would look like if he cut it all off. Not that I wanted him to. It was just one of the frequent random *what if* thoughts I had about Graham Scott.

"Sorry it took me so long. Backup on I-35."

"No worries. Ms. Hathaway kept me company—sort of."

"Who?"

"The school secretary."

He laughed. "We have one of those. Mrs. Waterstone. Ever notice how they always seem to have three-syllable last names?"

"Yeah. I think our no-nonsense, single-syllable names are the better choice." I kicked off my shoes, put my feet on the dashboard, and wrapped my arms around my knees. "And together they make a decent name. Scott Earle or Earle Scott. But can you imagine being named Hathaway Waterstone?"

"Seriously," he said.

We took turns trying out the name with a variety of accents—English, Irish, Scottish, and Australian—and fell into tear-filled fits of laughter.

WE PULLED INTO THE parking lot of House Park, and as I opened the car door, we were greeted by the familiar sound of wheels rasping against concrete.

"I see him," Graham said, pointing in the direction of boys in motion. "He's still doing practice runs, but he'll kick into his routine in a few."

He took me by the hand, and we walked past a herd of sweaty guys to a chorus of boards crashing on concrete, backed up with shouts of "Fuck," "Dude," "Yesss!" and "Nailed it!"

We settled on a spot in the spectator stands. His hand rested on my thigh, and I slung my arm over his shoulders. It amazed me how at ease and secure I felt with him after just a few short weeks. He still hadn't pressured me for sex, which to my mind increased his level of hotness by a factor of ten.

"Yo, Rocket!" Graham yelled.

Rocket stopped, popped his board up and into his hands, and waved in our direction. "Dude, watch this!" He pushed off again, headed toward a steep ramp, and catapulted into the air before he and his board returned safely to solid ground.

"Jesus!" I said, breathless.

"Fucking amazing, right?"

My phone vibrated, and I reluctantly pulled away from Graham to dig it out of my purse. It was Karin. She desperately needed to get away from the house.

"We're at House Park. See you in a few." I hung up and turned to Graham, sighing. "That was Karin. I told you about her bizarre parents? Well, I think they've finally jumped off the high dive. To punish her, they make her recite this Bible verse over and over." She'd told me so many times that I had it memorized. I crossed my arms over my heart and looked to the sky. "For this is the will of God, your sanctification, that is, that you abstain from sexual immorality."

"What the fuck?"

"I know, right? They made her say it every morning before she left for school, telling her that her virginity was precious. But now they're making her recite it over and over, like writing, 'I will not cheat' on the blackboard a hundred times. Anyway, it sounds like something else has happened, and she needs to vent. I told her to meet me here. She lives really close."

"No worries." He jumped up, cupped his hands around his mouth, and shouted, "Go, Rocket! Show 'em how it's done, dude!" Graham was transfixed. "Here it comes. Watch this."

With his legs pulled close to his chest, Rocket was literally flying, separated from his board as it rotated in the air once, twice, three times—I lost count. He and his board were completely disconnected from gravity. Then in a freaking miracle, they reconnected, his feet planted firmly on the board. Together, they came back down to earth, and I was able to breathe again.

"Did you see that shit? It's called a seven twenty double-kick flip. I hope he can pull it off again when he's up," Graham said, gazing at Rocket with admiration. "Man, I'd give my left nut to be able to do that." He tore his eyes away from Rocket and looked at me. "Uh, sorry, babe."

"Shouldn't he be wearing a helmet and, like, kneepads or bubble wrap or something?"

"What? Oh, yeah. It's required during competition, but he's just practicing."

I opened my mouth, ready to point out Rocket's recklessness and Graham's lame justification. Then I heard my name and saw Karin waving frantically from the parking lot. "I'll be right back," I said and headed over to her.

Despair emanated off Karin like heat vapors on asphalt. I'd been with her through tons of ups and downs—the downs always traceable to her parents. I steeled myself for another tale of emotional wounds from an unwinnable battle and hugged her tightly. "You okay?" I whispered.

She pulled back and wiped a tear sliding down her makeup-free face. "No, actually, I'm not. My parents' lunacy has increased exponentially." Even in times like this, Karin's vocabulary was notable.

"What happened?"

"It's like they're a cult of two, and they're trying to brainwash me to join them." She took a shaky breath.

Karin glanced in Graham's direction.

"It's okay." I pulled Karin with me to sit on the hood of her parents' car.

She told me she'd grabbed the keys and bolted—another infraction she'd be severely punished for when she got home. She roughly wiped away more tears with the back of her hand. "They went through my desk drawers and found my acceptance and scholarship letter from UT."

"Oh shit!"

"When I walked in the door, they were both standing there, letter in hand, blocking my way. They dragged me to my room, with me kicking and screaming, and..." She sputtered. "It was awful, Amanda. I'm so ashamed."

"If you don't want to talk about it, that's fine. Whatever you want. I'm here." I wanted to hurt her parents... no, what I wanted was for them to stop hurting her.

"No, I need to say it out loud," she said. "When they pulled me into my room, there was newspaper on the floor with rice sprinkled on top of it. I was so confused."

Had they made a mess for her to pick up? Did they want her to count the grains?

"My mother pushed me down on my bare knees on top of the rice and pressed both hands on my shoulders. My father stood there with an open Bible, reading text and drilling me on passages."

"What the...?"

"They kept me there for an hour, until my knees bled."

She lifted up her long skirt to show me. The cuts had stopped bleeding, but her knees were red, swollen, angry.

"Oh, Karin. Shit." Tears dribbled down my cheeks. "Do you want to stay at my house?"

"No, they'd come after me. I mean, the only thing that's kept me sane and functioning over the summer was the knowledge that I got a full ride to UT."

"You've been accepted, and it'll all be covered. You can get a part-time job for spending money. You can—"

"I'm still a minor, Amanda." Karin's lip trembled. "I skipped ahead, remember? I won't be eighteen until next year. They wouldn't sign off on it. UT is number one on their hit list of 'smutty schools.'"

"Okay, so maybe it's just for a few months, and then you can reapply."

She cocked her head at me. "I would lose my spot. If I don't accept, who knows if I'd get in again and get the same package." She stared off into the distance. "They want me to attend St. Anthony's in Abilene. They've already arranged for a full scholarship through the church. I just thought I'd, you know, figure it all out once it came time for classes at UT to start."

I felt guilty as I thought of going to NYU, buying pizza by the slice, attending art exhibits in Brooklyn, and catching underground indie bands in dark clubs while Karin was trapped in a prim uniform at St. Anthony's with morning and evening prayers, Bible class, and lights out at ten p.m.

"What are you going to do?" I asked.

"I don't know. Run away from home?" Her laugh lacked even a glint of humor.

"Okay, I feel weird even saying this, but I'm going to anyway—Graham's dad is a lawyer. Maybe he might have some ideas."

"About what? Legally emancipating myself from my parents?" Karin's voice cracked. "God, has it really come to that?"

"No, you're right. I'm sorry. That was stupid and insensitive."

Karin shook her head and sighed. "No, *you're* right. I know that. If I'm going to have a life, a real life, I'll need to explore all options, even legal ones. It... it just makes me so sad, you know?"

I hugged her again and mumbled, "I know." But I didn't know. I couldn't even imagine.

"Do you think his dad would even talk to me? Maybe he wouldn't want to get in the middle of all this."

"Let me ask Graham and see what he says."

I wasn't comfortable with giving hard-core advice, but for this crisis, I was going to make an exception. "Karin, you deserve to have some say in your future. I mean, it's your life. You should get to choose what you do with it."

Karin took a deep, bracing breath. "You're such a good friend." She glanced in Graham's direction again. "So, enough about my so-called life. You going to introduce me to your skateboarder?"

I locked arms with her, and we headed to where Graham waited. As we approached, he stood.

"Karin, this is Graham. Graham, Karin."

"Hey, um..." I could see him debating whether he should ask Karin if she was okay or move on. He opted for moving on. "I hope Amanda has at least mentioned me," he teased.

"Uh, yeah. More than mentioned."

"Excellent."

He was clearly pleased, and I was pleased he was pleased, but I was unsure how to move the conversation along, my mind still seizing from Karin's life-altering story. Rocket's sudden appearance, his board dangling from his hand, his scraped knuckles on full display, saved me.

"How'd it look?" he asked.

"Awesome!" Graham and I said in unison.

Before I could make introductions, Rocket said, "Hi, I'm Rocket, a friend of Graham's."

"Karin, a friend of Amanda's," she said, studying the ground as if she expected it to open up and reveal life's answers to her multiple-choice questions.

"Cool," he said. Karin was understandably shy, the kind of shy that was excruciating to watch, but Rocket, undeterred, took a step closer to her, forcing her to look up. "You like skateboarding?"

In a notch above a whisper, Karin said, "Um, I don't really know. I've never watched."

"Okay. A skateboarding virgin. I can fix that. It's about to start." When he winked at her, she looked as if she might spontaneously combust. But she never took her eyes off him as he straightened his man bun, grabbed a water bottle, finished it off, and jogged back to the concrete park.

Graham cleared his throat and, with arched eyebrows, turned to me and whispered, "What just happened there?"

"Shush," I said, jabbing him with my elbow.

Rocket made it back to the arena just in time to take his spot for the last round of the competition. The three of us whistled, yelled, and clapped as Rocket displayed his wicked skill set. When he was done, sweat trickling down his temples, he ran over, took off his helmet, and addressed Karin alone. "So?"

"Quite impressive," she managed to say.

Graham held him in a headlock and roughly kissed the top of this head. "You're the man!" he said as they wrestled.

Rocket got loose and flashed his winner's check. "I'm starved! So, are we going to get something to eat or what?" he asked, oblivious to Karin's underlying anxiety. "It's on me!"

"I thought we could go to my folks' café. Amanda hasn't been yet."

"You up for vegan cupcakes and sustainable coffee from the deep, dark jungles of Vietnam?" Rocket asked. I couldn't help but notice that he was directing his question at Karin.

She looked at me and nodded. Then she turned off her phone, disabling the tracking app her parents had installed. I knew what a huge deal this was for her, but she needed to be around people who weren't trying to brainwash her or lock her into a chastity belt and throw away the key. She needed to have fun.

"Ro-o-o-cket! Where are you, ba-a-a-by boy?" The slurred, disembodied voice filled the air as we gathered our things to leave.

"Fuck!" Rocket froze in place and jerked his head to scan the area, desperate to locate the source.

Graham nodded in the direction of a seldom-used entrance to the recreation building behind the skate park and whispered, "She's over there."

A short, stout woman with bright-red hair, wearing a half-buttoned housecoat and fuzzy slippers, slid down the brick wall in slow motion, calling out his name, stretching and slurring each nearly unintelligible syllable. "Ro-o-o-ck-e-e-t!"

Rocket's face matched the hue of his hair, and his entire body was cloaked in anger and humiliation. He dropped his chin to his chest, heaved a sigh, and looked up at Karin. "Really sorry. Next time for sure. Later, guys." He stuffed the check in his pocket, tucked his skateboard under one arm, and jogged in the direction of the woman, who was now slumped on the ground.

"Is that his mom?" I hoped I'd guessed wrong.

"Yeah, unfortunately."

The three of us were voyeurs, rubbernecking a heartbreaking scene, as Rocket tried to bring his mother to an upright position. Without a word, Graham ran over to help, and for a minute, I thought the three of them might end up splayed on the ground, but they got her up and carried her out of sight.

Wide-eyed, Karin said, "Wow, I feel so bad for him."

"Graham told me that Rocket had a 'situation' at home, but I had no idea."

"I guess I'm not the only one with screwed-up parents," Karin said, her eyes welling up with tears again—whether for Rocket or for herself, I wasn't sure.

One thing I was sure of—Graham and I were lucky. Really lucky. My less-than-grateful attitude toward my mom had to stop. I vowed to do better.

Chapter 19
Deb

I'd always loved the crisp, fresh smell of newspaper in the morning, paired with a steaming hot mug of just-brewed French roast. Amanda had gleefully pointed out to me more than once that reading the paper was horribly old-school, but as I folded the page and leaned back in my chair, I was content to be out of step. My father was an old-time newspaper guy. As ridiculous as it might sound, reading the paper felt like I was creating a connection we'd rarely had when he was alive.

The chair scraped the kitchen floor as I stood, slapped the paper on the table, and marched to the front door. Whoever was knocking at eight o'clock in the morning would pay the price for disturbing my peace. I was fully prepared to yell through the door to leave the delivery on the front step or voice my refusal to sign yet another petition to save the planet from itself. But instead, I flipped the deadbolt and opened the door.

"Merritt, what are you doing here?"

Clutching her purse, she cocked her head and breezed past with an expression that said, *That's how you greet me?*

"I... I'm just surprised, that's all," I said, trailing after her as she headed to the kitchen. "Want some tea?" Merritt wasn't much of a coffee drinker. Her aversion to it had increased with each pregnancy, pounding the final nail in the coffee coffin.

"Sure, that would be great." She'd already turned the corner and was out of sight.

I followed her to the kitchen, fixed her English breakfast tea, and sat across from her at the table, where she'd already settled in. She stared at the mug for a few seconds. "How are things?" she asked before lifting the steaming mug two-handed, blowing ripples across the surface, and taking a cautious sip.

"Same as yesterday when we talked. What's wrong?"

She bit her lip. "Maybe I... just... needed to see you."

I pushed the newspaper aside, leaned forward, and placed my hand on hers as I tried to intuit what was so incredibly urgent that it couldn't wait until our regular ten o'clock check-in. "I'm glad you're here. You want a bagel or toast or something? Won't take but a second."

"No. Thanks."

I hesitated. "We can just sit here if you want."

"That would be good."

I squeezed her hand before letting go. I thought about suggesting we go for a walk, before the heat settled in. Richard had brought me those new walking shoes he'd just gotten in at the store and—

"Deb?" She was staring into the cup again. "You're the only one I can really talk to who will understand, but I know you're the last one I should be talking to about my feelings about this. You know, the thing with Jess."

Of course it was hard for her to talk to me about it. About when I was seventeen. And pregnant. When our mother couldn't wrap her head around the reality that her teenage daughter had had premarital sex—had committed a mortal sin. She forced me to go to confession, to cleanse my soul, but when I had an abortion without her consent, she couldn't forgive me. My father drove me to the clinic, waited for me, and kissed me on the forehead as he tucked me in bed after—his one great fatherly gesture. She never forgave him either.

But I wanted her to know it was okay. "You know you can tell me anything, Merritt. What's bothering you?"

"I didn't tell Wes," she said. "I planned to tell him when he came back from that conference in San Diego but couldn't find the right time. Deb, it's eating me alive."

"Geez, why? I..."

She sighed. "I know it doesn't make sense, but it's like if I don't talk about it with Wes, it never happened."

I could certainly vouch for that approach. "But do you really think Wes wouldn't accept it?"

"No, I think he'd say it was the right thing to do."

"So, I don't understand."

Her jaw tightened. She clasped her hands together and stared down at them. "It's just that... I think it was a mistake." She looked at me, her eyes filled with tears. "A terrible, terrible mistake."

The sheer intensity of her emotions took my breath away. I slumped back in my chair. Her regret seemed directed at me as well as Jess. I couldn't think of anything to say that didn't sound defensive. But I felt defensive... no, I felt betrayed.

She wiped her eyes with her napkin. "But now I feel like I *have* to talk about it. And I don't know how to say this without sounding like I'm judging you, judging your decision, but..."

"Jesus, Merritt, that was over twenty years ago. I forgave Mom a long time ago. I've forgiven you."

"Forgiven me? What the hell for? What did I do?" She leaned back, appraising me.

"Dad told me that you felt guilty for not being there—"

She cut me off. "I have nothing to feel guilty about. You're the one who should feel guilty."

"Really, Merritt? Really?" My fight-or-flight response had kicked in, but this was my house, and I didn't want to fight with my sister.

She sighed and clicked her tongue in regret. "I'm sorry. I shouldn't have said that. But don't you ever think about it and wish you hadn't done it?"

When Merritt told me about Jess, I thought she had accepted it or was at least resigned to it. But now regret was written all over her face. Had Merritt's distress over not being there to support me all those years ago been bullshit? My father told me that she really wanted to be there for me, but she already had three kids under the age of three and a part-time job and just couldn't get away. It had made perfect sense at the time.

I swallowed hard. "No. Never." I insistently shook my head. "I was a kid. My life would have taken a completely different direction—and not a good one."

Merritt jumped up, rushed to the sink, poured out her almost-full mug, and began vigorously scrubbing it as if she were determined to wipe the bright-yellow flowers from its surface.

"Merritt, look at me."

She set the mug in the sink and slowly turned to face me.

"Why are you asking me this now?"

"I miss Ray," she said apropos of nothing. Before I could respond, her mouth knotted. "I just... I just wonder..." Her words spilled out in rapid succession, keeping time with my hurried heartbeat. "Even if she didn't want to be a mother, she could have given them up for adoption and made some family really happy." She paused and looked me in the eye, her voice firm. "Instead of taking the easy way out."

I heard myself gasp. Clearly, she wasn't just talking about Jess. I impulsively delivered the uppercut I knew would hit the mark. "Easy? You have no idea what I went through. Everything about it was hard. Really hard. You weren't there. If you're having regrets about helping Jess get an abortion, that's on you, not me!"

Blood buzzed in my ears. Had she been sitting on that for two decades, waiting for the opportunity to throw it in my face?

Her tears began to flow in earnest. Her voice cracked even as it grew louder. "That would have been my first grandchild. What if it were Amanda? You can't tell me you wouldn't have at least some doubt, some regret, losing your first grandchild."

My gathering anger was disrupted by memories of Mom beaming with all her grandchildren gathered round—all but the one I'd chosen not to have. "God, Merritt, are you *trying* to be cruel, or are you just being a bitch?"

Her chin trembled, and her back stiffened. There would be no long count where she readied herself for the next round. "It was a mistake for me to come here."

"I think you should leave. Now." Even as the words left my lips, I regretted them.

She abruptly stood up and backed away. She took a deep breath, the festering anger and frustration barely contained in her voice. "You think because that's what you did, that makes it right."

I was too filled with anger, self-admonition, and—yes—guilt to defend myself or stop her before she rushed out of the kitchen. I yelled something. I couldn't remember whether it was conciliatory or accusatory. Afterward, the only other sound was the slamming of the front door. I stood there, stunned, the sound reverberating in my head. It was identical to what I'd heard when my mother, shaken and unable to speak, ran to her bedroom and locked the door after my father told her what I'd done. I could hear her wailing and pacing the floor like a caged animal. She thought my life was over and that, by default, her life was over as well. After my father jimmied the lock, I watched, disbelieving, as her carried her out and drove her to the hospital. She was in shock. When she came back home two days later, she never spoke of it again. Not to me, not to Merritt, not to my father, not to anyone. Our fractured relationship limped along for years, never fully healing—an injury I was determined to never inflict on Amanda.

My throat tightened as I poured my coffee into the sink, tossed the newspaper in the trash, and stared out the kitchen window at the empty birdfeeder.

Chapter 20
Amanda

Graham was my designated superhero, showing up every day for the last two weeks to protect me from my nemesis, Jack Offerhaus. While Jack was making himself scarce, Janette had shown up in the school office more than once and had evidently resurrected me from the dead, making honest-to-God eye contact and giving me a heavily lip-glossed almost smile. I seriously suspected her motives. But after a few times, I stopped questioning her change of heart. I told myself I shouldn't judge her based on her brother's creepy behavior. Ms. Hathaway had gotten used to my daily appearance and stopped asking me if I needed anything. She paid about as much attention to me now as she did to the Texas-shaped paperweight on her desk.

As soon as Graham texted me, I grabbed my things and rushed to the parking lot. We were going to his parents' café again. When Graham and I first met, he told me his parents were cool. I thought, *Yeah, sure*. But I quickly discovered they weren't typical parents. Navy and Cade were long on listening and short on reprimands. Unlike my parents. Still, I felt bad for not inviting Graham over to meet my dad for a meal or a barbecue like Graham's parents had done for me. But after Graham came to the door that first time to take me to Rocket's practice, and I saw the look on my mother's face, I made sure I always found an excuse for why I would just meet him in the driveway. He hadn't questioned it, and I was relieved.

The bell above the door of the café tinkled as Graham held it open for me, and the blinds clacked against the small glass panes. We stepped in, and I breathed in the aroma of freshly brewed sustainable coffee. *Funky Austin* was the only phrase that came to mind to describe the place. The rickety stairs at the entrance led up to a converted 1950s house with creaky wide-paneled wood floors. The walls were decorated with the latest monthly art display alongside T-shirts with the coffee shop's logo, a medical-clinic sign that said, in bloodred letters, Urgent Café—Walk-Ins Welcome. The barista was a gray-haired guy wearing a single dangly earring and a knee-length plaid kilt. The only waitress was a willowy refugee from Nigeria with a lilting accent and skin so dark it was almost blue. Her name was Adaolisa—she told me it meant "God's daughter." She had escaped horrific conditions and made her way to the States with the help of Graham's parents. But she hadn't told the whole story of her perilous journey to anyone, not even Navy and Cade, and said she never would.

"Thanks, Adaolisa."

"Lisa," she corrected me. Her given name was too difficult for most Americans to pronounce, so she insisted everyone call her by the nickname. I liked being one of the few who were able to say her name correctly, but I promised myself I would try to respect her wishes.

Navy slipped her arm around Lisa's shoulders as she asked us, "So, what'll it be today? The usual?"

"Same?" Graham asked me. I nodded, and he turned to his mother. "Same."

Lisa turned and strode to the kitchen. I watched her walk away, wondering what awful truths she kept hidden away, secrets too terrifying to share—what life-distorting, mind-bending decisions she'd had to make to survive.

The bell above the door gave a tentative tinkle. Karin strolled in and sat at our table. "Hi." She gave a tiny wave in Graham's direction. While she and Rocket had been hanging out every chance she could grab to get out of the house, she was still shy around Graham. It was unusual for Karin to just show up without any preplanning.

"Hey, what are you doing here?"

"Rocket said he would meet me here after his practice." She looked at Graham. "I hope that's okay."

"Sure," Graham said. "When is he supposed to show?"

"Any minute now," she said, a big smile spreading across her face. "I was able to get away. I've got about an hour before I have to return home." She was taking bigger and bigger risks to be with Rocket, and she was giddy at the latest opportunity to spend even more time with him.

Karin and Rocket had become a couple at warp speed. They celebrated their anniversaries in weeks, not months. He brought her daylilies—her favorite. I'd never seen her happier. And I was happy to see my best friend and Graham's best friend together and in love, like us. But she was defying her parents more and more and enduring their increasingly harsh punishments. The last time, they'd locked her in the bathroom with a Bible and no food for twenty-four hours to "atone for her sins." *Karin sin?* It was such a joke, except it wasn't the least bit funny.

Graham had filled me in on Rocket's situation and why he spent so many nights at the Scott house. His mom had what Graham called "bipolar light." The actual diagnosis was cyclothymic disorder. She would get manic and plan trips she would never take, buy things they couldn't afford, then gradually sink into depression and not get out of bed for days, sometimes weeks. She refused to take prescription medications and instead self-medicated, mostly with alcohol and the occasional downer—when she could trick a clinic into prescribing them. When things weren't going well, she berated Rocket, blaming him for her misfortune, while sticking to him like Super Glue. Her disability check didn't go far, and they were always one step ahead of eviction. Rocket's part-time, minimum-wage jobs and his winnings helped but not enough. Graham said if Rocket got sponsors for his boarding, he might be able to dig them out of the financial hole they were in and get his mom the help she needed, even if she didn't want it. Karin and Rocket shared a desperation to have normal lives, or at least something that more closely resembled normal.

Navy wiped her hands on her apron and began rubbing my back, making small circles on my shoulder blades. She was a toucher, and her touch soothed me. "Good to see you again, Amanda."

I'd assumed that his parents were like that with everyone, but Graham had told me more than once that his parents liked me. A lot. "I just love this place. It's so... awesome."

"Well, you're welcome to drop in anytime. You know, I—"

She was interrupted when Cade burst in from the kitchen, double doors sashaying in his wake. "It's Rocket," he said, his voice shaking. "He's had an accident." He paused to take a breath. "He's in the hospital. We have to go."

I glanced at Karin. Her face flushed. "No," she whispered. "No, no, no." She rested her clasped hands together on the table, her nails digging into her palms. I put my hand over hers, but there was nothing I could say to undo her panic.

The next few minutes were a blur of activity as Cade announced to everyone huddled over their laptops, sipping on lattes, "Sorry, everyone, but we've had a family emergency. Going to have to shut down for the day."

Amid the slowpokes and grumblers were well-wishers, regular customers expressing genuine concern over Cade's announcement. As I watched Cade and Navy's warm smiles, double-handed handshakes, and pats on backs, it was clear to me why Graham was such a good person and such a good boyfriend. If it had been me, I would have wanted to shove everyone onto the street and lock the door behind them. Cade and Navy calmly ushered customers out while Lisa rushed around, turning off the espresso machines and shutting down the kitchen. I offered to help, but what could I do?

After the last customer had finally collected his things and gone, the place was deserted, and the footsteps echoed on the creaking hardwood floors. Cade worried his fingers through his thinning hair as Navy flipped off the lights. Graham turned the sign over to "Sorry, we're closed."

KARIN AND I LEFT WITH Graham in his car, and Navy and Cade left in theirs. I'd never spent much time in hospitals. People were sick in there. Some were really sick. People died in there. Just the thought made me woozy. I knew there was a morgue somewhere, probably in the basement. ID tags dangling from lifeless big toes, corpses covered in white sheets, lying in refrigerated lockers. In horror movies, the bodies always came back to life to go on a killing rampage. I shuddered. But Rocket was in this hospital somewhere, and Graham's Wite-Out face and hitched breath told me I needed to stay close. Graham was the first to reach the ER reception desk, pushing ahead, ignoring the crowd in the waiting room.

Karin straggled behind as if slowing the pace might alter the outcome. "We're looking for Rock—James Preston. He was brought here by ambulance maybe a couple of hours ago?"

James Preston?

"Are you family?"

Cade stepped up. "Yes."

The woman looked as exhausted as I suddenly felt. She slipped on her bright-blue readers, clicked the mouse several times, and squinted as she leaned into the computer screen. "Yes, he's in the ER."

There was a sudden stillness as the shock settled in. I glanced at Graham, his face frozen in dread.

She handed us visitor passes. "Down the hall on your right. Follow the signs."

We sprinted down the hall in a single line, Graham leading the charge, and craned our necks around each curtain. The antiseptic smell burned my nose. The occasional moan turned my stomach.

Graham took my hand and squeezed hard. I wanted to cry out in pain and in fear of what his best friend might be going through. *What will it do to Graham—what will it do to Karin—if the situation goes south? What if Rocket is no longer in the ER?* I pictured him in the other elevator, going down to the basement, a sheet covering his face, strands of his unruly red hair spilling out.

Graham's breath was coming in choppy gasps. Cade wasn't faring much better. Their anxiety snapped and crackled in the air. Navy was the calming force, keeping everyone from falling apart. My imagined disaster was coming into greater focus—tubes snaking in and out of Rocket's body, machines surrounding the bed, a respirator covering his nose and mouth, forcing him to breathe in an unnatural rhythm.

Graham pulled a curtain aside and stood there, slack-jawed.

"Hey, dude. How'd you know I was here?" Rocket asked.

Graham looked down, hands on hips, and took a deep breath before shaking his head. "Rocket, you shithead! You scared the crap out of us!"

Rocket was sitting up in bed, drinking a Coke. His red hair was as wild as ever, his eyes just as crystal blue. But he seemed confused by our entourage. "What...? Are we having a party?"

"We're your emergency number, dude! Shit, we thought you were dead or something."

Navy, Cade, and Graham were Rocket's proxy family. When Rocket turned eighteen, he'd given them power of attorney. He leaned on them for support, for love, and they gave it one hundred percent, like they did with everything.

"I didn't even know they called you. I guess they have it on file from the last time. Anyway, I'm fine. Doctor says a mild concussion. I just have to stay here for a few more hours to make sure I don't fall asleep or anything."

Navy and Cade looked relieved, on the edge of tears. They came around to the side of the bed, and Navy kissed Rocket's forehead. "Don't do this to us, Rocket. You almost put *us* in the ER."

"Amanda?" Karin asked.

I stepped out into the hallway.

She'd hung back, not wanting to step behind the curtain. She slowly walked in and slapped her hand to her chest. "Oh my God, you're okay!"

"Just a mild concussion. I'm fine." He motioned her over.

She sat on the side of the bed, and he held her hand.

"I thought... I thought." Her lip quivered, and I felt her heartbreak, even though there was nothing to be heartbroken about. But her tears broke free anyway. She abruptly sat up and punched Rocket's arm. "Why weren't you wearing a helmet? I've warned you repeatedly about practicing without a helmet. Sequential concussions can cause brain damage. I've told you that. Promise me this is the last time."

He crossed his heart and raised his right hand, revealing the words on his T-shirt—Zombie Apocalypse Response Team. "Last time, babe."

While Karin and Rocket were wildly different in an opposites-attract kind of way, they shared a bond—they both had the shitty luck to be born to shitty parents and the unbelievable good luck to have found one another. They'd become each other's escape hatch from the hell of their homes. They were stronger together, their lives better.

"Has anyone contacted your mother?" Navy asked Rocket.

"I called her on the way over." Karin sighed. "I'm not even sure she comprehended what I was saying." She hesitated. "I know this makes me a terrible person, but I hope she doesn't show up."

Rocket lifted her hand to his lips and kissed it.

The doctor, a tiny Asian woman in aqua scrubs, her dark hair in a tight bun high on her head, came rushing down the hall, her white coat floating behind her, catching her tail wind. She gave a professional smile and held out her hand. "Hello, I'm Dr. Hannah Kwak."

Dr. Quack? I smiled.

"I'm the neurologist on call." She didn't look much older than me, but she oozed confidence. She turned to Cade and Navy. "Are you the parents?"

"No, but we have medical power of attorney."

She nodded.

"So, he's going to be okay?" Navy's voice was shaking. I'd never imagined her like that—so vulnerable. The strength that she'd projected up till that point had faded.

Kwak's MD expression softened. "He should be fine. However, according to our records, this is his second one in less than six months. The last concussion was more severe. He needs to refrain from skateboarding for at least six weeks."

"Six weeks?" Rocket yelled. "No way!"

Dr. Kwak didn't miss a beat. "Two to three months would be even better." She turned back to us. "I just want to keep him for observation for the next few hours."

"Thank you, Doctor," Cade said, offering her a firm handshake.

I knew what was going through Graham's head. He had to be wondering if Rocket would still be able to get back to skateboarding, go pro, and get a life.

Raised voices echoed in the hallway. We all shifted in the direction of the sound. With the sureness of someone who worked the ER every day, Dr. Kwak pushed the curtain aside and stood straight, ready to deal with it.

And there she was. "Where's my boy? I want to see my boy!" his mother yelled in the raspy, strained voice of a longtime smoker. She waved her arms wildly, demanding that only the best doctors take care of Rocket.

Dr. Kwak mouthed to the floor clerk, "Call security."

While she was dialing, a nurse cautiously approached. I could see him assessing the situation, deciding if Rocket's mom was dangerous, checking to see if she had a gun. But before he could get to her, she tripped and fell face-first with a thud and a crack.

I wondered if this was rock bottom for Rocket's mom. *I mean, how much further down can she go before she agrees to get help?*

"James! Please! I want to see my boy. You can't keep me away from him! Jamie, baby, I'm sorry, please!"

I cringed. I couldn't even imagine my mom being barred from seeing me if I were in the hospital. I glanced at the ER desk clerk, who simply shrugged.

Rocket swung his legs around to the floor, but when he tried to stand, he fell back down in the bed. "Man, I'm so freaking dizzy." He looked in the direction of his mother. His contorted face revealed everything he was thinking, the pain he was feeling. The beefy nurse with the big biceps was in complete control as he helped her up. She stood straighter and tugged at her shirt as a trickle of blood from a cut above her eyebrow streaked her cheek. He escorted her down the hall to another room—to stitch her up was my guess.

She screamed, "Jamie, I'm sorry, Jamie. I just need to know you're okay..." Her voice drifted off. Maybe they'd given her something to calm her down.

"Surely she didn't drive here," Karin said.

"She got here the same way she got to the recreation center that day, the same way she's able to go buy booze—Lyft," Rocket mumbled. "I'd better go see if she's okay."

He gingerly stood with Karin's help and shuffled out of the curtained room. Karin had both hands over her mouth to stifle her sobs. She would have her own rock bottom when she went home to face her parents.

Navy whispered to no one in particular, "I'm going to check on her." She put her hand up when Cade started to follow. "I think it's better if I go, you know, talk to Beverly, mother to mother."

Graham had been hugging the wall, silently watching the scene play out. He turned to his dad. "Cade?"

"Yes?" Cade lightly touched Graham's shoulder.

"I think I want to go home for a while... tell Rocket I'll be back." There was a hitch in his voice. "I'll be back later. You and Navy going to stay for a while?"

"I'll wait for your mother." He stepped forward and hugged Graham tightly. "Take it easy, son."

Karin didn't want to leave, but she said the longer she stayed, the worse the punishment would be. She kissed Rocket goodbye and smiled at him. "You look good for someone who almost split their head open like a ripe melon."

Rocket chuckled. "Funny girl."

They held hands, then fingertips, letting go one finger at a time before breaking the connection. Then Karin backed away from the bed. We gave her a ride home. She was super quiet, even for Karin. I turned to her in the back seat. She was staring blankly out the window, her hands clenched in her lap, all color drained from her face.

"Karin," I said.

She didn't answer, didn't move.

"Karin."

She slowly turned toward me.

"Why don't you come with us to Graham's?"

She sighed and shook her head, defeat written on her face. "I'm going to have to face the consequences sooner or later. I might as well expedite the inevitable."

"You want me to go in with you?" I offered, though the last thing I wanted was to come face-to-face with the Dobsons and enter their sad house.

I'd done that only once before, and it was one time too many. Her mom called me a "Jezebel" as if I were trying to lure their daughter away from the light and into a life of sin. The worst thing was when they asked me if I was a virgin. I still couldn't believe it had happened. I'd never been treated like that before. After that encounter, I immediately went home and took a scalding-hot shower to wash away the filth they had projected onto me. I could only imagine the cruelty she was about to face.

As we turned onto her street, I said, "Text me, and let me know you're okay."

"Like I'll have a cell phone after this."

"Well, contact me as soon as you can."

"If you have any news about Rocket—if anything changes—come knock on my window after nine thirty. They always go to bed at nine thirty. I just don't know when I'll be able to see him again." She took a shaky breath. "But I'll crawl out the window if I have to."

We pulled into her driveway. Her parents stood sentry on the porch, brows furrowed, arms crossed. Karin reached for the door handle.

"Wait," I said. "Just stay with me. My parents won't mind."

"I can't." She looked back at her parents. Her father stepped into the yard. "I can't get away. Not yet."

She was out the door before I could ask what she meant. I watched her march defiantly to the porch. Her parents didn't scream or hit her. But her mom shot daggers my way before disappearing inside, her father close behind. Karin didn't look back. She simply followed them into the house and softly shut the door behind her.

Chapter 21
Deb

I hadn't dropped by the store in a couple of months. It was halfway across town, and Austin's traffic being what it was, going there required a precious three-hour chunk of my workday. Besides, Richard always seemed too busy to stop and have an impromptu chat if I just showed up. So I'd texted him that it was important and asked if he could spare the time to actually leave the store and have lunch with his wife. I hadn't shared anything with Richard about my argument with Merritt a couple of weeks before, and it had been festering. I just needed a distraction—a better one than writing about the dangers of type 2 diabetes.

I pulled into one of the four reserved parking spots in front of Richard's store. Correction, *our* store. Twelve years before, we'd placed an all-or-nothing bet on its success. When we rented the space, it was a mess. The previous tenants had left in the dead of night without bothering to clear out their stuff. The landlord was thrilled we were willing to take over the lease "as is."

It took us three months to get rid of the smell of fried chicken and french fries, all the time paying rent and sinking borrowed capital into our vision. Amanda joined us every day after school, excited to paint the storeroom—up to the four feet she could reach. She carved her initials with the date in the baseboard, claiming her space. After the store opened, she loved to sit in the storeroom and read. But around the time she turned twelve, she'd decided that hanging out at Dad's sporting goods store was no longer fun, no longer cool. Richard had told me that sometimes he still expected to walk into the storeroom and find Amanda curled in the corner, a book in her lap.

We'd fretted over what to name the store, almost as much as we'd fretted over naming Amanda. After much deliberation, we launched Monday Morning Sports with a magnum of champagne and the sky-high hopes and expectations that only two twentysomethings possessed. We were gambling our little family's future on the chance that the store would take off. My hope was that it would provide Amanda with more than I had growing up—more money, more of my time—and eventually the gift of attending the college of her choice. As always, we were looking ahead and seeing the best that life could offer.

Our gamble paid off—in spades. Monday Morning had become an Austin fixture, even a bit of a tourist attraction. The walls displayed Richard's collection of sports memorabilia. His dad had started him with baseball cards when he was a kid, and he was hooked. He'd gotten lucrative offers for the collection but refused to part with any of it. He built a back room with a shelf full of retro radios—Emerson, Admiral, Zenith, several encased in Bakelite—where customers could tune in to classic sporting events as if they were live. They could listen to the 1980 Olympic "Miracle on Ice," the Ali vs Frazier 1971 match, or the 2016 Cubs' win. I thought it was an odd idea, but Richard clearly understood his clientele.

"Looking good, Mr. Earle." I surveyed the shop. He'd moved a display of performance supplements front and center, some of which I recognized from his stash at home, along with a new shipment of high-tech impact-monitoring helmets. I'd written an article about sports-related head injuries. It seemed like a smart invention and a good addition to the store.

"You're here." Richard stepped out from behind the counter, looking more apprehensive than happy about taking his wife to lunch. He kissed me on the cheek. I knew that face. Something was on his mind. You learn things about your husband over nineteen years.

"Hi, Ms. E.," Jeff, the assistant manager, said. "It's about time he took a lunch break."

"You're telling me." I turned to Richard. "Where to, husband?"

Before he could answer, the bell above the door jingled, and in walked a twentysomething with a baby carrier strapped to his chest and a drooling doe-eyed infant peeking out. I was suddenly starving but not for lunch. Smiling at the sweetness, I glanced Richard's way, expecting a shared "Awww." We'd done that often enough over the years.

Instead, he froze like the scared opossum that occasionally appeared atop our backyard fence. He cleared his throat. "Welcome to Monday Morning Sports. Jeff, can you help this gentleman?" Richard turned to me. "There's a new Tex-Mex place down the street. I've heard good things. You hungry?"

"Starved."

"I've got it under control, Mr. E." Jeff was a sports fanatic and a loyal employee. A few years before, a hot water tank burst on the fourth of July. Water was everywhere. Jeff actually left his friends on Town Lake and came to Richard's aid, calling every emergency plumber until he found one willing to work on the holiday. Richard had promised a percentage of the profits to Jeff if he ever sold the place, as long as Jeff was still employed there. The papers were at his lawyer's office, almost ready to be signed. But Richard was nowhere ready to sell anytime soon.

Richard nodded. "Call if you need anything. I'll be just down the street."

"I'm good," Jeff said. "Y'all enjoy." He turned his attentions to the customer with the baby, and as we walked outside, I heard him say, "Are you looking for something for yourself or the future athlete you've got there?"

"It's only four blocks from here, but it's so hot. I think we should drive."

We got in the car, and as Richard was backing out of the parking space, my phone dinged with a message from Amanda: *Just left the hospital.*

I gasped. "Richard, wait. It's Amanda!"

He slammed on the brakes.

Amanda: *I'll be late. Went with Graham to visit a friend.*

"That child, I swear."

"What?"

"Said something about the hospital, and I had a moment of panic. She actually went with Graham to visit a friend. She could have led with that."

"When am I going to meet this Graham boy? Seems like she's been hanging out with him a lot."

"I've only seen him a couple of times myself. Maybe we should invite him over for dinner."

He nodded, apparently satisfied that he was going to meet "this Graham boy." He was looking at me expectantly. "Was there any special reason you wanted to have lunch?" he asked, his brow furrowed.

I stared at him blankly until I could have sworn an actual light bulb materialized above my head. "I'm... I'm not pregnant, if that's what you were thinking." The relief on his face angered me. "What—did you think I was plotting an 'accidental' pregnancy?"

"No, Deb. It's just the way you said you wanted to meet me and the way you were looking at that baby, I just thought—never mind."

I thought of Jess, of the father. *Has she told him? Does he care? Is he relieved she got an abortion?* I thought of myself and my boyfriend at seventeen. Neither one of us had been anywhere near ready to become a parent. And I was acutely aware, even at that tender age, that it was my body, not his. I'd stuck with my decision—for better or worse. I wondered if, when he looked back, he felt the same enormous relief that was evident on Richard's face.

Richard snapped his fingers in front of me. "Hey, Deb? We're here. Where are you?"

I hadn't even realized we'd left the store parking lot. "Sorry, I drifted."

Inside, the restaurant was typical Austin—small, cozy, with the aroma of peppers, cumin, and freshly toasted tortilla chips in the air. Vintage posters, license plates, flyers for bands and artists, and T-shirts lined the walls. Maybe we were pushing forty, but we'd claimed Austin as our home before we even turned twenty, and the youthful vibe still felt like ours as we slid into the purple vinyl booth.

"Okay, so what *did* you want to talk to me about?"

I hesitated. "Merritt and I had a big fight."

"What about?"

His question set my heart pounding. "It was stupid. You know, it's not worth repeating. I'm just glad we're here to take my mind off of it."

"You and Merritt will trip over each other apologizing, and things will go back to normal in a day or two. You two never stay mad long." Richard was well versed in how Merritt and I sometimes butted heads and always came back together.

"Yeah, maybe."

He shrugged.

So accepting. A change of subject seemed in order. "Listen, when we're done, do you want to go for a walk on the trails around the lake? There are plenty of shaded areas."

He leaned back and sighed. "I'm beat. I was actually thinking of knocking off early, coming home."

"Really?" This made the second time in a week.

"I'm not twenty-five anymore," he said. "Another reason why having a baby is a bad idea."

Chapter 22
Amanda

As we stepped into Graham's house, the first thing I noticed was the familiar smell of incense. The second thing was the quiet. When Cade and Navy were there, the house had such a positive energy. Empty, the house felt flat.

"You want something to drink? Eat?" Graham asked as I curled up on the loveseat.

"Just water."

He handed me a glass of ice water from the kitchen and stood looking down at me.

"What?" I asked.

"I'll be right back," he said before heading up the stairs.

I set the water on the side table, walked over to the sliding glass door, tugged the curtain, and looked in the backyard. The barbecue, the table and chairs, the quarter-moon wind chimes—everything was exactly the same.

"Amanda." Graham stood on the landing, a can of WD-40 in his hand. He unscrewed the bottom and showed me the three perfectly rolled joints nestled inside.

"Where'd you get that?" I smiled.

"Amazon. You can get anything on Amazon—except the joints, of course. Got those from Corey." He laughed. I laughed. It released my leftover anxiety from Rocket's trip to the ER.

He sat next to me on the sofa, our elbows touching. Even that little skin-to-skin contact warmed me all over. Graham pulled a joint and a lighter from the container, lit up, and silently passed it to me. I was never a regular user, so after a couple of hits, I'd had enough to feel like I was becoming one with the loveseat.

"That's it?" he asked.

"Yeah, I'm good."

"You sure?"

"Positive."

He inhaled deeply one more time, snuffed out the joint in a seashell on the coffee table, and laid his head on my lap, closing his eyes. I fiddled with his dreadlocks. I remembered how badly I'd wanted to do that the first night we met.

I leaned over and softly kissed his forehead. He pulled me down, cradled my face in his hands, and kissed me softly. Then again harder.

He took my hands and kissed my palms. Still holding my hand, he slowly stood up. He looked six feet tall as he locked eyes with me. My heart was about to explode. I thought this had to be what love felt like.

From the day we met, I'd known my first time would be with Graham. But I thought I'd have a chance to prepare. I would get a pep talk from Hadley and Karin beforehand. I would shower and wear a new Victoria's Secret push-up bra and matching thong. But somehow it felt right at that moment—no, it felt perfect.

As we made our way up the stairs, my senses were on high alert, picking up every detail. I was conscious of my bare feet on the hardwood floors, of the breeze from the fan overhead, of the taste of his lips still on my tongue. He stepped back to let me go into his room first. It looked the same as the last time I'd been there but felt radically different. Static electricity bounced off the walls. He slid his arm around my waist, pulled me toward him, and kissed me. I wanted to remember this forever. I shivered as he let go.

"You okay?" he asked.

"Yeah, just nervous. You sure your parents won't be coming home anytime soon?"

"I'm sure." He smiled as he lifted his T-shirt back to front in that uniquely guy way and pulled it over his head.

I was lightheaded. I'd seen his bare chest before, of course, but here in his bedroom, just the two of us, with emotions high and lights low, it felt wildly erotic, forbidden. He took a final step toward me.

"Your turn," he whispered. He reached out and lightly grazed my arm with his fingers.

I let the straps slip from my shoulders. I trembled as my sundress slid down my body and puddled on the floor beside the bed. I stood in front of him, a good girl in a black bra. His breath quickened, and I tried not to look at the barely contained bulge in his jeans. Up until that point, there had been a lot of fumbling in the dark. I always felt it pressing against my thigh, but this—this was different. I closed the space between us, wrapped my arms around his neck, and kissed him hard.

He reached around and fumbled to unfasten my bra. I slipped my arms out of it and let it drop to the floor. He stepped back, transfixed, and I had to fight the urge to cross my arms over my chest to shield myself from his stare. Jack had roughly squeezed my breasts under my shirt, played with them like they weren't attached to my body, but he'd never reacted like this.

Graham erased my intrusive thoughts of Jack when he leaned over and kissed each breast and then stood back up and kissed my mouth, his tongue exploring. "You're beautiful."

I hooked my fingers in his belt loops to bring him even closer. He stepped back and removed his jeans and boxers with startling speed. Only my barely there thong stood between us.

"You're sure about this?" he asked. It made me want him more.

"I'm sure," I whispered.

"Take it off," he said, his voice a rumble.

I stepped out of it and tossed it on top of my bra, and he guided me to the bed, laid me down, and kneeled over me. I pulled his face to mine and softly ran my tongue across his bottom lip. He peppered me with kisses on my neck, my arms, my ribs, my belly button, but when he started to go *there,* I pulled him back up. My breath was coming in little gasps. It was too much.

"Now?" he whispered, his breath hot in my ear. I nodded. He reached for the bright-red foil packet in his nightstand drawer, and I watched as he expertly slipped on its contents. I was staring, dizzy with anticipation.

He whispered instructions in my ear. "Spread your legs a little more... lift your hips... is this good? Let me know if it hurts... okay, relax."

Relax? He's totally kidding, right?

And then it was happening. But it wasn't... what I had expected... what I'd been breathlessly waiting for. Far from it.

Shit! It hurt. It hurt a lot. I bit my lower lip as a distraction.

He stopped and looked at me, his eyelids swollen with lust. "You okay?"

"Yeah, I'm good."

Man, all those movies with women moaning and writhing in ecstasy were full of shit. It was a crushing disappointment. It was as if I'd been offered a mouthwatering slice of chocolate cake, took a bite, and found that it tasted like mud. Before, I couldn't wait for this to happen. Now I couldn't wait for it to be done. I started moving my hips.

"God, Amanda, don't. I can't..." He let out a guttural noise, and he relaxed, his entire body weight on top of me.

I counted to five. "Graham, I can't breathe."

He lifted himself in a push up, leaned down, kissed me, and rolled over to the other side of the bed. "I'm sorry. You started moving, and I couldn't hold it back any longer."

He sat up, pulled off the condom, and threw it in the trash. As I sat up, my eyes went to the blossoming red spot on the sheets. I wanted to cry. Not exactly the dewy afterglow I'd envisioned. I quickly sat up, my head in my hands. He put his arm around me, pulling me close.

"Graham, I feel so... I don't know what I feel, but I don't feel good. I expected it to be so different—good different. And the sheets... *shit.* I wanted to so bad, and I thought it would be amazing. But... I don't know. Maybe something's wrong with me."

"It'll get better, I swear."

Right then, I had zero desire to find out.

He placed the palm of his hand on my back.

I turned to look at him.

"How about I throw the sheets in the wash, and while that's working, we can have a beer or some wine? Or another joint? It'll relax you." He lifted my chin up.

He looks so, so... shit! I felt the same gripping in my stomach as before. I wanted to run my fingers down his chest and kiss his full red lips.

"I'm okay," I said. "Really."

His phone dinged. He grabbed it from the nightstand. "It's Navy. They're discharging Rocket. Come with me?"

I was gathering my underwear and getting ready to make a pit stop in the bathroom before exiting the scene of the crime.

"Amanda?"

When I didn't answer, he took my hand and pulled me to the edge of the bed so I stood between his legs. He pulled out a handful of tissues and began gently wiping the blood from my inner thigh.

I ripped the tissues from his hand. "I've got it."

"Amanda?"

"What?"

"I'm sorry it wasn't what you expected."

"I'm sorry that you're sorry," I said.

"But I'm not sorry. Not about being with you. I promise, it'll get better."

"You already said that." I looked away, clutching my sundress to my chest.

"Amanda, look at me, please."

I sighed and looked into his sad blue eyes.

"I would never do anything intentionally to hurt you because... I love you, you know. I mean I really love you."

Chapter 23
Deb

I kicked off my shoes, welcoming the cool of the house. Fall was right around the corner, but somebody had forgotten to tell that to the summer gods, who apparently were angry. I headed to the kitchen for a cold glass of lemonade made from a recipe handed down from Richard's grammy with love, an Earle-family summer tradition. The clink of the ice triggered a rush of relief, and I gulped the first glass then poured another. After carrying the glass upstairs to my office, I sat at my desk, opened my laptop, and checked my email, With the glass to my lips, I choked on the last sip.

From: Timothy Roi.

I opened it and began cautiously reading.

Amanda's grade in calculus has dropped dangerously low, and the school requires that we contact parents and offer a conference when there is a precipitous drop, as it would likely affect her class ranking. I'm available any day this week after 4:30, room 234.

Professional and to the point. I breathed a sigh of relief. I couldn't help but wonder if he felt as awkward sending the message as I did reading it.

I wrote back, *Today at 4:30 works for me.*

Even shorter and more to the point. I stared at my response for a few seconds more before hitting Send. While seeing his name was a shock, I shouldn't have been surprised at the subject. Ever since

Amanda met Graham, she'd been distracted. *Obsessed* was more like it. She spent every spare minute with him.

I raised my feet off the floor, pushed away from my desk, and rolled toward my restocked cigarette stash. I lit up, staring out the window at the quiet street below, blowing smoke into the still air outside, and watching the glowing embers with a weird fascination. I hadn't seen Amanda enough lately to exchange even two sentences, much less pin her down on her college applications. She was so late getting the applications done, and I was afraid that if she didn't get with the program, she was going to miss out.

What will be her next move? Community college? A far cry from her dreams of NYU.

Maybe a conversation with Tim wouldn't be a bad thing. He had years of experience dealing with high school drama, angst, and of course, young love. We'd had several wordless encounters at back-to-school nights over Amanda's high school years—never more than a nod or a stilted smile, never up close, but I would sit in the back of the classroom, making sure I was the last one in and the first one out. Now the thought of sitting across from him, looking him in the eye, having a conversation, and wondering what he was thinking filled me with an unexpected combination of anticipation and dread.

THAT AFTERNOON, I PULLED into the parking lot of the school, where only a few cars remained. They probably belonged to teachers trying to catch up on grading and students staying late for club meetings and sports practice or begging said teachers to round their grades upward. It had been a while since I'd set foot on the school grounds. Once Amanda and her friends got their drivers' licenses, my shuttle service was no longer required.

I scanned the building. It always reminded me of a prison. Built in the 1970s, the institutional architecture was typical of the decade, but I found it intimidating rather than welcoming.

I slipped the silver windshield shade in place so I wouldn't burn my thighs when I got back in the car, something every Texan learned the hard way. Even though summer was officially over, it was still flesh-meltingly hot. I adjusted my sunglasses, pulled my phone from my purse to check the email with the room number, and popped a breath mint. I looked at the time—4:25 p.m. *No more dawdling.*

I opened the heavy door to the front office, and despite the more than two decades that had passed, I was back in high school. The adolescent angst came flooding back, muddying my thoughts—the cliques, the jocks, the cheerleaders, the goths, the teacher who was fired for getting a bit too chummy with a boy in his class, the girl in my chemistry class who'd committed suicide.

"Can I help you?" said a young voice from behind the counter. She stood up.

I thought I recognized her from Amanda's middle school. *Yes, she and Amanda used to study together.*

"Oh, Mrs. Earle. Hi! Remember me? Jennifer Middleton."

"Of course I remember you. How are you, Jennifer?"

"I'm good."

"So, senior year, huh? What are you doing after graduation?"

"I'm going to Texas State." She was all youthful enthusiasm. "Has Amanda heard yet?"

"No word yet." I smiled, but I couldn't admit even to Jennifer, a girl I barely remembered, that Amanda hadn't yet applied to any colleges. "I have an appointment with Mr. Roi. Do I need to get a visitor's badge or something?"

"Just sign here." She handed me a name tag to fill out. "Do you need me to look up his room number?"

"Thanks. I've got it. Room 234."

"Tell Amanda I said hi. I haven't seen her in a while."

Me either, I thought. "I'll be sure to tell her."

Jennifer had provided a much-needed distraction from my purpose for this visit, but climbing the stairs to the second floor, I had to talk myself down from a full-fledged panic attack. It didn't make a bit of difference that I knew I was being ridiculous. My history with Tim was just that—history. Ancient history. Sometimes it felt more like a forgotten dream. But my fight with Merritt had brought it all back. Meeting with Tim would convert it to a full-color high-resolution memory.

Room 234. I wiped my sweaty palms on my skirt and peered through the glass panel of the door. He was at his desk, reading. I stood for a few minutes, trying to reconcile my memory of an Adonis in algebra class with this grown man with a slightly receding hairline and glasses on the tip of his nose.

As if he sensed my presence, he looked up, and I quickly ducked out of sight. *God*, I really was back in high school. After chastising myself, I straightened up, knocked twice, and sheepishly opened the door.

Chapter 24
Amanda

While I waited in the office for Graham to pick me up after school, I scrolled through Hadley's Instagram posts of yin-yang symbols. She was in a spiritual phase and had recently gotten into astrology and throwing Tarot cards. I was avoiding the college-application links my mom had forwarded to me. Again. The more she pushed, the more my motivation went underground. I thought about how my own life had taken on a distinct yin-and-yang flavor—the darkness and the light.

Graham was my yang, of course. He made me happy, made me smile. And he was supportive. He was encouraging me to get my college applications done. I didn't resent him for that, but just thinking about leaving him behind filled me with anxiety. His plan was to stay in Austin, help with the café, and eventually take over when Navy and Cade retired for real. It wasn't what they wanted. They wanted him to go to law school. Actually, I was pretty sure that was what he wanted, too, but his parents were getting older, and he felt a responsibility. He was determined to keep Urgent Café going and to keep hiring people, like Adaolisa, who needed help getting their lives on track—just like Navy and Cade had always done.

I racked my brain, trying to think of a realistic way for us to stay connected when we were separated by 1,743 miles and the price of a round-trip ticket. I tried to picture him in the café, serving lattes, while I attended classes at NYU, wandered around Greenwich Village, and hung out in Washington Park. In my university fantasies, I was always a seriously lonely girl walking the streets of New York City, snow falling, with nothing but my textbooks to keep me company. I just knew that one of those days, he'd be working the espresso machine, and the real girl of his dreams would walk in and smile at him as she ordered a caramel latte, and my heart would be ground up and scraped into the compost heap with that day's coffee grinds.

But for as long as possible, he would be my yang. My yin at the moment was Karin—not Karin herself but the weight of her sadness. It was so fucking unfair. There was her unbelievably shitty—and increasingly scary—situation at home. She was my best friend, and I worried that—

"Hon, I'm going to run to the bathroom. I'll be back in the shake of a lamb's tail."

I wasn't sure why Mrs. Hathaway was checking in with me about her trip to the girl's bathroom, but whatever. I watched her swish her way down the hall and disappear around the corner.

"Amanda!"

I looked up, and there was Janette, giving me a perfectly aligned toothy smile like I was her long-lost BFF. "Hey, Janette. How's it going?"

She stood directly in front of me. "Good. Great, actually. I got a new car! Woo-hoo!" She struck a well-practiced—two hours every day after school—cheerleader pose.

Of course you did, I thought. "Cool! What kind?"

"You wanna come see?"

"I really can't. I'm waiting for someone to pick me up."

She pouted then replaced it with her bright smile. "It'll just take a sec. It's right around back."

I checked the time. Graham probably wouldn't be there for another ten minutes, and she seemed so excited. I reminded myself that it was Jack I was mad at, not Janette.

I shrugged. "Sure, why not. Just for a sec." I grabbed my stuff and followed her out to the vacant alcove behind the art building that was under construction. It was the only shady spot in the whole parking lot. A real find.

"Voilà!" she said, sweeping her arms as if introducing me to a bachelor offering a rose.

Forget a bachelor. This was way better—a brilliant-blue BMW Series 4 convertible. A surge of resentment and envy washed over me against my will. Janette was three years younger than me. I didn't even have a hand-me-down Kia waiting in the wings.

"Wow! Just wow!"

"Wanna go for a quick ride?"

"It's awesome, but really, I can't."

She put her palms together as if she were about to fall down on her knees and pray. "Please, please, please? I haven't gotten to show it off yet."

I'd never get another chance to ride in a sweet car like that. "Maybe just around to the front parking lot? My friend usually parks there."

She pressed the key to unlock the doors, and when I opened the passenger side, the new-car smell wafted out. It smelled like money. I sat down and took in the two-tone black-and-saddle interior, the soft leather steering wheel, the notebook-sized screen, and the control panel. I ran my hand over the smooth leather of the seat, let my head relax on the padded headrest, closed my eyes, and took a deep breath. This was what Jack's life was like—all leather and luxury and entitlement.

"Amanda." His voice was a vise on my chest. He was settling into the driver's seat.

"What the hell?" I whipped my head around to scan the parking lot. "Where's Janette?" I looked up to see Janette walking away, mission accomplished. "Jack, seriously? You convinced Janette to do this?"

"She knows we need to talk."

I grabbed the door handle and heard the distinctive click of the door lock. "Jack, let me the fuck out of here!"

"Amanda, you and me, we belong together. You have to know that!"

"*We*? Shit! What is wrong with you? How many times do I have to say it? There is no 'we.'"

His eyes had taken on a dark, desperate look, the look that made my throat close and my stomach curdle. I took a deep breath, turned to him, and as calmly as I could, said, "Jack, it's hot in here. Let's go outside, and we can talk."

He turned the ignition. Janette must have handed off the key to him as she offered me up as a sacrifice. Or maybe she didn't know this side of her brother like I did. The air conditioning blasted my face. Chill bumps rose on my arms.

"Open the door, Jack. Now! Graham'll be here any minute."

"I don't get what you see in that little douchebag, and it looks like he's fucking late, but I'm here. I want you, Amanda, and I love you more than he ever could."

He smiled at me. A wave of nausea washed over me. "He'll be here." I heard myself. I sounded as scared and desperate as I felt.

"Well, he's not here now, is he?" He lifted a strand of my hair and wrapped it around his finger and leaned in close, our noses almost touching. "You two fucking yet?"

My stomach clenched. *Can he tell?* Fear and embarrassment kept me silent.

When I said nothing, he lunged without warning. His hands were everywhere—under my skirt, down my bra. I heard my skirt rip. He feverishly climbed over to the passenger side, hitting his head on the roof. "Fuck!" he growled, his teeth clenched. With his full weight on top of me, the seat began to recline in slow motion. As I struggled, my thigh rammed against the gearshift. I screamed until my throat was sore, but the BMW was designed to keep out road noises—and keep in my screams. I kicked, I scratched, I drew blood, but I was a welterweight, and he might as well have been the heavyweight champ. When his hands slid around my neck, I made the split-second decision that my only chance of making it out of this nightmare alive was to just let it happen. He pressed his left arm against my neck as he tried to unzip his fly with his right. I couldn't move. Jack's heavy breathing was like the roar of a jet overhead. I closed my eyes. He was going to kill me.

"Open the fucking door, you fucking piece of shit!" It was Graham's muffled voice. I opened my eyes as Jack jerked his head toward the window. Graham's face was scarlet, his knuckles white from the grip on his skateboard. Jack released his hold on me, and I gasped, coughed, my hand on my neck.

"Graham!" I rasped. My attempt to breathe was cut short by the explosive sound of the skateboard hitting the car then glass cracking. I fumbled for the door lock, but it was just out of reach. After one more violent swing of the skateboard, icy fragments of glass rained down on us. Hot air rushed in along with the ear-piercing sound of sirens. Jack jumped out of the car and left me there, my skirt hiked up, my legs sprawled. His weight lifted, I took a half breath, triggering a coughing fit. I grabbed the door handle with both hands and pulled myself up. My tears blurred the scene, but I could see two officers hurl themselves out of a squad car, guns pointed at Graham. *Who called the police?* Jack was frozen in place.

"Drop it! Now!"

Graham threw down the skateboard, and one of them rushed forward and grabbed him, forced him to the ground, and handcuffed him then pulled him back up. Stunned, I tugged at my skirt, my fingers trembling.

"This dude is crazy!" Jack yelled, pointing at Graham. "He said he was going to kill me!" Graham was in shock, at least what I imagined shock would look like—pale, wide-eyed, breathless. The officers had released their grip on Graham, but Jack wasn't done. He inched closer. "He just destroyed my sister's new car!"

Graham locked his jaw and rushed toward Jack in a headbutt, but the officer built like a linebacker blocked him. "Whoa, whoa!"

"He was trying to rape her!" Graham sounded on the verge of a breakdown. "She was screaming!"

"She wanted it! She's *my* girlfriend, dude!" Jack yelled.

"He's a fucking liar!"

"Okay, okay, that's it! Everybody just calm down." The officer shoved Graham into the back seat of the squad car and ordered him to "Stay," as if speaking to a dog. The linebacker charged back and pushed Jack aside. Then he bent down, hands on knees, to peer into the car. "Are you okay, young lady?" His face softened. "Are you hurt? Do you need to go to the hospital?"

Am I okay? I felt a huge bruise blossoming on my thigh, and my skirt was ripped. I brought my hand to my neck, my throat hurt. And I had just learned my ex-boyfriend was a wannabe rapist. I started to speak but barked a cough instead. I shook my head.

He turned to Jack. "You," he commanded, "come with me."

A second squad car arrived, and Jack was dragged to the back seat and questioned out of earshot. I was still trying to process what had just happened and what had almost happened when a delicate hand reached out. I looked up, and relief rushed through me to see a woman in uniform. Shaking like it was twenty below instead of well above one hundred, I dropped my feet to the concrete, straightened what was left of my skirt, and stepped out of the car, holding onto her with one hand and the car door with the other. She lowered me onto the curb and sat down beside me.

"I'm Officer Spencer. And you are...?"

"Amanda."

"Your last name?"

"Amanda Earle."

"Amanda, are you okay? Can you tell me what happened?"

I began to cry. I'd needed a female presence to admit that I was absolutely nowhere near okay. *How could I possibly be okay?* The words spilled out as I told her everything, from Janette's invitation to Graham's skateboard shattering the window. With each word, I felt a sense of control returning—less like a helpless victim and more like myself.

"Whatever she says, she's lying," Jack yelled.

"You, shut up!" she yelled back.

"I need to call my mom."

"Where's your phone?" the officer asked.

"In my purse."

When my mom answered on the first ring, I told her only that I needed her to come get me. "What's wrong, Amanda?" She sounded panicky.

"Just come get me, Mom. I'm in the back parking lot."

Jack was still shouting, pointing a finger at Graham, when I heard my mother's voice. "Amanda!"

I was so confused. *How did she get here so quick? What's happening?*

"Why are these students being detained?"

And Mr. Roi? Nothing made sense.

Another officer approached Mr. Roi. "And you are...?"

"Timothy Roi. I'm a teacher here." He looked at me then at my mom.

The officer pulled him out of earshot, and my mom rushed to my side, wrapped her arms around me, and pulled me close. "Mandy, sweetie, what happened? Are you okay?" That was the third time I'd been asked that question when the answer should have been obvious. Before I could speak, she turned to the female officer next to me. "What the hell happened here?"

"That's what we're trying to find out, ma'am. Are you her mother?"

"Yes."

She took in the scene—Graham in handcuffs and Jack being questioned, both in the back seat of police cars—and then zeroed in on the rip in my skirt. She grabbed my chin and looked me in the eye, her voice laser sharp. "Was it Graham, Mandy? Did that boy hurt you?"

Chapter 25
Deb

Despite the litany of questions squirreling around in my head, Amanda's fragile state prevented me from asking anything more of her, and little was said on the ride home from the police station. The police had already asked enough questions—questions I wasn't privy to, questions I was craving answers to myself.

Officer Spencer had gently pulled me aside. "Ms. Earle, your daughter would prefer that you not sit in while we interview her."

I was appalled. "What? I have a right to..."

"Ma'am, she's seventeen. She has a right to make that decision."

But she was just a child. *My* child. To hell with legalities. She needed me. *Will she be too afraid to tell them what really happened? Will they twist her words and trap her? Will they even believe her?*

I watched the hem of Amanda's torn skirt flutter as another officer escorted her into a room and closed the door, severing our connection. It felt as if she'd been ripped from my arms. I sank into a backless wooden bench pushed against the wall, gripping the metal bars designed to cuff suspects and prevent escape.

Amanda was too young to rent a car, to sign a lease, to vote. Most institutions understood that she was still a child needing her mother's guidance. Everyone except the police. This was wrong. I called Richard again and again, but he wasn't answering. I left a message, trying to unsuccessfully channel calm as I watched the cast of characters being dragged into the station. I wouldn't go to the bathroom.

I wouldn't get a sip of water. I wouldn't budge. I wanted to be the first face she saw when the door to the interrogation room opened. My thoughts festered. Whoever was responsible for hurting Amanda would pay. And I had a gut feeling that none of this would be happening if Graham weren't involved.

The door to the station swung open, and an officer walked in with... Graham. I had a moment of panic as I thought they might cuff him on the bench next to where I was sitting. His head down, his hands cuffed behind his back, he looked every bit the part of a drug dealer. He cut his eyes in my direction as they pulled him toward another room. And then he was out of my sight.

Next in line was Jack's father and another man who, based on his Brooks Brothers suit, I could only assume was a lawyer, who strolled in side by side, commanding attention. The lawyer was talking to one of the officers, his back to me, his voice low.

Moments later, an older man with a gray ponytail, wearing overalls and flip-flops, burst in and asked for Graham. "I'm Graham Scott's father."

He looked old enough to be *my* father.

"You need to take a seat, sir."

"And his lawyer."

Amanda needed a lawyer. *Did I screw up by not contacting one for her?* I had a new source of churning angst.

An eternity passed before she walked out of the interview room, Officer Spencer right behind her. "You can take her home now, Ms. Earle."

I pulled Amanda to my chest. She held onto me as if letting go would drop her off the edge of a jagged cliff. She was trembling.

I stared at Spencer. "So?" I demanded.

"I'm afraid we have conflicting accounts of what happened. We're taking everyone's statements, and the investigator will review them tomorrow, and we'll have to take it from there." She shifted her feet in an apology, everything on her duty belt shifting with her, before she said softly, "I have a teenage daughter, too, Ms. Earle. We'll do what we can to get a clear picture of what happened."

ONCE WE WERE BACK AT the house, Amanda beelined up the stairs and into her room.

"Amanda, wait, do you want to talk?" I asked, desperate.

"I just want to go to my room."

"Amanda, please. I need to know what happened, what the police said."

"Mom, not now." She started to cry. "I'm so tired."

The sharp words escaped before I could stop myself. "Amanda, was it Graham?"

She stopped midstep, her back to me. "No," she whispered. "He wouldn't hurt me."

"So, what... are you telling me it was *Jack*?" I heard the incredulity in my voice.

She hesitated before turning around. Her fists were clenched. "Jack tried to rape me. Graham stopped him."

I grabbed the banister to steady myself and collapsed on the bottom step. Jack Offerhaus in the Oxford blue button-down collar seemed so wholesome, so genuine, so *nice*. How could it be that just a few days ago, he was in the driveway, waving and asking me how I was doing? I'd let Amanda be alone with him day after day, night after night.

Has anything like this happened before? I felt sick. I could almost hear the gears stripping as I tried to shift my perspective. I thought I knew Jack well, but I clearly didn't know him at all.

"Well... well, then, we *will* press charges, Amanda." I crossed my arms. My jaw clicked with tension. "He has to pay."

She sighed with the resignation of a world-weary octogenarian. "I don't think so. He's got serious connections. His uncle is a federal judge, and his dad is CEO of Blue Sails. You think anyone's gonna believe me? Believe Graham?"

"But, Amanda, if he did this, he can't just get off scot-free!"

"If? See, even you're doubting the truth."

I shook my head. "I'm sorry. That's not what I meant, and you know it."

"All I know is, I'm not going to put myself or you and Daddy through all that. Or Graham. Anyway, just think for a minute. A trial? Lawyers? Mr. Offerhaus is a big deal. It would be all over Reddit and Twitter, not to mention the local news. There's no way Jack would go to jail even if I did press charges. So it stops here."

"But was anyone else around? Were there any witnesses?"

The front door flung open, slamming the doorknob against the wall in the entryway, leaving a permanent notch in the sheetrock. Richard looked at me then up at Amanda. "I went to the station, but they said you'd gone." Still breathless, he asked, "What the fuck happened?" It was the first time I'd heard Richard use the f-word in front of Amanda. He took the stairs two at a time and enveloped her in a hug designed to shield her from all the evils of the outside world. "Mandy, sweetie, are you okay?"

"Yes, Daddy, I'm okay," she said before dissolving into convulsive sobs. Richard looked at me as if he expected me to telepathically transmit the day's events. I motioned to the kitchen. He took Amanda by the hand and led her to her room. I stayed at the bottom of the stairs, listening to the muffled sounds of their exchange. When I heard her bedroom door close again, I went into the kitchen and waited for him.

"I tucked her in. I think she was asleep before I even closed the door. So..." He stiffened, shrugged one shoulder, and twisted his neck until it cracked. "What happened? The police weren't at all helpful.

They said it was an 'alleged assault.' What the hell does that mean?" He leaned in. "Was she...?" He cleared his throat and shifted in his seat. "Raped?" He whispered the last word, imbuing it with the gravity it deserved, his eyes filled with genuine terror.

"No... no." I put my hand on his forearm to comfort him, only to realize how much I needed his touch, our connection, to steady me.

He looked at the ceiling and exhaled in relief. I filled him in on the facts as I knew them, complete with Graham using his skateboard as a weapon, the shattered glass, the police, Jack declaring his innocence, and Amanda declaring his guilt.

"Thank God Graham was there," he said.

I was still having a hard time casting Graham as the good guy in this scenario.

"So, what was Jack charged with?" he asked.

"Nothing yet."

"What—everyone just went home like nothing happened?" His booming voice rose with each question. "Fuck that shit."

"Richard, shhh. You're going to wake Amanda." I had a flashback to when Amanda was a baby and every conversation or argument ended with me saying, "Richard, shhh. You're going to wake Amanda."

"She's been traumatized. That son of a bitch is going to jail. I'm calling Christopher."

Christopher Becker was the lawyer who helped us set up everything for Monday Morning, but he wasn't a trial lawyer. Amanda was right. The word *trial* triggered vertigo.

We both jumped at the sound of my cell. I didn't recognize the number. I stared at it on the table as it rang three more times, rumbling ominously against the wood.

"Answer it, Deb."

I hesitated before picking it up. "Hello?"

The commanding baritone on the other end belonged to the Brooks Brothers suit. I mouthed to Richard, "Jack's lawyer." The conversation was mostly one-sided as I listened, pacing the kitchen, Richard on my heels.

"What's he saying? Tell him we're going to press charges," he growled, his face reddened with anger and frustration. When I hung up, Richard locked eyes with me, eyebrows raised, looking like he would implode waiting for me to fill him in. "So?"

"His name's Stephen Vega."

"What did he say?"

My fingers trembled as I set the phone back down on the table. "Shit, I can't believe it."

"What? What did he say?"

"He reminded me—not so subtly—that Jack's family is well connected. And he made it very clear that attempted rape is next to impossible to prove without witnesses—a he-said-she-said situation."

"This Vega is threatening us? He could be disbarred trying to pull something like that."

"But do you really want to put that to the test? Plus, Jack is her ex-boyfriend, and he's saying they had sex when they were together, this was just more of the same, and she's angry at him for breaking up with her."

"What? I thought she broke up with him!"

"She did."

"And the police saw Graham break the window. He could be charged with aggravated assault."

"Jesus!" Richard stood up, his hands balled into fists, and he began pacing.

"*And* he said Jack could easily cast doubt on the situation—maybe Graham was jealous and went crazy when he saw Amanda and Jack together. Maybe Amanda didn't want Graham to know that she was seeing Jack again and concocted this story that

Jack attacked her. They have a few options that let Jack off the hook and make Amanda look like a liar."

Richard slumped back down in his chair and began shuffling his supplement bottles on the table like chess pieces. "That is seriously screwed up."

"Yes, it is." My stomach churned. Because of Jack's horrifying behavior and his parents' obvious disregard for Amanda, I had to protect her from all things Offerhaus. *Better late than never?*

Chapter 26
Amanda

I stayed home for two days, trying to sleep away the trauma. It didn't work. I was tired down to my bones, as my gran used to say, and my stomach was on a slow boil. I had quietly shuffled to the bathroom and dry heaved—twice. I couldn't eat.

Hadley came by after school both days and sat on my bed, trying to make me feel better. "Okay, I am now your personal bodyguard, your own Secret Service detail. Your code name is Dragon Tattoo."

"What?"

"The girl with the dragon tattoo! She was badass."

I'd laughed, but the thought of going back to school had my heart racing, even if Hadley would be my security detail.

My phone dinged. It was Graham. I hadn't seen him since... since it happened. My mom made sure of that. Even his heroics hadn't been enough to convince her that having him in my life was a good thing.

"Amanda, I think that boy is a disaster just waiting to happen. He's evidently hanging out with a bunch of rowdy skateboarders, and I don't know anything about his family. I mean, I saw his dad with the ponytail and tattoo sleeves. I just don't think—"

I yelled back, "You don't know anything! You're just being prejudiced. You don't know any of them. I do!" I'd slammed my door in her face, dropped on my bed, and cried myself breathless.

When I didn't answer, Graham texted again: *Amanda? You okay? I miss you. When are you going back to school?*

Me: *Tomorrow*

Graham: *Great. I'll pick you up. Can't wait.*

I slunk back in my pillow and stared at the screen.

Graham: *Babe still there?*

Me: *My mom says she's picking me up from now on.*

Graham: *WTF? When can I see you?*

Me: *Sorry. My mom is being weird. Says she doesn't trust you.*

I didn't trust myself. I wasn't sure what my reaction would be the first time he put his arm around me, leaned in to kiss me, and breathed on my neck. I waited. He wasn't typing. I waited some more. Finally a single word popped up.

Graham: *So?*

Me: *I'll figure something out. And I miss you too.*

"What'd he say?" Hadley asked.

That was all it took for me to begin bawling again. I'd cried more in the past three days than I had all year.

WHEN I WENT TO SCHOOL the next day, I was welcomed back with ugly notes stuck to my locker.

You're a lying cunt.

Fucking whore.

I hope you die.

Jack was a basketball superstar. I was just a girl who had been rejected by the senior hottie and was out for revenge. I ripped them off, stuffed them in my purse, and walked away without getting my books.

On my way to first period, I spotted Jack down the hall. My heart stopped. This was a million times worse than when he'd started spreading those sick rumors about me. That was immature. What he had done to me in the car turned him into a psychopath. I turned and walked as fast as I could in the opposite direction to the bathroom, into the only empty stall, and leaned over, thankful I hadn't eaten breakfast. Maybe this would be the routine for the rest of the school year—see Jack from a distance, take evasive action, and puke.

That afternoon, as I sat in the school office waiting for Graham to walk through those doors, Ms. Hathaway looked at me, a sympathetic tilt to her head. "How are you, hon?"

"I'm good, thanks."

She hesitated, stood up, swished in my direction, and leaned over the counter between us. "I... I heard what happened. I'm so sorry."

Jesus, everyone knows.

"I hope you know none of it is your fault."

I shifted uncomfortably in my seat.

"If you need anything, anything at all, you let me know."

I pushed my hair behind my ears and nodded.

"Don't let this whole thing taint your senior year. I know that family. Just don't let them get to you. Okay?" She leaned in farther, spilling over the counter, and locked eyes with me. "I know exactly how you feel." She took a breath and straightened. "My understanding is that there weren't grounds to suspend Jack, but he won't be a problem after this week. Don't you worry."

"Amanda?" Ms. Gordon, the school counselor, was summoning me to her office. She must have figured it was her job to counsel me.

All the seniors had been to see Ms. Gordon at some point. Counseling was mandatory. She would say things like "You have great potential," "We're so proud of the work you're doing," and "Is anything getting in the way of your success at school?" Her canned responses left people more irritated than when they walked in and sat down, staring at the photo on her desk of her three bratty kids. I only hoped she wasn't going to focus on what had happened to me.

"Amanda, I'm so sorry to hear about the incident earlier in the week."

Here we go. "Incident"? Is that what we're calling it now?

"However, I'm glad to see you back at school. How are things going?"

Awesome, just awesome. "Fine."

"I just wanted to let you know that Principal Sherman spoke both with the police and with Jack's parents and..."

Oh? I feel so much better. "Thank you, Ms. Gordon."

"If you need anything at all, feel free to drop by anytime."

When hell freezes over. "I appreciate that, Ms. Gordon."

I heard my mother's muffled voice mixing with Ms. Hathaway's. "My mom's here. I should really go." I stood, gathered my stuff, and turned to the door, ready to make my escape from her claustrophobic office. My phone dinged. I pulled it from my pocket and glanced at it—the third text from Graham since I'd walked into the office.

"Amanda?"

I turned back around. "Yes, ma'am?"

"I really do have an idea of what you're going through." Her eyes were glistening. "I mean it when I say I'm here anytime you need to bend someone's ear."

I mentally groaned, not because she wasn't being genuine but because I really did have a terrible talent for misjudging people.

Chapter 27
Deb

It had been a few weeks since Merritt and I talked, so I was surprised when she answered on the first ring. "Deb?"

"Look, Merritt, I know we're not in a good place, but..." My voice cracked.

"What's wrong, honey?" The boundless concern in her voice reminded me that we were sisters. Always. There was no reason to rehash our fight or exchange apologies. It was understood.

"Merritt, I..."

"Is everyone okay?"

"No, not really. I'm not even sure where to begin." I choked on my words.

"Take a deep breath, and then just let it out."

"So, you remember Jack, Amanda's boyfriend from the summer?" I stood and paced my office as I told Merritt everything—about Jack and Graham, about the skateboard, about the police.

"Shit, Deb. Shit, shit, shit! But Amanda's okay?"

"Physically, yes, but this has had an effect on her."

"Of course, it did. And on you too. How's Richard handling it?"

"You know Richard. He wants to 'fix' everything."

"So, what happens next?"

"Nothing. The Offerhauses' lawyer made it crystal clear that, without witnesses coming forward, they were prepared to sue Amanda for falsely accusing Jack and causing—wait for it—'emotional distress.'" I let that sink in. "And Graham could be sued for damages to that seventy-five-thousand-dollar car and—"

"Jesus! Who in their right mind gives a teenager a seventy-five-thousand-dollar car?"

"The Offerhauses, apparently. Anyway, pressing charges would mean thousands and thousands of dollars in legal fees and the potential of a bankrupting lawsuit with little chance of winning. So it ends here. And anyway, Amanda is refusing to press charges or cooperate even if the prosecutor decided to press charges."

I could hear Merritt's breathing speed up.

"Merritt?"

"God, that pisses me off. I told you, I never liked that whole Offerhaus crew. Wes dealt with them when they were filing construction permits for Blue Sails's new headquarters. He said Geoffrey Offerhaus was an overbearing asshole, a real piece of work. He and his lawyer are joined at the hip, always ready for a lawsuit. And his wife, well, she's just a bitch."

There was a brief pause as we both regained equilibrium. I heard her chair scrape against the kitchen tile as she pushed it back and then the splash of water from the faucet into the electric kettle. I pictured her pulling her favorite mug from the cabinet and spooning out the tea leaves—she always gave me a hard time for my Lipton tea bags. She was settling in for one of our talkathons. Though it was unspoken between us, all was forgiven.

"I'm sorry it's under these circumstances, but it's really good to hear your voice, Deb. I've missed us."

"Me too." I walked over to the window, my contemplation corner. "There's something else I wanted to tell you," I said, apprehension washing over me. "I was there when it happened—on campus."

"On campus? You were there?"

"I was in a parent-teacher conference with..." I lowered my voice. "Tim Roi."

"Wait. *That* Tim Roi?"

"Yep."

"Was it weird?"

"Pretty weird."

She hesitated and took a sip of her tea before lightening the conversation. "How does he look up close?"

"Oh, Merritt, stop."

"I'm serious. Richard doesn't have to know."

"A little less hair, and he's got glasses now, but... he looked really good." I whispered.

We giggled like a couple of teenagers gossiping about the boys on the football team. And it felt good to think about something other than what had happened to Amanda.

"I remember him being a real cutie-pie. Is he still a good guy? I remember that too."

I'd never told Merritt about his harsh words back then, and I didn't want to relive our recent conversation. I hadn't sorted it all out myself. "Yeah, I think he is."

"Married?"

"Merritt, stop it!"

"Just asking," she said in a singsong voice.

"Divorced, no kids."

"So he's single?"

"Enough," I said sternly, sapping the humor from the conversation.

"So... did you talk, you know, about what happened between you two?"

I hesitated. This was an emotional minefield. We were talking again, and I didn't want to have it blow up in my face. But her question was about Tim and me, not Merritt and me.

"I think he wanted to get things off his chest, but then we heard the sirens, and our conversation was cut short. Probably for the best."

I'd expected to feel relieved after we hung up. But whatever space in my heart had been freed up by our mutual unspoken apology was replaced with growing concern for Amanda and whether she was handling everything, whether it would leave a deep emotional scar. I grabbed a cigarette, lit it, and gazed out the window at the quiet street.

My infinite capacity to worry, especially when it came to Amanda, frightened me. Had my tacit agreement not to press charges under threat of lawsuits sent the wrong message to her? Or maybe she thought we didn't care enough to insist that charges move forward.

My emotional load was over capacity. Thinking back to my meeting with Tim wasn't helping—how he'd immediately stood when I walked in, papers fluttering to the floor and the hydraulic door closing in slow motion behind me with an amplified whoosh.

"Hi, Debby," he simply said, his voice deeper than I remembered. Ray was the only other person to call me that.

"Hello, Tim." Despite his age-appropriate appearance, I could still see the boy my mother detested—the long hair, the scraggly wannabe beard, the pierced ear, the tattoos. But the coup de grâce for her had been that he was the lead singer in a band that performed in bars he wouldn't have otherwise been allowed to enter.

My soles were glued in place. My heart pounded. I wanted to turn and run. I hated myself for having any kind of reaction at all. What happened with us was nothing more than an outdated hangover.

"Look, I know this is a little strange—for both of us. We haven't spoken in years—decades, even—and, well..." He motioned to a chair, and I spotted the edges of his tree-of-life tattoo peeking out from his sleeve. "Please, Debby, come and sit down."

I nodded before walking the perimeter of the classroom and sliding into one of the students' chairs positioned in front of his desk. I set my purse down and patted it in place as if commanding it to stay.

"How have you been?" he asked.

"For the last twenty-two years?" I chuckled.

"Well, yeah, give or take." His warm smile hadn't changed.

We exchanged stats—colleges, marriages, jobs. When the small talk began to slow, I said, "So, I understand Amanda's having some trouble in calculus. Do you think I should hire a tutor?"

He sighed. "Debby, can I just say something first?"

He was that seventeen-year-old boy again, minus the long hair, crying and asking how I could do something like that without telling him first. But I had, and it was too late. "You're a selfish bitch!" he'd yelled before he turned his back on me and stormed away. I told Merritt and my dad that Tim and I had decided together. That was a big, fat lie. A few months later, his dad was transferred to Houston. I'd never spoken to Tim again.

Until now.

I knew he'd moved back a few years before and that he was Amanda's teacher throughout high school. We'd exchanged nods of recognition from a distance at PTA meetings, but I'd done everything in my power to avoid the awkwardness of a face-to-face encounter. But there we were.

"I've wanted to say this for years," he said, not looking at me. "I wish I'd reached out and said this to you long ago. Or at least when I moved back to Austin." He swallowed hard. He looked like he was in physical pain. "I'm sorry for everything you went through. I was insensitive, and I—"

"Tim, you don't have to do this. Really. I'm the one who was insensitive. I mean, I should have talked to you beforehand. But I was panicking, scared out of my mind. You know how my mother was. I just didn't see another way."

"She didn't know?"

"She found out after." I took a breath and tried to smile. "That's a whole other story."

He placed his elbows on his desk and steepled his fingers against his lips, pulled back, and cracked his knuckles. "Debby, I'm with kids all day who are the same age we were, and yes, they make astoundingly stupid decisions and say really insensitive things. Believe me, I know stupid." He chuckled. "Still, I shouldn't have said those things to you, of all people. I may have been a kid, but I really did love you." He smiled. "Like only a seventeen-year-old boy can."

At first, I was taken aback. But then I was touched that he recalled the intensity of his adolescent feelings for me. "Tim, if we're being totally honest here, I didn't tell you because... because I was afraid you'd talk me out of it. I was crazy about you, too, and... well, neither one of us was anywhere near prepared to be parents. We were just teenagers, for Chrissake." I shook my head.

"Can you please just accept my apology?"

To me, the events of all those years ago was fetid water under the bridge, but he needed absolution. I nodded before looking him in the eye. "Yes, I can do that. If you can somehow accept mine."

"Deal." He exhaled as if he'd been holding his breath all those years. He sat up straighter, pulled a file from a pile on his cluttered desk, placed his hands palms down on top, and took a deep breath. "So, about Amanda," he said, his tone shifting to teacher mode. "She's a really bright student. It's not that she doesn't understand the material. It's like something else—"

That was when we heard the scream of sirens. The "something else" was in the parking lot, smashing the window of a seventy-five-thousand-dollar BMW.

Chapter 28
Amanda

I couldn't sleep. When I closed my eyes at night, I was nose to nose with Jack's angry, twisted face spitting disgusting words in my ear, his hot breath on my neck, his precious senior ring digging into my skin. My mom tried so hard to make everything better, bringing me tea with lemon and honey, making me mac and cheese, but she couldn't get in my head, see what I saw, feel what I felt. And I didn't want her to. Not just her—I didn't want to share the details with anyone. If the police hadn't gotten involved, I wouldn't have even told her. I just wanted it to go away.

The ringing of my phone was a welcome distraction. Hadley's breathless voice was on the other end. "Did you hear about Jack?"

He was the last person I wanted to hear anything about, but I dutifully said, "What about him?"

"He's been shipped off to a military academy in Connecticut!"

I felt relief, sadness, regret. This was proof, at least to me, that his family knew who, or what, he really was. But they didn't want him to have to pay the price, to ruin his perfect future, to be branded a sex offender. Maybe most important of all, they didn't want him to be a stain on the family name.

Later that day, Janette called, on the verge of tears, to tell me what I already knew. And to apologize. She'd thought she was playing matchmaker. "Amanda, I really thought he just wanted to talk." She said she'd hung back to see our happily-ever-after reunion. But when she saw what was happening, she called the police. Anonymously, of course—Jack was still her big brother. My tangled feelings stopped me from offering up the forgiveness she clearly wanted. Yes, if she hadn't called the cops, there was no telling how it would have ended. But if it weren't for the part she played in the beginning, none of it would have happened at all.

Jack might have been physically gone, but he'd staked a claim to a space in my head and made it dark and dirty. I wasn't going to let him erase the bright and shiny space that belonged to Graham.

MY BIRTHDAY WAS COMING up—October 31. I always loved celebrating the twofer by dressing up as Maleficent, the sorceress in *Sleeping Beauty*. When I was a kid, it was a cute little number with black ruffles and a horned hat. As I got older, it morphed into a sleek black gown, black nail polish and lipstick, cat eyes, and unnaturally long false eyelashes. I would prowl the neighborhood, handing out candy corn and cackling until my throat hurt.

This year, the night presented an opportunity to be with Graham for more than just a few minutes. To steal those few minutes with him, I'd been telling my mom I was going to after-school tutoring and that she needed to pick me up late. Graham and I would sit in his car and kiss like we were starving vampires. But each time I had to ease into it. As much as I wanted to be with him, I had to constantly remind myself that Graham wasn't Jack. Graham was a cuddly warm-blooded mammal. Jack was a reptile. Graham would never force me to do anything I didn't want to do. Still, that feeling of strong hands on me, even when they were Graham's, triggered an instant of panic, and I had to fight my primal instinct to push him away.

I knew he could feel me tense up because he'd pull back and whisper, "It's okay, Amanda. Just tell me if you want to stop." But I didn't want to stop—I just wanted to wipe my mental slate clean of Jack.

Each day, when the alarm on my phone would go off, it was time for Mom to pick me up. I would run around to the front door, and there she'd be with that *I want to make it all better* smile. She would say, "You look flushed, sweetie. You okay?"

I would answer, "I was on the other side of campus, so I had to run" or "The heat was turned on way too high in my last class" or "Yeah, I'm not feeling so great." I rotated my reasons for having rosy cheeks.

She hadn't exactly said Graham was off-limits, but she would inevitably come up with some excuse as to why we couldn't get together. She was always hovering, always checking, always watching the clock. Graham and I hadn't had a chance to be alone without a time limit in weeks.

When she finally let him come over, we watched a movie in the living room while Mom sat in the kitchen within earshot. I nodded in her direction and whispered, "This sucks. I'm really sorry."

"Yeah, me too." He gave me a lopsided smile. "God, I wish we could be alone," he whispered. He glanced in the direction of the kitchen before cradling my face in his hands and kissing me as if we were actually alone.

At the sound of footsteps, he quickly pulled away and positioned a suede throw pillow in his lap. A second later, my mom leaned into the room. "You two want some popcorn?"

On Halloween night, it was hard to miss the extreme arch in my mom's eyebrows when Graham came to the door dressed as the devil, complete with red horns and a forked tail. As I walked out the door, she slipped a pink canister of pepper spray in my hand. "Just in case," she whispered. She was arming me against the wrong guy.

As we wandered the neighborhood, Graham and I handed out individual packages of candy corn and oohed and aahed over the kids' costumes. My favorite was the little angel with wings, her pink outfit dragging the ground. She was too young to say "trick or treat," so she would just walk up, open her bag, and smile, her mom standing an arm's length away. In between candy deliveries, Graham would stop and pull me to the dark side of a house, kiss me hard, and press his body against mine, always asking first, "Is this okay? Are you okay?" I could feel the rough brick pressing against my back through the thin fabric of my costume and his excitement pressing against my stomach.

Mom wanted me to come home in time to go out for a birthday dinner—just her, my dad, and me. She made it clear, without coming right out and saying it, that Graham was not welcome. But Daddy had other ideas.

Chapter 29
Deb

Richard insisted that we invite Graham to come along and to let him take Amanda out after dinner, as long as they were back by eleven o'clock.

"Like it or not, Deb, we can't let what happened to Amanda rule her life. And I don't see how any blame falls on Graham."

"But—"

"Can't you see that by trying to cut Graham out, it'll just make her want to be with him that much more?"

"Yes, but—"

"Deb, it's her birthday! Besides, I want to meet the guy. She's been seeing him for a while, and I'd like to make my own judgment about him."

There was a silent break before he lowered his voice. "This is not an I told you so, but I always had my doubts about Jack. You were just so impressed with him that I—"

He was rubbing blame in my face. As if I weren't berating myself enough for colossally misjudging Jack. My footsteps pounded the stairs as I headed to the bedroom and slammed the door.

Richard and I weren't fighters—not until the baby thing. We'd always been sharers, peacemakers, the couple who never went to bed angry. So I had little practice suppressing hurt feelings with him. But no matter how hard I tried to push my resentment away, it pushed back with surprising strength. I never understood how marriages survived constant bickering, name-calling, and accusations—the constant battle of wills.

But Richard didn't understand the underpinnings of my feelings about Graham or Jack.

How could he? I'd never told him about my ongoing battle with my mother when I was Amanda's age. She'd made a judgment about Tim, based on his appearance and the well-worn guitar he always had slung across his back. And now I had judged Jack, and I'd been so wrong. *Was I wrong about Graham as well?*

Amanda's eighteenth birthday. Who decided that adulthood begins at eighteen? Amanda was still a child. It was such a tired cliché, but I couldn't help but ask myself, *Where did all those years go? Wasn't it just a couple of years ago that Amanda was folding her little arms against her chest, stomping her feet, and crying because she suddenly hated socks and insisted on going to preschool barefoot? Wasn't it just a couple of months ago that she came home from third grade, so proud of her ribbon for perfect attendance, only to be crestfallen when she learned she wasn't the only one? It was certainly yesterday that she tried out for the dance team her freshman year after spending the summer in the Texas heat, practicing drills.*

Hadley had made the cut, but Amanda hadn't. She was destroyed. She'd gotten over it, but I never had. The memory of that look on her face could still ruin a good mood.

"I'll get it!" Richard yelled from downstairs. I'd been so deep into my thoughts that the chiming doorbell hadn't registered.

I heard Amanda bounding down the stairs and the lilt in her voice. "Daddy, this is Graham. Graham, my dad."

"So, I finally get to meet *the* Graham Scott," Richard said.

I pictured Amanda's blush and the mano-a-mano handshake. "Thanks for inviting me, Mr. Earle."

"Of course, call me Richard. Everyone else does."

I shook my head. That meant Graham would be calling me Deb. I heard the smile in Richard's voice when he called up the stairs for me to come down.

"I'll be there in a minute!"

We were about to gather for a birthday celebration for Amanda. But because of Graham, in all his dread-headed glory, I didn't want to go. I would have to fake it—smile and make pleasant "parent conversation," as Amanda called it.

I stared at myself. "Mirror, mirror on the wall, who's the most narrow-minded of them all?" I stuck my tongue out before practicing my welcoming smile and heading downstairs.

I stood on the last step of the stairs and scanned the scene. They were still in their costumes. Amanda looked deliriously happy standing next to Graham, and Richard looked pleased with himself for being the reason she was so happy.

"I'm so glad you could join us," I said, smiling. Richard cut a glance in my direction, and I smiled at him too. He put his fist to his mouth and cleared his throat as he tried not to laugh at my forced graciousness.

"We're going to that new Italian place downtown," Richard said to Graham. "Hope that's okay."

"Sounds awesome," Graham said, his dreads flouncing as he nodded and pulled Amanda close. I thought I was doing a pretty good job of fixing a smile on my face, but when Graham looked at me, he stepped away from Amanda... and I was pleased with myself for creating even that small wedge between them.

THINGS WERE GOING AS well as could be expected when, somewhere between the prosciutto bruschetta and the chicken pesto, I brought up the subject of college. "Amanda is applying to

New York University." I looked at Amanda. "If it's not too late to apply."

"Mom, come on. Not now."

"Okay, we won't talk about your college plans. What about you, Graham? Where are you planning to go?"

He shifted in his seat. "Well, Ms. Earle, I'm actually not applying right now. I don't know if Amanda told you, but my parents own Urgent Café, a place near the university, and they want to retire, so I'll be taking over, at least for a while."

"Oh. No school?"

"It's an awesome place, really," Amanda interjected as she leaned in to Graham. "Sustainable coffee and all-vegan menu. I love it."

"Well, that sounds great, Graham," Richard said, clearly trying to put a positive spin on it. "As a business owner, I can tell you it can be exhausting, but it can be really rewarding too."

I glanced at Richard. He *looked* exhausted.

"And for me, being my own boss has been reward enough. We've each managed to be our own boss for almost twenty years, right, hon?"

"Yes, *after* college."

My comment was followed by a thorny silence. Maybe this *was* a good thing. Graham would be in Austin, and Amanda would be fifteen hundred miles away and living a new life in New York City. Graham would likely be relegated to the "high school boyfriend" she might tell her own daughter about as she warned her about first loves. For a second, I felt better.

Amanda reached out and gently placed her hand over Graham's. The young waiter's timing couldn't have been better as he approached the table, stood at attention, and began belting out "Happy Birthday" in operatic Italian. Amanda buried her blushing face in her hands but not before shooting pretend deadly daggers at her father.

When the song was done, the waiter took a bow and handed out dessert menus.

"Oh good. Anyone care to split a birthday tiramisu?" Richard asked. "Amanda?"

There would be no more talk of colleges or Urgent Café. Dessert was the wordless clinking of forks on plates until Richard leaned into me and whispered, "I'm going to the bathroom." I nodded, and he scrambled away, almost knocking a serving platter from a waiter's hands.

After a prolonged segment of fill-the-space conversation, I stood. "I'm going to check on your father. I'll be right back."

I knocked on the men's bathroom door. "Richard?" No answer.

A man who had been seated at the table next to ours was about to go in.

"Excuse me, could you check on my husband? He's been in there awhile. His name is Richard."

"Sure."

As he pushed the door open, I craned my neck to look inside—all I could see was a row of empty urinals. I heard the man calling, "Richard?" then the mumbling of male voices before the man opened the door to let Richard out. "He looks a little pale."

"Thank you. Richard, are you okay? What's wrong?"

"I'm really not feeling so hot. I need to go home." He took a bracing breath before shuffling back to the table.

"Daddy? What's wrong?"

"I think maybe it's all this rich food. Not used to it." He was trying to look less sick for Amanda, but I could tell he felt bad. Really bad. I asked for the check, and Richard pulled his two-percent-cash-back credit card from his wallet.

We were standing to leave as Graham politely thanked us for dinner and said, "Let me give you a gift card for Urgent. Maybe you can drop by when you're feeling better." I almost felt sorry for him, so anxious to impress at least one of Amanda's parents.

"That sounds great, Graham." Typical Richard. He felt like crap but was still making nice with Amanda's boyfriend.

Graham whipped his wallet from his back pocket and removed a bright-blue card, pulling a shiny red square foil packet along with it—the exact color of his devil costume. I watched in horror as it fell in slow motion into the middle of what was left of my tiramisu. The light from the candle on the table made the foil sparkle like a Christmas decoration. Time stopped as Richard and I stood, staring at it. Graham got the clock ticking again when he swiped it off the plate and shoved it back in his wallet, not even bothering to wipe it clean of mascarpone.

Chapter 30
Amanda

As we drove away from the restaurant, Graham and I laughed until we cried, mimicking my parents' expressions over the condom drop. "Your dad looked like he was about to puke, and the look on your mom's face... well, I'm not sure how to describe it. Shock? Embarrassment? I don't think she could have looked more horrified if I'd thrown you down on the table and ripped off your clothes."

I felt myself blush at the thought. "Yeah, I know. I can't believe she didn't say anything. I think it was just too much for them to process."

If they had tried to renege on their permission to let Graham and me go out alone after dinner, it would have been like saying they knew Graham and I were going to do it as soon as we were out of their sight. The irony of it all? Graham and I had only had sex the one time. I didn't even know he was carrying the condom around in his wallet. It wasn't like we were going to do it in the back seat of his microcar. And I was still trying to put Jack and what he'd done to me in the past.

I barely noticed when Graham slowed, pulled onto a side street, and put the car in park. "What are we doing?"

"Just a sec." He reached in the back seat and handed me a card. Colorful butterflies covered the front. Inside, it read, *What's a butterfly garden without butterflies? Happy Birthday!*

I broke into a grin. "Am I the butterfly in this scenario?"

"The only one, babe." He gently ran his fingers through my hair and pulled me toward him until our lips met. It was a perfect birthday kiss. When he pulled back, he said, "Wait, one more thing." He reached back to the floorboard, hauled a huge box to the front, and set it on my lap.

"Wow. Did you wrap this yourself?"

"Pffft. Yeah, right. Open it."

"What the...? It's so heavy." I ripped off the paper and stared at the writing on the box. I frowned. "Are you serious?"

"I'll teach you."

I managed to remove the skateboard from the box. It was decorated with an amazing black-and-white varnished image of a butterfly-like creature with an elephant's trunk and tusks. "What is it?"

"It's a take on the Hindu god, Ganesha, the god of beginnings."

"Very cool," I said, though I was really thinking, *Me on a skateboard*?

"I don't expect you to do tricks." He laughed. "But it would be awesome if you could go with me sometimes. Just a little. It's something we could do together."

I ran my fingers over the smooth surface of the board. "That's so sweet, and it's beautiful. I appreciate it, I really do. But..."

It really was a thoughtful gift. *The god of beginnings.* Maybe I would begin to be more adventurous. I loved him for trying so hard to hide his disappointment in my hesitation. I leaned over and kissed him. "Okay, okay, when the weather warms up, I'll do it." I hesitated. "I think it's probably best if we keep it in your car, though."

THREE WEEKS HAD PASSED since my eighteenth birthday, and Karin had been on lockdown the entire time, only permitted to go to school and back. She was freaking out, her situation reaching DEF-

CON 1. I always let her use my phone at school to call Rocket, and I watched her crouching in the corner, whispering to him, her voice cracking. It made me want to cry. But she rarely cried. She had lots of experience covering her feelings with an invisibility cloak. She could have just caught the bus and headed to wherever Rocket was, but the consequences she was sure to face when she got back home kept her feet firmly planted in place. More than once, I watched her wait at the bus stop, take a step toward the door, then hesitate.

"You getting on?" the bus driver would ask. She would shake her head as she stepped back and watched the bus pull away.

Since Halloween and the fateful condom drop, Graham and I had spent more time talking and texting than touching. I'd long since realized that we hadn't been a hookup—we were in it for the long haul, despite my parents doing their best to keep us apart. I pouted and grumbled my way through Thanksgiving dinner, and I came close to a complete mental meltdown at Christmas when Mom and Daddy created a united front to forbid me from spending it with Graham. But Daddy was not his usual joking self, and I didn't want to upset him, so I figured I'd better not bitch about it too much. Maybe I was legally an adult in the eyes of the law, but those rules didn't apply at home.

Does Mom actually think her restrictions are going to foster my Christmas spirit? It was, hands down, the worst Christmas ever. And I didn't even want to think about New Year's Eve.

Another month had gone by before Graham called with a way for us to be together. I didn't ask for specifics. I just said, "Yes!"

"You haven't even heard what I'm going to say yet."

"Doesn't matter. I'm in." My heart fluttered just thinking about his bare chest pressed to mine, his whispers in my ear, asking me what I wanted, what I liked. I knew that this time would have more pleasure and less pain. And I wasn't going to let my monstrous memories of Jack get in the way of my happiness with Graham.

"I hope you're not expecting me to seduce you with poetry and champagne, because it's more likely to be weed and beer."

"That sounds perfect."

"So, my parents are going to be out of town this weekend for a couples' retreat. They go to these things all the time, and they always stay for the whole weekend."

"Are you inviting me for a sleepover?" I giggled.

"Yes, as a matter of fact, I am."

"Should I bring my sleeping bag?" I teased.

"Will it fit two?" His voice rumbled, and I knew he was conjuring the same image as I was—the two of us pressed together in a single sleeping bag.

I swallowed hard. "It sounds amazing. How exactly do you think I can pull this off?"

"Can you get Hadley to pick you up and say you're sleeping over at her place? I mean, I haven't met her, but you trust her, right?"

"One hundred percent."

"Good. I really want to be with you again, Amanda."

I felt my face blush hot. "Me too." I tried not to sound too anxious, when what I wanted to do was jump through the phone, wrap my arms around him, and not let go.

"WOW!" HADLEY SAID. "You sure you're up for that? I mean, you know..."

"I refuse to let Jack fuck up my relationship with Graham." Tears threatened. I stood up and began pacing my room, the phone pressed hard to my ear. Lately, my anxiety had a hair trigger. My breath came in short gasps.

"So, the whole house to yourselves. What are you going to do for twenty-four hours—besides have lots of torrid sex?"

Her words pulled the trigger, and against my will, I began to seriously second-guess our plan. "I don't know." I laughed nervously.

How will we spend the rest of our time together? Watching movies? Listening to music? Getting stoned? Skateboard lessons? I just knew I wanted to be with him, no matter what that meant.

"So, you in?" I asked.

"Hell yeah! I'll be there to get you tomorrow around five o'clock?"

"I'll be ready."

MOM WAS HOVERING IN the doorway to my bedroom as I packed my overnight case. "So, Hadley is picking you up?"

"For the sixth time, Mom, yes." I wanted to pack my new thong and a teddy that Hadley had loaned me. I needed her to leave.

"And you'll be back tomorrow at what time?"

I turned around. My eye roll was as uncontrollable as a hiccup. "It's not like I have to clock in. Whenever I feel like I want to come home, Hadley will drop me off."

"Mandy, look, I'm just worried, okay? I don't think I'm being unreasonable here."

I was irritated by her questions—maybe because I was lying.

She matched my eye roll with an exasperated sigh. "Okay, listen, I'm going to run some errands today. Do you need anything? Shampoo, toothpaste, face wash, tampons?"

"Nope."

She backed away and, without another word, headed downstairs.

And I felt like shit.

Chapter 31
Deb

Amanda was safe at Hadley's, but sleep was still playing hard to get with me. I slipped out of bed so as not to wake Richard, went into my office, and turned on my laptop to check the latest headlines, my Twitter feed, Facebook posts, and my overflowing email inbox. I checked my spam folder for the first time in weeks. It was full of a ton of miracle cures for impotence, creams to take twenty years off no-longer-youthful skin, and surefire ways to make a million. And then there was this:

To: Deborah Earle

From: Timothy Roi.

It was from his personal email, not his school account, and it was dated after our meeting, the day Jack... I double-clicked.

Debbie, first I wanted to see how Amanda was faring. She seems fine in class, but I know that's no indicator of what's really going on in her head. I understand Jack has been shipped off to Connecticut and that no charges were filed. He got off way too easy. I'm truly sorry for that. I just hope Amanda is able to deal with everything and can move on with her life. She's a wonderful young woman, and she has a terrific future ahead of her.

And of course, I wanted to see how you were coping. I know how devastating this must have been for you. I'm sorry we didn't get to speak afterward. Since that day, I've gone over and over our conversation, and I hope I didn't overstep by bringing up the past. I know it's "ancient his-

tory," as you put it. But sometimes it feels as if it were not so long ago. It makes me happy to know that you have a lovely family and the career you wanted. I so clearly remember us sneaking off to Mt. Bonnell late at night to look up at the stars and how you talked about your fantasy of becoming a writer. You made it happen.

Anyway, if I can help you or Amanda in any way, please don't hesitate to let me know.

With Affection,

Tim

I stared at the screen. Why did I feel guilty? Maybe because I was glad to hear from him. Maybe because I had no intention of telling Richard who Tim Roi had been to me. Or maybe because I had my fingers on the keyboard, ready to respond.

When I finally crawled back into bed an hour later, I obsessively ruminated over everything that had happened to my baby girl. Our decision not to pursue charges so as to protect her from the Offerhauses' well-funded revenge filled me with an unspeakable helpless rage. Over the last few months, I'd mentally rehearsed a dozen different conversation starters that might get her to open up to me, to share her pain. But they all fell flat in my mind. If I couldn't be her confidante, I was hoping that her spending time with Hadley would help.

I eventually dozed off and dreamed Jack was behind bars, screaming his innocence, his red face twisted in anger. I was about to scream back at him when Richard's low moan pulled me from sleep. He was sitting on the side of the bed, gripping the mattress, rocking back and forth, his shoulders shrugged to his ears. I glanced at the bedside clock. The bright-green digital numbers said *11:30.*

"Richard, are you okay?"

He didn't answer.

"Richard?"

"I need you to take me to the emergency room."

I leapt out of bed, rushed over to his side, and sat down next to him. Richard hated doctors. Hospitals were on a whole other level of loathing. He moaned again as my movement jostled the bed. His forehead was dotted with beads of sweat, his breathing shallow.

I touched his chest. "Richard, you're burning up. Are you in pain?"

"My stomach. It's killing me." He placed both hands on his stomach. His well-toned abdomen was swollen. "And I have this god-awful taste in my mouth."

I threw on some clothes, helped Richard into sweatpants and a T-shirt, and slowly guided him down the stairs that he usually took two at a time. I eased him into the passenger seat of the car, gently buckled him in, and jumped into the driver's seat. Then I pulled the keys from my purse and, with shaking fingers, turned the ignition once, twice, three times. "Shit!"

Richard slumped toward me, and the familiar scent of his tea tree shampoo triggered a jagged fear of the unknown. "Deb," he whispered.

"Shhh." I caressed his hand. "Shhh."

I stomped on the gas pedal with the ferocity of squashing a roach and turned the key one more time. When the motor rumbled, I cried in relief.

"It's okay," I whispered to myself, wiping away my tears. "It's okay, Richard. We'll be there in just a few minutes."

Richard was normally a terrible backseat driver. He'd say things like "Why did you stop so far from the stop sign?" "Whoa, you're too close to the car in front of you," or "Don't go so fast!" But as we headed down the street toward the hospital, he simply lowered his head and closed his eyes.

At a red light, I silently stared at the sight of him doubled over in pain. The headlights cut a path through the sludge of darkness. The streets were empty, peaceful, a stark contrast to Richard's moans and the war of worry going on in the car. I ran the red light without a second thought.

Richard was never sick. I told myself it was just a stomach virus, or maybe his gallbladder was acting up. There were so many benign possibilities. But I'd also written about countless potentially deadly diseases, mostly with comfortable academic detachment. Now they felt all too real.

It was midnight when we pulled up to the emergency room. Richard squinted against the bright lights of the ER canopy. "Stay here," I said. "I'll go get a wheelchair."

"It's okay. I can walk," he mumbled

"You can barely talk. Just stay here."

The automatic doors opened with a whoosh and a blast of refrigerated air.

I ran up to the desk. "My husband is in the car. He's in a lot of pain, and he's got a fever."

"Do you need a wheelchair or a gurney?"

"Either one. Just hurry, please."

I glanced out the door. Richard, who always outran everyone and was always in control, had his cheek pressed up against the window, the glass fogged from his breath. The woman at the reception desk requested assistance over the PA system, and a man in green scrubs purposefully stepped through the swinging doors, pushing a wheelchair, and followed me out to the car. It took maximum effort from both of us to get Richard out and lower him into the chair.

"Sorry. We're shorthanded. Shift change."

I simply nodded. I wouldn't have cared if a raging fire had been snapping at our heels. I just wanted Richard inside and a doctor telling me that it was a bad bout of gas and he would be all better by morning.

His whimpering moan transitioned to a guttural grunt and reverberated off the walls of the ER cubicle as the nurse tugged on the curtain for the illusion of privacy and I helped him get Richard in bed. I pulled a chair next to the bed, where Richard had curled himself into the fetal position. The fluorescent lights cast a sickening pall on his face... or maybe his skin really was turning the shade of a ripe mango.

"Where's the doctor?" he mumbled.

As if to answer his question, a voice came over the PA system. "Dr. Comrey, please report to the ER. Dr. Comrey to the ER."

The same overworked nurse took Richard's temperature, blood pressure, pulse, and oxygen level. He asked about medications, symptoms, and medical history and gave him an ID bracelet. The five minutes it took for Dr. Comrey to appear felt like no less than an hour. As she pushed the curtain aside and stood by the bed, I breathed in with renewed certainty that everything was going to be okay.

"I'm Dr. Comrey," she said calmly with a trace of a French accent. She was statuesque, with deep-ebony skin and close-cut gray hair. "Are you Mr. Earle's wife?"

"Yes," I said, my voice cracking as I uttered that single word.

She turned to Richard. "Mr. Earle, can you tell me where it hurts?"

He barely opened one eye. "My stomach," he moaned.

"Mind if I take a look?"

Richard nodded.

"Can you roll over on your back for me?"

He shook his head.

"Okay, that's fine." She listened to Richard's heart and lungs. When she pressed lightly on his swollen abdomen, he wailed. She looked at his chart and then turned to me. "He's not on any medication?"

"No." I told Comrey how over the last few weeks, Richard had been exhausted and had developed a mystery rash. I told her about how weeks before, he'd had to leave Amanda's birthday celebration early and how he'd complained of a stomachache for the last few days but had refused to go to the doctor.

"I'm going to order some blood work and a CT scan, and we'll take it from there. But I'm fairly confident it's not his stomach."

Fairly confident. I'd interviewed countless doctors while researching topics for health articles. Their responses were always couched in similarly well-rehearsed qualifiers—"Maybe," "We're not sure," "It could be," or "It depends." I always found their cautious responses thoughtful, worthy of admiration, and incredibly quotable. But in that moment, I wanted to throttle Comrey with my shoe until she spat out a diagnosis.

"How long will that take?"

"I'm calling it in now and something for the pain, but we'll have to wait until morning for the scan." She reached for her phone in the pocket of her lab coat and stepped out into the hall.

I returned to Richard's side. "Richard? Richard?"

His eyes were closed. His breath hitched each time he tried to breathe in.

"God, I feel like I'm dying," he said with a strained breath, and I died a little inside.

His grunts slowly became wails of agony. I had never heard the sound before—certainly not from Richard. Queasy, I bit my lip to stifle the nausea. I was sinking into a steaming tar pit of panic.

Amanda! I needed to let Amanda know. "Richard, I'll be right back." I kissed his fevered forehead, brushed his hair back, and ran my fingers across his bristly cheek. He didn't respond.

I stepped into the corridor, still keeping an eye on him, and called Amanda. No answer. I left messages. I texted her. *Dad's in the hospital. Call me!*

I didn't have Hadley's cell number, but Hadley's mom, Jacqueline, and I had exchanged phone numbers when we volunteered together for the end-of-the-school-year party a few years before. I checked the time. It was almost one in the morning, but maybe she was still up. My fingers trembled as I scrolled through my contacts. Jacqueline answered on the first ring.

"Jacqueline, this is Deb, Amanda's mom. I'm sorry to be calling so late, but could I speak to Amanda? We've had a family emergency. Her dad is in the hospital."

She hesitated. "I'm sorry, Deb, but Amanda's not here."

"What? Hadley picked her up this afternoon, and she said she was spending the night at your house."

"Hold on." I could hear the television blaring in the background. "Hadley, where's Amanda?"

I heard Hadley's voice. "Huh? What?"

"Amanda's mother is on the phone, and she says you picked her up today and said that she was spending the night with you. She needs to get in touch with Amanda."

Then there was silence. "Jacqueline? Jacqueline?" I said. She'd muted the phone.

The waiting was interminable.

"Ms. Earle?" Hadley's voice was uncharacteristically unsure, cautious.

"Where's Amanda, Hadley?" I didn't realize I was screaming until the words were already out.

Her shaky breath echoed in my ear.

In a more measured tone, I said, "Hadley, please. Amanda's father is very sick. He's in the emergency room at St. Joseph's. If you know where she is, you have to tell me."

"She... she's at Graham's. Ms. Earle, I'm sorry. I... I..."

"The address! I need his address."

"I can get her and bring her to the hospital, if you want."

"Yes, you do that."

"I'm really sorr—"

I hung up. I wanted to hurl the phone against the wall, but I stuffed it in my jeans, ripping the pocket, and returned to Richard's side. This was all too much. The night's events triggered a realization with an unmarred clarity—I had been ridiculous to think about having another baby. I just needed for Richard to be okay and for Amanda to be with me.

I had Amanda, and I had Richard. That was all I needed. All I would ever need.

Chapter 32
Amanda

My head lay on Graham's chest, and I listened to the in and out of his breath, the rhythm of his heartbeat. He'd been so right. It did get better. No, it got good. Really good. I was in that sweet twilight space just before I drifted off to sleep, remembering the feel of his strong hands on me and looking forward to the next time and the time after that, when insane pounding on the front door downstairs jerked me awake.

"Jesus!" he mumbled as he lifted his phone from the nightstand and the screen brightened, shedding light on our nakedness. "It's after one. Who the hell could that be?" We both sat up and listened, debating whether to dial 911 or just pray that they'd go away.

Then I heard Hadley's voice. "Amanda! It's me! Answer the door!"

We both jumped out of bed and grabbed our clothes from the floor. Graham pulled on his jeans, I slipped my sweater over my head, and we ran down the stairs. Graham unlocked the door and swung it open. Hadley paused as she took in our half nakedness.

"Amanda, why didn't you answer your phone? Your mom called my mom, and I had to tell her where you were." She took a breath. "Your dad's in the hospital."

"Oh God! What happened? Is he okay?"

"She just said he's really sick and for me to come get you. Here, use my phone." She pulled it from her back pocket and handed it to me.

Mom answered before the first full ring.

"Mom? Is Daddy okay?"

"He's in a lot of pain, and he's got a fever, but they're running some tests. We probably won't know anything until morning."

"I'm sorry, Mom. I—"

"Mandy, I just need you here. Your dad needs you."

"Okay. I'm on my way." I hung up and turned to Graham, who was hovering.

"Let me take you," he said, looking at me with concern.

Hadley and I locked eyes as I handed the phone back to her and turned to Graham. "It would only make things worse, you know? Hadley'll take me, and I'll call you later."

I sprinted up the stairs and into Graham's room, quickly dressed, grabbed my purse, and glanced at my overnight bag. It was best if I didn't bring a reminder of where I'd been and what I'd been doing. I rushed back downstairs. The front door was still open, Hadley was standing on the welcome mat, and Graham hadn't moved a centimeter. Despite being shirtless, he seemed oblivious to the cold air wafting in.

"Amanda, I'm so sorry," he said. I knew that was as much for my dad as for the colossal trouble I would be in. "Let me know how your dad's doing."

"I will." I gave him a quick peck on the cheek and, trailing Hadley, jogged to the Volvo. The key was still in the ignition, the motor rumbling.

Graham stood at the top of the driveway, watching us drive away, his hands shoved in his pockets, hopping from one foot to the other on the freezing concrete. Things had spun so far out of control. My heart was going to burst with shame and remorse. Bad things really did come in threes—my dad sick, my mom knowing I lied, and me leaving Graham all alone. Tears spilled over.

"Amanda, I'm sure your dad will be fine. He's the healthiest old guy I know."

And that was what worried me. Whatever had sent him to the emergency room had to be something serious.

BREATHLESS, I STEPPED out of the car, pulled my phone from my purse, and dialed as I stared at the hospital entrance. "Mom, I'm here. Where are you?"

"Wait in the ER. I'll come get you."

"You want me to stay?" Hadley asked.

"Thanks, but you know, I think I should probably go in alone. I'll let you know."

Her phone rang. "It's my mom. She's going to give me hell for my part in this."

"Thanks for coming to get me. For everything." I hugged her tightly.

She stepped back and shrugged. "What are best friends for?" She walked away, her phone to her ear.

As I went through the automatic doors, I turned to see Hadley watching me, making sure I made it in okay. I looked around. The waiting room wasn't crowded, but everyone there looked sick, sad, defeated, or all three.

Mom came flying through the double doors, her red hair wilder than usual, her eyes just as red and just as wild. She must have realized how crazy she looked, because she suddenly slowed, brushed her hair back, and took a deep breath before she walked up and threw her arms around me.

"Mandy," she whispered in my hair.

"Is Dad okay?" I asked, my voice muffled against her shoulder. She smelled like Finesse shampoo and coffee. She smelled like home.

"I don't know yet, sweetie. Come on. He's asking for you."

I nodded, and we walked hand in hand through the double doors. The unsettling sounds and antiseptic smells took me back to when we rushed to the hospital, worried that something awful had happened to Rocket. But Rocket was okay. Daddy would be okay too.

Through the quiet clamor, I heard him. *Daddy!* I ran toward the moaning and pulled the curtain aside to see a sleeping elderly woman. I heard his voice again in the cubicle next door. As I rushed in, I was hit with shock at how bad he looked.

"Mandy..." he moaned. Under the glaring fluorescent lights, the whites of his eyes were the color of piss, and his skin looked like it did that time he'd gone on a juice cleanse and drank carrot juice every day for a month.

"Daddy," I whispered. I took his hand and kissed his cheek. "How are you feeling? You don't look so good."

He managed a really weak laugh.

The doctor stuck her head in. "Ms. Earle, can I speak with you a moment?" She motioned for Mom to follow her.

"It's okay. This is our daughter."

Dr. Comrey nodded and stepped in all the way. She looked at Daddy. He had drifted off. "Well, we've gotten some blood work back, and your husband has severely elevated liver enzymes."

Mom's eyes had taken on that crazed look again. "His liver?" she asked, her voice strained.

"I've ordered the CT scan and more blood work."

"So, he has liver damage? Nonalcoholic fatty liver disease, maybe?"

The doctor looked at Mom like she was speaking a language she hadn't expected her to understand.

"I write about health topics for a living."

The doctor didn't look at me. "Well, that's a possibility, but based on his medical history and his overall good health, I would be surprised if that were the diagnosis. I would like to wait for the CT scan and the additional blood work to come back. Nothing's going to happen right now. I suggest you go home and get a few hours of sleep."

"I want to stay, I—"

"You'd best get some rest now, while you can. You can come back in the morning, and we'll have more information for you. He'll be sedated. He'll be comfortable for the next several hours."

The images of every medical show I'd ever watched raced across my brain. And it was not good. Mom and I walked to the car in silence, got in, and sat staring into the poorly lit parking garage. She looked at me and blinked twice. I thought she was going to say something to assure me, tell me that everything was going to be okay. Instead, she laid her head on the steering wheel and sobbed.

Chapter 33
Deb

On the ride home from the hospital, Amanda asked me in her most little-girl voice, "Mom, how sick do you think Daddy is, really?"

"I don't know yet, sweetie." I couldn't share with her what I was really thinking, what made my head feel like it had been invaded by a colony of angry fire ants—that elevated liver enzymes could be a sign of any number of horrible, even deadly, diseases or conditions. Or the fact that my period was late.

Amanda turned to stare out the car window as the reflective white stripes flew by on the dark highway. As we entered the newly paved overpass, she turned back and reached out, gingerly placing her icy fingers on my arm. I stopped myself from recoiling from the cold. "I want you to tell me everything the doctor says. Promise?"

I patted her hand, keeping my eyes on the empty road. I couldn't chance a glance in her direction, certain it would trigger more uncontrolled sobbing. "Promise."

"I'm sorry, Mom. You know... lying about being at Hadley's."

I sighed. "I don't have the energy to talk about that now, Mandy. But we *will* talk later."

I OPENED THE FRONT door, and Amanda beelined to her room without a word. I watched the light that spilled out from under her door disappear. The sun would be coming up in just a handful of hours. I wanted to collapse on the bed—coat, jeans, shoes, and all—and disappear into an amnesiac sleep. But I had to wash off the hospital smell that permeated my clothes and transported me back to Richard in the ER and my palpable panic.

As I stood in the shower, the scalding water beating down on my back, I was grateful that when I'd left, Richard had been heavily sedated, unaware. I could have used something myself, but I'd never been one for sleeping pills. I was all too aware of the downside. Richard always said I knew just enough medical information to scare the bejeezus out of everyone around me. I smiled at the memory, then it hit me like an anvil dropped on my head from five stories up—the possibility of my life without Richard. My panic came in waves, receding, swelling, and crashing again. Impossible images flashed across my brain—his liver failing, a donor never found. Richard's funeral, his beautiful body laid out on white satin, makeup smeared on his face to hide its urinous tint.

I gasped. *Stop it! Just stop it now!* I shook my head and turned toward the shower spray to wash away my tortuous thoughts. I was shattering over something that hadn't even happened and, I prayed, never would.

I stepped out of the shower, wrapped my body in a towel, and opened the cabinet below the sink. I calmly took the box, ripped it open, pulled the stick out, and stared at it. I'd bought the pregnancy test when I felt sure Richard would be on board with having another baby. When he said no, I almost tossed it in the garbage. But I'd kept it stashed in the back of the cabinet in the hope that he would change his mind.

The last time I was this late, I was pregnant with Amanda, and when I peed on the stick, I was bubbling with excitement. I was twenty-one and naively confident that this parenting thing would be a piece of cake, that I would be a wonderful mother, and that Richard would be a phenomenal father. Sharing the news with him had only amplified my joy. He placed his hand on my stomach and whispered, "We're going to be a family." I'd been ridiculously young and ridiculously happy.

I sat on the toilet, peed on the stick, and set it on the counter. My brain was barely functioning, but the rapid thumping of my heart was visible beneath my skin. I washed my hands, sat on the toilet seat, and set the timer on my phone. Just a few months before, I would have hoped for a plus sign. Now I was hoping—no, I was fervently praying—that a minus sign would magically appear. But if it was a plus sign, well, I would deal with it.

Along with everything else.

Three minutes later, the timer went off. I held my breath and shook my head as if that would give me the result I needed. My hand shook as I reached for the stick. Negative. I breathed a sigh of relief and promptly burst into sobs.

As my head came in contact with the pillow, I mentally repeated the mantra—*Richard will be fine. Richard will be fine. Richard will be fine*—until I slipped into a troubled unconsciousness that barely resembled sleep.

WHEN THE SUNLIGHT SEEPED through our annoyingly sheer IKEA curtains, I stretched and moaned as I rolled over to Richard's side of the bed. Cold. I quickly scooted back to my warm spot as it all came flooding in anew. Richard was in the hospital, sick. Really sick.

I wanted troubled sleep to possess me once again. I wanted Richard there in our bed, his strong arms around me, telling me that he loved me, whispering, "Come here, baby." He still called me baby when we made love.

I glanced at the clock. Seven o'clock. Thoughts of the night before, when I'd tracked down Amanda and caught her in a lie, invaded my brain. But I still wasn't strong enough to deal with that. *Not now.*

Once I returned to the hospital, Richard and I might have to wait hours before being granted an audience with the hepatologist that Comrey had referred us to. I'd been warned by a floor nurse that the esteemed Dr. Armstrong came and went at will—sometimes at first light, sometimes long after twilight. No warning. *Doctors.* I'd interviewed enough of them to ID his self-absorbed profile. I chided myself. I was being unfair. It wasn't his fault Richard was sick, but he made an excellent scapegoat for my growing anger and dread.

I went down the hall to Amanda's room, passing family portraits that hung on our walls. One photo stopped me cold. I hiccupped a sob as I reached out to touch the image—a three-year-old Amanda perched on my lap, Richard standing over us, smiling down at our bright future. The perfect little family.

Crap like this doesn't happen to perfect little families.

Only it does.

Every day.

I pulled myself together, stood up straighter, and tapped on Amanda's door. When there was no answer, I slowly opened it to find her sitting on edge of the bed, her phone pressed to her ear, cradling it with both of her hands, whispering urgently.

"Amanda, honey?"

She whipped her head up, her eyes red and puffy.

"It's time to get up, sweetie." It was the best business-as-usual voice I could muster for my daughter's sake.

"Any news?" she asked, her voice full of heartbreaking hope.

"No, but that's a good thing," I said, as much to convince myself as to reassure Amanda. "I'm going to get dressed and head over there now."

Amanda seemed to suddenly remember the person on the phone. "Yeah, okay. Later," she said before dropping the phone onto the bed. She heaved a leaden sigh.

"Are you okay?" I asked.

She looked up at me with bloodshot eyes. "Well, Daddy had to go to the hospital in the middle of the night, and he looks like he's dying or something"—her voice cracked—"so, actually, no, I'm not okay."

A boulder-sized lump in my throat threatened to choke me. I couldn't swallow. I opened my mouth—to say what, I wasn't sure—and just as quickly shut it. I stiffened as I worked to gain control of my emotions. "There's really nothing for you to do at the hospital. Maybe you should stay home and rest."

She looked at me like I had lost what was left of my mind. I backed out of the room before our exchange took a turn for the worse and closed the door behind me. Her gentle sobs gutted me. My initial instinct was to return, sit on the bed beside her, stroke her hair, kiss her forehead, and tell her everything was going to be fine and Richard was going to be okay—that we were all going to be okay. I looked at my watch, a gift from Richard. He'd said he couldn't deal with me always digging through my luggage-sized purse for my phone to check the time. It was seven thirty. I hurried down the hall to the bedroom, washed my face, threw on some clothes, grabbed my keys, and tapped on Amanda's door before opening it again.

I hesitated as I reconsidered. "Mandy, why don't you come with me?"

Richard had made me promise that I wouldn't let Amanda worry—not yet, anyway—but I just couldn't let her stay home, imagining the worst. I closed my eyes, nodded once. She was up and dressed in record time.

During the short drive to the hospital, there was an unspoken agreement that I could turn up the music to a hearing-loss decibel level like Richard always did. I didn't know who was singing, but it was one of those irresistible pop songs that everyone loved to ridicule—especially Amanda—but I just knew that when critics were alone, they danced around the room to the beat. The bass pounding through the speakers drove out all thought, and I found myself singing along, lifted by the music. *Karaoke therapy.*

Amanda was giving me a pass. By the time I pulled into the hospital parking lot, I was in a more manageable frame of mind, ready to celebrate good news or be better equipped to cope with the unthinkable. As we stepped out of the car and headed to the hospital entrance, Amanda reached for my hand and squeezed.

I thought back to the times Richard had broken a rib, a finger, or a toe, and he'd had his appendix out just five years before, but he always bounced back in record time and was working out, running circles around everyone else. Okay, maybe he liked to complain about minor physical ailments, but I never took it seriously. I was always sure Richard would outlive me. Now I was reluctantly mulling over the possibility that I could be the one left behind.

WE STOOD OUTSIDE RICHARD'S door. I ran through the lyrics of the last song on the radio, threw back my shoulders, and put my arm around Amanda's shoulders before pushing the door open. Richard was propped up in bed, the IV still dripping. His color seemed a bit better.

"Good morning, handsome. How's my favorite husband?"

"Morning."

My Little Miss Sunshine act hadn't worked. I walked over and kissed him softly on the lips.

"Hi, Daddy." Amanda went around to the other side of the bed and kissed his stubbly cheek. Richard normally shaved every morning, even on the weekends. I noticed a few gray hairs in his scruff that I hadn't even known were there.

I lowered the rail and sat on the edge of Richard's bed while I held his hand, waiting for Dr. Armstrong to show up, deliver the full report, and tell us about treatment options. Richard was silent.

I reached out and patted his leg. "Honey, I'm sure it'll be fine."

He turned to look at me. "I hope you're right." He hesitated. "But," he whispered, "I feel like shit." The television was playing reruns of *Friends* on a seemingly endless loop as Richard stared out the window at the gathering storm clouds. "Come sit by your dad, Mandy." He patted the bed, shaking his IV bag in the process.

She gently lowered herself onto the side of the bed. Though I'd tried to convince myself otherwise, he didn't look good. His skin was a sickly shade of yellow, like his eyes. His voice—the voice that always felt like foreplay—was weak and raspy.

The doctor walked in, bristling with efficiency and purpose, a chart in his hand. "Good morning... Ms. Earle?"

I nodded, but he didn't introduce himself. He glanced at Amanda, giving an obligatory smile, before approaching Richard on the other side of the bed. I watched Amanda scurry away.

"Mr. Earle, I'm Dr. Armstrong. How are you feeling today?"

"Well, I'm hoping better after you give us the results."

I saw dread, hope, and anticipation in his eyes, and one by one, those feelings reverberated in my chest. Dr. Armstrong opened Richard's chart, glanced at it, and sighed. He made eye contact with me then looked in Amanda's direction.

"It's okay," I said. "Go ahead."

"Richard, I'm going to be honest with you. I'm afraid the news isn't good."

I felt my heart take a long jump to my throat. I reached out, and Richard squeezed my hand until the bones in my fingers ached.

I mentally repeated his words. *The news isn't good.* In doctor speak, that meant it was really, really bad.

"Not only are your liver enzymes dangerously elevated, certain proteins in your blood are at abnormal levels as well. And the CT scan shows extensive scarring in your liver—cirrhosis."

Richard pushed the button on the bed's remote control to raise the bed another notch and look the doctor in the eye. "So, what does that mean?"

"It means that your liver is severely damaged and isn't functioning the way it should. In fact, it's barely functioning at all. You're in liver failure."

I gasped. I was torn between comforting my daughter or my husband. But how could I comfort them when I couldn't even comfort myself?

"My liver? But I barely drink, and I don't do drugs." He glanced at Amanda and lowered his voice. "Well, not since college, anyway."

"There are any number of things that cause liver damage—hepatitis, immune disorders, medications, infections."

"How long will it take to heal?"

I wanted to put a force field around Richard. And around Amanda. I wanted to shield them from what I knew Armstrong was going to say.

The doctor didn't miss a beat. "It won't heal, but we want to identify the underlying cause. In the meantime, we'll get you on the transplant list."

My first instinct was to check in with Amanda. As we made eye contact, she slapped her hand over her mouth and turned away. Her shoulders were shaking.

"A liver transplant?" Richard's words flew out with the force of a fist.

My love and empathy were ping-ponging between Amanda and Richard. They both had to be in shock, in pain—and in denial. I'd written about transplants and organ-donor lists. This wasn't like having an appendix removed. It was major surgery with a lifetime of medical monitoring—if a donor became available. Still, the whole thing seemed ridiculous. Richard was the healthiest thirty-nine-year-old man I knew.

"I'm afraid so," Armstrong said with zero empathy. "As I said, a large portion of your liver has developed scar tissue. You don't have enough healthy tissue left for your body to function properly."

I'd seen that expression on Richard's face only once before—when the call came with the news that his father had died on what would have been his parents' thirtieth anniversary. I couldn't allow him to see the same anguish reflected in my face.

He turned to look at me, and I fumbled over the words. "Richard, let's try not worry about something that hasn't happened yet." I turned to the doctor. "Right?"

"I think you should prepare yourselves. We'll talk about options more when I make my rounds this afternoon."

"So, are there other treatments besides a transplant?" Richard was like a kid asking if he could have a pill instead of a shot.

My chin quivered as I fought back tears. He was waiting for Armstrong's answer with a desperate kind of hope. But all hope had an element of desperation woven into it. I couldn't let him see mine.

The doctor patted Richard's shoulder and flashed a patronizing smile. "A transplant is your best option."

He turned and quickly exited, the tail of his white coat flapping behind him. He had dropped a two-ton bomb on my family and escaped before it detonated. I hated him.

Chapter 34
Amanda

Mom was staring at the closed door when Daddy turned to me and motioned for me to come closer. "Well, it seems I'm sicker than my good looks would lead you to believe, sweetheart." He pushed himself up in the bed and grimaced.

A nurse marched in. "Mr. Earle, I've got something that will help with the pain and let you get some sleep."

"Oh, good. Drugs." He gave her a weak smile.

As she plunged the needle into his IV line, he mumbled something that made no sense and closed his eyes. He looked so helpless. It made me want to turn away. And that made me ashamed.

The nurse silently slipped out of the room. Mom had wandered over to the window. Raindrops splattered then slithered down the glass.

"Mom?"

She slowly turned around. She was crying. I went to her, and she wrapped her arms around me, and for just a few seconds, my mommy was keeping me safe from harm, safe from heartbreak.

"Daddy's out," she said, roughly wiping away her tears, "so why don't you stay here, and I'll go downstairs and get us some coffee. It's extraordinarily bad, but I'm desperate. We'll talk when I get back."

I sighed. "Sure."

I'D ALREADY WATCHED an episode of *Friends*, the one where Monica and Chandler slept together for the first time. They were so happy to have finally found one another. The laugh track was pissing me off.

I looked at Daddy. He was still out of it, his breathing slow and steady. *How long does it take to get bad coffee?* I held his hand for a few minutes and kissed his forehead before heading downstairs to the cafeteria. Just stepping out of his room and into the hall made breathing easier. But dread hovered over my head like a tracking drone.

I stopped at the nurses' station to let them know Daddy was alone, and I stepped into an empty elevator. Just before the doors closed, a man with two kids, probably middle schoolers, stepped in. None of them looked like they'd slept recently. Their clothes were rumpled, and the smell of oily hair and stale coffee breath followed them in. It didn't take a mind reader to know that someone they cared about was lying in a bed somewhere in the hospital. I'd never had a fear of enclosed spaces, but when the doors slid shut, I could feel their grief sucking all the available oxygen. I stared at the digital countdown and tried to think of Monica and Chandler.

When we reached the cafeteria on the ground floor, I motioned for them to go first, but the dad shook his head and pressed the button for the floor below. As soon as I stepped out, my phone dinged. I glanced down. Graham was checking in. By the time I looked up, the doors had closed—the family and their grief had gone. I texted him back, took a shaky breath, and followed the arrow on the sign that read Cafeteria.

I looked around. I didn't see Mom, so I got a Styrofoam cup and filled it with freshly burned coffee from a giant urn on the table shoved against the wall and took a sip. It was god-awful, even worse than she'd made it sound. I went to the station with the cream and sugar and added a healthy dose of both, took another sip, and shuddered. I scanned the room again. I still didn't see Mom, but thanks to really bad acoustics, I heard her.

"Merritt? Yeah, I'm so sorry about the telephone tag. It's been crazy. I can barely think straight. Okay, so the doctor came in this morning. He said... he said... a liver transplant... no, no other possible treatments. Oh, Merritt, of course you're family, but I don't think you understand what's involved. It's not like you're offering to donate blood... Amanda? No. Absolutely not. I wouldn't want her to undergo such a risky surgery, and neither would Richard. Anyway, he said that a donor would likely to be found before any of us could get through all the testing and screening..."

Testing and screening. Liver transplant. Risky surgery. I hurried to a table before my legs buckled. When Mom came into view, her sunken expression told me everything I didn't want to know. She sat down and stared at the fake-wood tabletop.

"What did Aunt Merritt say?"

She jerked her head up.

"I overheard."

She shook her head. "Just that she'll help however she can."

I wrapped my hands around the coffee cup. "So, you really think he's going to need a new liver?"

Thunder outside grumbled an answer. She sighed and looked out at the pouring rain. Her voice quivered. "Yes, I do."

"Aunt Merritt was offering?" I didn't know much about organ transplants, but I figured the odds of Aunt Merritt being a match were no better than a random stranger pulled off the street.

She reached out for my hand and looked me in the eye. "There's no way to know for sure, but Armstrong said the odds are better for getting a 'deceased donor.' It usually takes longer to arrange for a living donor."

I leaned into her, about to drown her in questions, when the table rocked, spilling my coffee. As the coffee ran over the edge of the table and into my lap, my stomach soured. I jumped up, sending my chair crashing to the floor. I ran to the bathroom and puked up the only thing in my stomach—that disgusting coffee.

Chapter 35
Deb

I knocked frantically on the bathroom stall. "Amanda? Are you okay?"

She retched and flushed. She was really sick. "Ugh. Hold on, Mom."

The door to the stall opened, and Amanda staggered to the sink, splashed water on her face, and rinsed out her mouth. Placing both hands on the hospital-white countertop, she leaned in to look at herself in the mirror. She was as pale as I'd ever seen her.

"What's wrong, sweetie?"

She wiped her mouth with a paper towel, tossed it in the direction of the trash, and missed.

"Stress and crappy coffee."

I picked up the paper towel from the floor and threw it away. "Let me take you home. You didn't get much sleep last night." I hesitated as I tried not to think about the other reason for her lack of sleep. "There's some anti-nausea stuff in the medicine cabinet. You can rest, take a nap."

She turned to face me. "Graham's going to pick me up."

I breathed out my displeasure. "Okay, but he drops you off, and that's it. I don't want the two of you in the house alone." As soon as the words left my lips, I realized how foolish I sounded. Obviously, that metaphorical train had already left the station.

She cocked her head. "Seriously, Mom?"

"Yes, seriously."

In spite of my disappointment about her lie and my anger at Graham, I was relieved that I wouldn't have to leave Richard alone. I never in a million years thought I'd be standing in the bathroom of a hospital cafeteria, worrying about both my daughter's virtue and my husband's survival. Everything about this moment was dizzyingly wrong. Resting my uncomfortably idle hands on my hips, I looked down to hide the tears erupting.

Amanda closed the space between us. "Daddy's going to be okay." She wrapped her arms around me and squeezed. "I promise."

I nodded in silence, soaking up her sweet but impossible-to-keep promise.

"Let me know if you hear anything else from the doctor. I'll keep my phone nearby."

She softly kissed my cheek, just like she'd done when she was little but without leaving traces of peanut butter and jelly, and walked out the door. As Amanda left, another woman walked in, and we exchanged knowing looks. Everything about this place was oppressive. And that feeling was written in indelible ink on everyone's faces. Sure, it was a place of hope and healing, but it was also a place that reeked of helplessness—the kind of helplessness I felt right then, waiting for my feet to propel me back to Richard's sick bed.

WHEN I PUSHED THE DOOR open, a nurse was changing his catheter. He was awake.

She said, "We'll be a few more minutes."

I turned my back to him. I'd seen Richard naked thousands of times, seen him stand and pee enough times. I'd even walked in on him masturbating once, when he thought I was out. But this... this was even more intimate, more private and, knowing Richard, far more humiliating.

"That wasn't so bad, was it?" she said.

"If you say so," Richard mumbled as she marked her completed task on the whiteboard hanging on the wall next to his bed, gathered her equipment, and left to torture her next victim.

"Hey," he said as I lowered myself onto the beige Naugahyde chair beside his bed and it squeaked under the pressure. His eyes turned in the direction of the door. "Where's Amanda?"

"She wasn't feeling well. Graham's going to take her home."

He exhaled. "Okay." He shifted his position and glanced at one of the machines monitoring his bodily functions. "Babe, I think we need to talk about what if—the worst-case scenario. You know, what you would do about the store—Amanda's future."

My throat closed. I furiously shook my head.

"There are detailed instructions in the lock box at the bank, life insurance, a will. You know where the key is."

"Richard, don't. I really don't want to have this conversation. You're going to be fine."

"Yeah, well, you know me... better... safe... than..." he said, the strength of his voice dwindling with each word. His eyes fluttered. He was out again.

That was so Richard. Even as he drifted off, he was worrying about having all his ducks in a row rather than about the possibility of having his liver ripped out and replaced with one from a dead man. Not wanting to think about his last words, I pulled my phone from my purse and checked my neglected emails. Despite the pressing drama in my life, deadlines loomed. Some editors would understand. For others, nothing short of a global apocalypse would be an acceptable excuse for missing a deadline. I answered a few emails, explained my situation, and mentally set priorities—what was possible, what wasn't, what I cared about, what I didn't. The truth? I didn't really care about anything except Richard. And Amanda. I reached for

Richard's hand, laid my head next to him on the bed, and closed my eyes.

"Ms. Earle? Ms. Earle?"

I jerked my head up, blinked twice, and wiped the drool from my cheek with my sleeve. It was Armstrong.

"Sorry to wake you."

"Oh, no, no, it's fine. I just dozed off."

He glanced at Richard's sleeping form, then at me. "Maybe we should step out into the hall." He opened the door, gesturing for me to go first.

I stepped outside and shivered. The hall was far colder than the room. He got right to the point as he held Richard's chart tight against his chest.

"All the tests indicate that your husband is a good candidate for a liver transplant. He's on the waiting list."

"How long does that usually take?"

"There's no way to know, but he's been placed on the priority list."

I felt my face go slack with the shock of it, but based on Armstrong's unchanging expression, he might as well have been giving me directions to the vending machines, not telling me that my husband had a life-threatening condition that might or might not be fixable.

"We still haven't been able to pinpoint the cause of the liver damage. I know we've already gone over this, but I have to ask again. You say your husband isn't a heavy drinker—"

"No, maybe a beer or two on the weekend, but that's it."

"What about drugs? Are you certain he's not using?"

I crossed my arms tightly against my chest. I had to look up to meet his gaze. I hated it. I leaned in and whispered, "No, my husband is not a drug user."

He bit his lip and looked off into space before focusing on me again. "Well, what about supplements? Does he take any vitamins or herbal supplements?"

I froze. My heart pounded against my chest. "Yes, yes. He takes several every morning."

"Can you bring those in today to have them tested? Some supplements, especially herbals, have been linked to liver damage. Depending on what he's been taking, that could be the culprit."

I knew that. Why hadn't that occurred to me? I pictured the little bottles I'd dutifully lined up every day without a second thought. *My God, has my lack of concern put Richard's life in danger? Am I to blame?*

Armstrong's voice echoed from a rapidly narrowing tunnel. "We're going to try to stabilize him until a donor becomes available."

I looked at him, trying to process his words, but my guilt was clogging the gears. "I want to be tested for compatibility."

"Do you know your blood type?"

"A negative."

He flipped through the pages of Richard's chart and shook his head. "Your husband's blood type is O positive. Incompatible. In any case, it would take at least a couple of weeks for a living donor to go through the screening process, and with any luck, we'll be able to find a donor before then."

He reached in his pocket and handed me a business card. I stared at it.

"Make an appointment with the transplant coordinator." He motioned to the card in my hand. "She'll let you know how the transplant committee works, and she can answer any questions you might have." He stepped back. Our conversation was coming to an end. "Of course, your husband will have to remain in the hospital until a donor is found."

"How long a recovery time?" I was already projecting into the future, but I could barely deal with the present.

"If there are no complications, he would be able to go back to work three to six months after surgery."

"Complications?" My brain was barely functioning.

He glanced at his watch. "We can talk about that before surgery. Have one of the nurses page me when you have those supplements." As he walked away, I wondered if he'd purposely left his white coat unbuttoned so that it flew in his wake—a caped crusader come to save the day.

I hesitated. I'd sent Amanda home to rest, to feel better, but I couldn't leave Richard. I texted: *Can you bring Daddy's supplements to the hospital? They're on the kitchen counter. It's important! Armstrong says they may be contaminated.*

The traffic jam in my head wasn't allowing me to move forward. I needed to update Merritt. And ask Jeff to take the supplements off the shelves until they had been tested. And ask if he could watch the store for the foreseeable future. And check with our health insurance. And make an appointment with the transplant coordinator. Instead, I went back into the room, sat by Richard's bed, and watched the steady rise and fall of his chest with each life-giving breath until I fell into a deep sleep.

Chapter 36
Amanda

The automatic doors opened, and I stepped outside under the canopy, protected from the crappy weather. The rain had turned to sleet, and my breath formed puffy clouds in front of my face. I shivered, pulled my jacket tighter, and hugged myself. I didn't know who that was in the hospital bed, but it wasn't my father. All that talk about liver transplants freaked me out. The disbelief and shock on Mom's face had only made it worse. But standing outside the hospital, all I felt was relief at leaving it all behind, even if just for a little while. I took a deep breath and felt the sharp cold bite my lungs.

Graham pulled up just as the hospital doors closed behind me, and he motioned for me to get in. I slid into the passenger side, and my whole body relaxed. He leaned over and kissed me. "You okay?"

I answered with an explosion of sobs. He put his arms around me, and I let myself feel bad for Daddy... for Mom... for myself. And I felt guilty for wanting to separate myself from it all. I didn't want to move. I wanted to stay right there, where Graham would make everything okay. Even better, I wanted to travel back in time and make it to where Daddy never got sick.

A tapping on the car window forced us apart. A security guard was leaning over, peering in the window. We turned our heads and followed his finger to the signs:

No Parking.

Patient Pickup and Drop-Off Only.

Graham nodded, waved, and put the car in gear, and we drove away.

BY THE TIME WE TURNED onto my street, the rain that had turned to sleet had stopped. I was really looking forward to curling up on the sofa with Graham and watching something mindless on Netflix—a two-hour therapy session before going back to the hospital and facing my new reality.

Three houses down from mine, I spotted a man I saw almost every day. We'd never spoken other than to say hi, but I was always amazed by his steel will. He had to be at least ninety years old. He made his way down the sidewalk using a walker, somehow managing the cracks in the sidewalk while holding his little Boston terrier on a leash. But that day, the dog had tangled himself and the leash around the legs of the walker, and the old man was stuck, frowning in concentration, frustration, and then panic, unable to rescue the dog or himself, unable to move forward. Graham stopped in the middle of the road, slammed the car into park and, without a word, jumped out.

My phone dinged with a message. I glanced at it, not wanting to take my eyes off the scene playing out in front of me. It was Mom. *Shit. So much for a couple of hours away from it all.* I looked back up. Graham was untangling the leash, righting the man's walker, and petting the dog. He was pointing at the car. The man shook his head. Like I said—willful.

Graham jogged back and jumped in the car, bringing a whoosh of freezing air with him. He held his hands in front of the heating vent. "Shit, it's cold out there."

"He's okay?"

He shrugged. "I offered him a ride. Said he was fine. He introduced me to his dog, Calvin."

A car came up behind us and honked. Graham rolled down the window and motioned for them to go around. The guy pulled up beside us and mouthed, "Fuck you!"

Graham shook his head as he rolled the window back up. "Nice. Fucking asshole."

I watched the man and Calvin slowly make their way home. "My mom texted me. She needs me to bring something from home to the hospital, so we can't stay long."

"Maybe just long enough to make some decent coffee?" He smiled.

"Decent coffee sounds awesome."

As I slid the key in the front-door lock, I felt Graham right behind me, his warm breath on my neck. We rushed into the house and threw our coats on the sofa, soaking up the central heating.

"The kitchen's this way." In all the time we'd been dating, he'd never made it past the living room.

He looked around before following me. "Your house is very—organized."

"Yeah, every place except my mom's office upstairs. It's a real fire hazard."

He sat down at the kitchen table in Daddy's spot. It somehow made my dad's absence that much more painful. I wanted to ask Graham to move, but I told myself that would be childish. I filled the coffee maker with water, grabbed a filter, and scooped the ground beans. While we waited for it to brew, our conversation took a weirdly formal turn.

"How long have you lived here?"

"Twelve years."

"Does your mom like freelancing?"

I shrugged. "She bitches about it a lot."

"What about your dad? How long has he owned the sporting goods store?"

The mention of Daddy triggered more tears. I turned my back to Graham so I could pull myself together and found myself facing Daddy's supplements neatly lined up against the granite backsplash. I ignored the sinking feeling in my stomach, poured coffee into two mismatched mugs, and set them on the table. I wrapped my hands around my mug, a warming anchor.

"Amanda, do you want to talk about it? It's, you know, okay if you don't."

I took a sip of coffee and lifted the mug in a toast. "Better than the cafeteria, at least," I said, forcing a chuckle. I did want to talk about it, but I didn't want to break down in front of Graham. Not again. *Who wants to deal with a whimpering girlfriend?* I wanted to be stronger than that.

"Okay, so what is it you need to get for your mom? Need any help?"

I stood up, walked over to the counter, and gathered up the supplement bottles and set them on the table. "Sooo... the doctor thinks these supplements my dad takes every day could be the reason his liver failed. Anyway, Mom asked me to bring them to the hospital."

He picked up a couple of bottles and read the labels.

"Shit! Seriously? I thought these things were supposed to be good for you." He frowned as he set them back down. "So if they find out that's what happened, they can treat it?"

"I don't think so. I don't know if he's going to be okay." I swiped my runny nose.

"Come here," he said softly. He held out his hands, inviting me to sit in his lap. "He's going to be okay." He slid my hair behind my ear and held my face in his hands before he kissed me.

I kissed him back. And like a blast of sunshine after climbing out of the icy waters of Barton Springs, it warmed me all over. I quickly shifted positions and straddled him in the chair and felt him hard against me. I pulled my shirt up and over my head, feeling in control for the first time in the last two days.

My phone dinged. I hesitated.

"It could be the hospital," he said, breathless.

I reluctantly picked up the phone and read the text.

Mom: *Amanda, where are you?*

Chapter 37
Deb

My phone vibrated in my lap. I glanced at the screen. I'd managed to ignore several text messages and voicemails from my siblings—Isabelle, Nicholas, June, and Janet. *Really? Now they want to talk?*

I didn't have the emotional energy to call each of them and go over the depressing details again and again, convey all the medical information, and explain what it all meant. None of us kids had stayed in touch the way Merritt and I had, and I wasn't ready to absorb their polite expressions of sympathy. They barely knew Richard. Or me, for that matter—not anymore. I figured Merritt must have been playing a depressing game of telephone tag with them, passing along the bad news. I breathed a sigh of thanks, happy to let her continue in that role.

Richard was still sleeping when I quietly slipped out of the room and headed to the nurses' station, the heartbeat of the fifth floor. I wondered if the men and women decked out in scrubs and clogs, crammed into this twelve-by-twelve laminated space, felt the weight of responsibility for their patients the way I felt the heaviness of Richard's condition. *How could they?* Writing about health issues had always been easy for me in a detached, clinical, *Isn't that interesting* sort of way. But these people dodged emotional bullets every day, responding to each code blue like they were running into a burning building, not knowing if there would be any survivors. For them, it was all too real, not easy words tapped out on a computer screen.

I approached a young woman in slate-gray scrubs, bent over a computer screen, the light from the monitor reflected in her red-rimmed glasses, her shoulders tightly shrugged, dark ringlets falling in her face. She was typing insanely fast, but when she realized I was hovering, she stopped, pushed her glasses onto the top of her head, and looked at me expectantly.

I leaned over the counter. "Sorry for interrupting. My husband, Richard Earle, is in room 504?" It came out more like a question than a statement. I pointed down the hall. "It looks like he's going to be here awhile, which means I'll be hanging around a lot." I forced a chuckle that was on the verge of segueing into an awkward sob. "And I thought it might be good if, you know, I introduced myself."

She smiled politely. "Sorry, Ms. Earle, but this isn't my usual station. I'm just filling in. Sarah will be here for the evening. She's the charge nurse. But if you like, I'll leave her a note that you stopped by."

"Oh, okay. Yes. Thank you." I turned to head back to Richard's room, and the typing started up again. The brief exchange had exhausted what little energy I had for social interaction and left me disappointed that my effort had been for naught.

I was halfway down the hall when I felt a tap on my shoulder. "Ms. Earle? Deborah?" I turned around. She reached out to shake my hand and placed her other hand on top of mine. "I'm Bethany. I'll be on until three. Just let me know if you or Mr. Earle need anything."

"Thank you." Her small gesture of genuine kindness and concern took my breath away. "Really," I said, nodding furiously as I fought back more tears.

AMANDA WASN'T ANSWERING my texts. I'd thought that after our mother-daughter bonding, even if it was in the cafeteria bathroom, she wouldn't be pulling a stunt like this, especially considering her lies from the night before. I needed those supplements. I had to know if I'd been an accomplice in Richard's downfall. The possibility presented a painful irony. I always fussed at him for not getting enough sleep and working too hard, and I always made sure he got his annual checkup and went to the dentist and the ophthalmologist. He rarely took medication, but when he did, I always Googled it to see what the side effects might be.

Why didn't I register the same concern over his supplements? I felt preemptive guilt and a burning shame.

The feelings resurrected a painful memory, one I seldom let see the light of day for fear it would burst into flames, leaving me in ashes. I'd never told anyone. Sometimes I was even able to convince myself it was a false memory—that time had remolded the events, warped the facts.

But it had happened. Everyone was out of the house—my father had run to the hardware store, my mother was shopping, and all of my brothers and sisters had scattered, as they did every Saturday, except for Ray. He'd been assigned babysitting duty of seven-year-old me. And he was ignoring me, just as any seventeen-year-old boy forced to watch his little sister would. He was holed up in his room, bomb blasts and gunfire from his video games echoing down the stairs. Ray told me not to bother him, to stay downstairs and watch TV, which I did.

Until I got hungry. "Raayyy!" I whined from my spot on the sofa downstairs. When he didn't answer, I stood at the bottom of the stairs, gripping the banister, and tried again. "Ray, I'm hungry!" I wasn't allowed to use the stove, and my stomach grumbled for a grilled cheese sandwich, Ray's specialty. He still didn't answer. Barefoot, I trudged up the carpeted stairs and pushed open the door to his bedroom. That image of him, like an old Polaroid that slowly developed, always came into dreaded focus.

Ray was sitting on the edge of the bed, tightening a tourniquet around his bicep with his teeth, a syringe poised above his arm. He was shirtless, sweat trickling down his chest. My seven-year-old brain wondered why he was giving himself a shot.

He jerked his head up, his eyes wild, unrecognizable. He was mad. Really mad. Crazy mad. "What the fuck are you doing up here? I told you to stay downstairs! Shit!"

Ray frequently ignored me or told me to get lost, but he'd never cursed at me or spoken to me with such vitriol. I thought he hated me. I was crestfallen. He dropped the needle onto the bed, snapped off the tourniquet, and stood, towering over me. He had always been my temperamental older brother, but I'd never been frightened of him. I took a step back. I was readying myself to run downstairs, out the door, and to the neighbor's house, when his face softened.

"Debby, I'm sorry. I'm so sorry." He swiped the back of his hand across the sweat glistening on his forehead. He used to come home sweating like that when he was on the track team, but he'd quit months before. "I didn't mean to yell at you like that." He plopped down on the edge of the bed, threw the sheets over the tourniquet and syringe, and motioned for me to come sit by him. "It's okay, Debby. I won't yell anymore." He smiled, and his lips trembled. "Promise."

I climbed on the bed next to him, deadly curious as to what I'd just witnessed. "Ray, what was that?"

He sighed and took my hand. "I'll tell you, but just you. You have to promise you won't tell anyone. Not Mom or Dad or even Merritt. Okay? Promise?"

I liked the idea of having a shared secret with my big brother. I knew he and Merritt had teenage secrets that I'd never been privy to. This was my chance. "Okay."

"Cross your heart and hope to die?"

I nodded enthusiastically as I crossed my thumping heart.

"Well, that was some special medicine the doctor gave me."

"Dr. Garrett?" He was our pediatrician. It didn't occur to me that Ray was past the pediatric stage.

"No, this is a different doctor."

"You're sick?"

"I was, but I'm getting better. I didn't want anyone to worry, so I kept it a secret. Now it's *our* secret."

I knew if Mom found out, I'd be in big trouble for not telling her—more trouble than Ray would be in if they found out about his medicine.

"Debby?"

"But... but won't we get in trouble?"

Beads of sweat had pooled on his upper lip. He grimaced. "Debby, they'll send me to a special hospital, and I wouldn't be here for Christmas. You wouldn't want that, would you?"

I thought of Ray's stocking not hanging beside Merritt's. I'd already decided what I wanted to give him. I loved my brother. I teared up. "No," I said, shaking my head, unable to look at him. Only years later would I understand just how illogical his justification for my silence was.

"Okay, so you swear you won't tell anyone?"

"I swear," I whispered.

He let out a sigh. "Good girl." He kissed the top of my head. "Now, go downstairs, and I'll come after a while and fix you a grilled cheese sandwich. How does that sound?"

I wiped my runny nose with my sleeve. "It sounds yum!"

He hugged me. He didn't smell like Ray. "Okay, kiddo. Get going."

I skipped out of the room and down the stairs.

And I waited.

He never came down.

We'd buried him three days later, and our family had fallen apart.

ON MY WAY. The text from Amanda rescued me from my destructive thoughts. Nurses and aides had come and gone with annoying frequency, checking Richard's vital signs, eyeing the beeping monitors, asking if he was in pain when he managed to open his eyes, changing IV bags, emptying his Foley bag. Nurse Sarah had become my least favorite person on the planet, pushing Armstrong to second place. So when the door opened again barely a minute after she left, I felt an irrational irritation overtake me.

But then I heard Amanda's voice. "How's Daddy?"

"About the same." I stood, hands on hips. "What took you so long?" I demanded, my voice louder than expected. I was primed to confront Amanda over her lies as well as her lackadaisical response to my urgent texts.

"Sorry, Mom. My phone died, and I charged it in my room while I was downstairs. I didn't see your texts."

"Really, Amanda? Really? I told you this was really important."

She was trotting out her favorite white lie again. She handed me a plastic bag filled with Richard's supplements, and I snatched it from her hand.

"It's everything that was on the counter by the sink," she mumbled.

I sat back down and smoothed out the bag on my lap to count the bottles—eight in all. "That's everything. Stay here with Daddy. I need to take this to the nurses' station." I had my hand on the door handle when Amanda came up behind me and touched my shoulder. "Mom," she whispered, "Graham is waiting in the hall."

I bit my lip as I reluctantly turned around. "Amanda, why would you bring him here?"

"He offered to keep me company while I get something to eat downstairs. I haven't had anything to eat today."

That made two of us.

"He's a good guy, Mom. Really." She shuffled her feet and cocked her head. "He cares about me."

And there it was. I saw it in her iridescent green eyes, the eyes she had inherited from Richard. She was in love. I remembered too well that all-consuming feeling that the other person was my oxygen, that I wouldn't be able to take a single breath without him.

I exhaled a weary sigh, clutched the baggie as if I feared a mugging, and opened the door. There he was, leaning on the opposite wall as he scrolled through his phone. Ripped jeans and a faded long-sleeved T-shirt. Blond scruff. His dreadlocks were pulled back with a hair tie. His gold earrings flickered under the fluorescent lighting.

He looked up, smiling expectantly, then straightened and slipped his phone in his back pocket. "Oh, Ms. Earle..."

I felt anger flush my face. I wanted to walk away and leave him hanging, but he looked embarrassed, remorseful. And so young.

"Yes, Graham?" It was as much as I could give.

He shifted his weight and slipped his hands into his front pockets. "I wanted to apologize... you know... for, um... for last night. It was... my idea."

"No doubt." *Does he think I don't know my own daughter?* "And your parents?"

"Oh, my parents were out of town, and I... we... Amanda and me..." His voice dropped to a deep whisper. "Don't be mad at her. Please."

He was begging. I wanted him to beg. "Graham, believe it or not, I was Amanda's age once. I get it. But you have to understand, this cannot happen again. Amanda is about to go off to college, and her father is sick. She doesn't need this right now, and I won't have her distracted by you. Do you understand?"

He looked down the hall, then at the floor, before locking eyes with me. "Ms. Earle, I would never do anything to hurt Amanda or her future. Can *you* understand *that*?"

I was taken aback by his steadfastness in the face of my roiling anger. I threw my shoulders back, standing straighter than I had in the last forty-eight hours. A head taller than Graham, I leaned into him, almost nose to nose. "Just so we understand one another." And without another word, I headed to the nurses' station, clutching the bag of supplements that rattled with each step.

Chapter 38
Amanda

Mom walked back into the room, her head lowered, her shoulder rounded. Her hands were empty, but she carried an invisible weight. I glanced into the hall before the door closed behind her. No Graham. Had she chased him away?

"Did they say when they'll know something about the supplements?"

She looked as if the life force had been sucked right out of her.

"Not long."

"They really think the supplements might have made Daddy sick?"

"They just want to exhaust all possibilities."

"But if it was the supplements, can't he just stop taking them, and they could give him medicine or something? Maybe he wouldn't need a transplant?" For a giddy second, I thought that it would all be fine.

She glanced at Daddy and protectively crossed her arms before looking me in the eye. "No, sweetie. He'll still need a transplant."

My fresh balloon of hope popped. "Then what the hell difference does it make what's in the supplements?" I hadn't realized I was shouting until it was all out there. "Sorry."

She put her arms around me, kissed my forehead, and said so softly I barely heard the words, "If it's the supplements, they can rule out underlying conditions that might need to be treated as well."

I nodded into her shoulder. We stood like that for a few seconds before pulling away and retreating to our separate corners. It was my turn to stare out the window at the needles of rain pelting the windows.

"So, you talked to Graham?" I asked.

"Briefly."

She was going to make me work for it. I turned to face her. "And?"

"And nothing. He said he was sorry he talked you into lying to me, and I told him it better not happen again."

I rolled my eyes and exhaled as loudly as possible.

She rushed to my side and stood over me, her energy restored, and spoke just short of a shout, "Amanda Grace, you are in no position to be giving me attitude right now, and I'm in no frame of mind to put up with it."

I opened my mouth to say something, but a groan from the bed stopped me. "Daddy?" I rushed to him and gently placed my hand on his arm.

Mom hurried to the other side of the bed. "Richard? How are you feeling?"

He opened his eyes. "I need to piss."

"Richard, you have a catheter. You don't need to go to the bathroom."

He shifted, and the bed pad crackled under the sheet. He mumbled, "Fuck," and closed his eyes again.

"He's okay. He's just doped up." Mom was doing her best to ease my growing fear.

My phone vibrated with a text from Graham. I looked at the message then at Mom and braced myself for an argument. "Graham says he's waiting for me in the cafeteria."

She simply nodded. She'd given up the battle, if not the war.

"You'll be okay, Mom?"

"We're fine. Just don't be gone too long, and don't leave the hospital—I need you here."

"Do you want anything?" I asked as a peace offering.

"No, thanks."

"Text me if you hear anything."

She nodded as she pulled the chair as close to the bed as possible and sat on the edge of the chair's cushion, as if those last few inches would somehow keep him safe.

I STOOD IN THE DOORWAY of the cafeteria and watched Graham shudder as he took a sip of coffee from a Styrofoam cup. It was a far cry from the freshly ground brew he was used to at Urgent Café. I couldn't help but smile. He was still there, drinking coffee drudge—proof that he loved me.

"Hey," Graham said as I pulled up the hard plastic chair next to him and the metal legs screeched in resistance. He fiddled with the cup, twirling it around in circles on the table. "So, how's your dad?"

"Same. They're testing the supplements."

He reached for my hands, clasped in my lap. "Amanda, I'm really sorry all this shit is happening."

"Yeah, me too." I took a breath before changing the subject. "I guess Rocket told you about his and Karin's 'great escape'?"

"Fuck. I meant to say something, but with everything that's going on, I seriously forgot. Anyway, I figured Karin had already told you everything."

"So, they're really leaving?"

"Yeah. Heading to Colorado. Getting married."

"What the...? You can't be serious." I fell back into my chair. Karin hadn't shared that last bit of information. "So, they're... eloping?"

That was not the Karin I knew. It had to be a mistake. Something had gotten screwed up in translation. Or there was one other possibility.

"Is she pregnant?"

Graham shook his head. "I asked, but Rocket says they haven't even done it yet. She wants to wait, you know, until they're married."

That I could believe. "What are they going to do for money?"

"Rocket's got some boarding friends in Denver. Says they can put him and Karin up for a while until they can get something going. He says he's in good enough shape to get back into boarding and maybe still get sponsors, and they—"

"I have to talk to Karin." I reached for my phone before the realization slapped me—again. Her parents had taken her phone away from her months before. "This is crazy stupid. You have to talk Rocket out of this."

"Amanda, listen. I already talked to Rocket. You know how things have been with him and his mom. He's finally decided he can't take it anymore. He can't help her, and she still refuses to get help or go into treatment. And you know better than me what's been going on with Karin and her parents. Rocket says she's afraid they might actually kill her if they found out about them."

I couldn't wrap my head around it. Karin was smart. Super smart. Couldn't she see the stupidity in this? But then, I'd never gone home afraid my parents might kill me.

Graham leaned back and cracked his knuckles. "There's more."

I gestured for him to get on with it.

"Hadley is going to help with their getaway."

"Hadley? How? When?" I was so confused. Hadley blamed Karin for not having the balls to report her parents to social services and make them pay for their abuse. And Hadley didn't even know Rocket. But my experience with Jack had left me more understanding of Karin's decision not to expose her awful secret—to spill all the details and end up in the courts and then who knew what would happen. Maybe she would be placed in a foster family. That was always a hard no. I could never blame her for wanting to get away from them.

While I was trying, mostly unsuccessfully, to process it all, my phone vibrated with another message from Mom: *I need you here!*

Chapter 39
Deb

Three unbearable days of watching and waiting had passed before Armstrong reported back with the results from the supplement tests. My mind was fueled by a high-octane blend of fear and anger over the news he dropped on me. The supplements were contaminated with high levels of selenium and epigallocatechin gallate, a compound found in green tea. For Richard, both were a matter of too much of a good thing.

"You just never know what you're going to find in these supplements—and in what quantity." He paused as if waiting for me to say something—maybe to defend myself. "Anyway, we'll be reporting them to the manufacturer and to the Food and Drug Administration. And we'll be moving forward with the transplant as soon as a donor becomes available. If you have any questions, you can call my office."

The lack of even a drop of empathy in his voice made my heart race and my teeth clench. I was blinded by a glint of bitterness I'd been ferociously trying to ignore.

The door had barely shut behind Armstrong when it swung back open with fresh force, bringing my torrent of racing thoughts to an abrupt halt. Merritt rushed in and wrapped me in a hug. I hadn't realized how much I needed it until her arms were fiercely locked around me.

"I'm here," she whispered.

I caught the whiff of freshly baked bread that always seemed to trail her, and I wished more than anything that I was sitting in her warm kitchen, buttering a slice, drinking coffee, and sharing news about anything but this. We stood, frozen in place, unwilling to unwrap ourselves from our embrace, sisters sharing past sadness and steeling ourselves for future sorrow.

I reluctantly put distance between us but held tightly to her hand, which was still icy from the outside chill. "Merritt, it's my fault." I stared at the chip in the floor tile I'd spotted to avoid looking Armstrong in the eye as he told me about the toxic ingredients in the supplements—something that I could have uncovered on my own with a simple keystroke if I had just been paying attention. "It's all my fault."

"What? You're not making sense, honey. Richard's sick. That's not your fault."

"Yes, yes it is." The words tumbled out in rapid succession as I told her everything. About Richard's daily supplement routine. About my uncharacteristic lack of concern. About Armstrong testing them for contaminants. As the words left my lips, I couldn't help but feel that my blurted confession to Merritt was a practice run for sharing my guilt with Amanda.

She pulled me back into a hug. "Deb, you can't blame yourself."

I abruptly pulled away. "No? Then who? Richard?"

She shook her head, the first signs of exasperation shadowing her face. "That's not what I'm saying."

"I should have known better. I should have checked," I said, ready to impose penance on myself. I turned away.

She tilted her head in sympathy. "Like Dad used to say, 'If you insist on blaming yourself, do it once, and then move on.'" She paused. "Deb, look at me." I did as asked. "Blaming yourself won't change anything," she said, "and you have to be strong right now. For Richard. For Amanda—for *yourself*, for Chrissake."

Merritt was good at telling me things I didn't want to hear—usually things I *needed* to hear. Tears welled up and blurred my vision before trickling down my cheeks.

"I know, you're right," I said, my voice hoarse. "I have to get it together. I need to—"

Amanda rushed in, breathless. She looked at Richard's still profile then at Merritt and me. "What happened?" She slapped her hand over her gaping mouth. My baby girl was panicked.

I backed away from Merritt and motioned for Amanda to come into my open arms. "Daddy's okay, sweetie," I said.

She exhaled in relief as she rushed to me.

"Dr. Armstrong was just here." I glanced at Merritt and cleared my throat. "He said they tested for several diseases that might have damaged his liver, like hepatitis C and some autoimmune diseases, and… I can't even remember what all, but everything came back negative, and—"

"So, what is it, then?"

"Well, he says a couple of the supplements Daddy was taking were… were contaminated with toxins that could have damaged his liver."

Amanda sank her head into my shoulder as if she could no longer support its weight, and I stroked her hair to calm her. The feel of her stubborn curls and the smell of her herbal shampoo soothed my fractured nerves.

"How could he not know?" She stopped breathing. She pulled back and cocked her head, her composure stark, as my culpability dawned on her. "How could *you* not know?" Her voice rose accusatorily. "Isn't that the crap you write about all day?"

"Amanda, I…"

When she was little, she'd loved me unconditionally. Mommy could do no wrong. I couldn't believe that now she was so quick to turn on me and declare me guilty. No defense. No extenuating circumstances. It was okay for me to blame myself, but it hurt like hell that my baby girl was pointing an accusatory finger at me. A throbbing in my temples kept time with my guilty heart.

"Mom?"

Merritt and I exchanged a look of understanding. She lightly touched Amanda's shoulder. Amanda whipped her head around, poised to focus her anger, maybe even her blame, on Merritt.

"Mandy, honey, I know you're hurting right now, but you have to know that your mom would have done anything—everything—to prevent your father from getting sick like this. You're going to have to cut her some slack. Right now, she's in a lot of pain too."

Amanda turned away from us both, lowered her head into her hands, and sobbed. I was immobilized, afraid that if I tried to comfort her, she would push me away, and I was in no frame of mind to deal with her rejection.

Merritt jumped in. "Mandy, I think we should focus on the positive here. If what Dr. Armstrong told your mom about the supplements pans out, it means we won't need to worry about treatment for some other condition after the transplant. Once he has a new liver, he'll be able to go home and live a normal, active life and go back to the store."

She turned around, wiping away tears. The flash of uncertain hope that brightened her face gutted me.

"They're making arrangements for the transplant now," I said, reentering the conversation, but even as I said the words, they didn't register as real.

I could see the fierce battle going on behind her eyes—a battle between relief and worry. She swiped the back of her hand across her cheek, smearing the remaining tears. "When?"

My brain was crowded with words and phrases but devoid of coherent thought. "When what?"

She cocked her head again, a note of irritation returning to her voice. "The transplant!"

I closed my eyes and nodded. "Armstrong said there's no way to know. We just have to wait and see."

Amanda's brow furrowed in thought. "So, someone has to die for Daddy to get a liver." It wasn't a question.

All three of us had checked the organ-donor box on our drivers' licenses, never imagining a real-life scenario in which our family would be grateful to a complete stranger for doing the same. It was a simple sure-why-the-hell-not stroke of the pen. Whoever was going to be Richard's donor was going to be our savior. Ordained a saint. And I already loved that person unconditionally.

Amanda might not have been asking, but I knew I had to provide an answer. "Yes, it's an awful reality," I said.

She shifted her body weight into a determined stance and glanced at Richard, who was still sleeping.

"But when someone who has agreed to be an organ donor dies, and they're a match, then—"

"I hope someone dies soon," she said.

Chapter 40
Amanda

Strain had carved deep grooves into Mom's face, but as I walked out of Daddy's room, I told myself I wasn't abandoning her in her time of need. She had Aunt Merritt. They could spend hours talking about livers and supplements on top of crap that had happened a hundred years ago that I'd already heard a thousand times.

But really, that was just me justifying my escape from the whole depressing drama. I couldn't stay in that freaking hospital room another minute, watching Daddy's slow breaths—each one feeling like it might be his last—dealing with Mom's exhaustion, and absorbing the sickening smell of disinfectant that made me want to run to the bathroom and puke. At least Daddy was out of it. He wouldn't even know whether I was there or not.

I was a shitty daughter. I was in such a rush to leave that I'd forgotten to ask for Mom's credit card so I could get a Lyft home. I checked my bank balance on my phone. Five dollars. *Shit.* I couldn't go back in there. I might be a shitty daughter, but even I knew that would be over-the-top thoughtlessness.

I texted Hadley.

Me: *Take me home? At the hospital.*

Hadley: *45 minutes? I have to talk to you.*

I knew Hadley's "forty-five minutes" would be at least double that.

I hesitated. Even in the middle of a family crisis, I did want to hear all the details of her role in Karin and Rocket's bizarre escape plan. It would take my mind off everything else, but I didn't want to hang around in a hospital lobby for—if she was true to form—two hours or more.

Me: *Never mind. Got a ride. We'll talk. Later.*

Hadley: *Cool, call me!*

Graham had left earlier to help out at the café, but I texted him anyway.

Me: *Any chance you can take me home when you get off?*

Graham: *Been slammed, but slowing down. Can you hang another 30?*

I knew Graham's thirty was solid.

Me: *Thank you! In the lobby.*

Heaving a too-loud sigh, I grabbed an ancient *People* magazine and plopped down in one of the hard industrial-looking sofas in the lobby. The fake rubber plants in oversized ceramic pots didn't make the place feel any homier, if that was the goal. I wondered if they cleaned the leaves with the same disinfectant that left a lingering odor in every square inch of this place. Mom told me once that one in every ten hospital patients got an infection during their stay. Some of them died.

I dropped the magazine on the table midsentence, imagining all the germy hands that had held it before me, jumped up, and began pacing. I'd never paid much attention to her shoptalk, and now I couldn't stop remembering it. I pulled out my phone again, hoping for a *Be there in 5* message from Graham. Nope.

I watched people being wheeled in and out, older faces worn out with worry and kids racing around, hopping like rabbits, totally unaware there was even anything to worry about. Mom's shaky voice buzzed my brain. The things I'd said to her left a sour taste in my mouth. She was worried. Super worried. And she was trying to be strong for me, for Daddy.

Why did I give her such a hard time? I'd all but accused her of making Daddy sick. Yes, I was still mad at her and her pissy disapproval of Graham, but that was no excuse for my bitchy behavior. Not now. Not with Daddy so sick.

I wished I could be more like Aunt Merritt. She always kept it together. The one-sided conversation I'd overheard in the cafeteria earlier that day made it clear that Aunt Merritt was tossing out the idea of being a donor—a living donor—and giving up a chunk of her liver to Daddy. That was so Aunt Merritt. She was my favorite of all Mom's brothers and sisters. When I was little, she would come over with Jess and keep us occupied—and sort of quiet—while Mom stayed in her office upstairs, working. Our favorite game was a big magnetic board of tic-tac-toe she would carry in her year-round straw beach bag—where she kept all her surprises—pulling them out one at a time like magic tricks. The pieces to the game were bigger than my hand, so she would help me place them on the board. Aunt Merritt always let us win, and then she would act super impressed because we were such masters of the game.

After we'd all defeated her, she would make us healthy snacks of hummus and carrot sticks, per my mom's instructions. But then she would slip us a few M&M's. "It's our little secret," she'd whisper as the red, blue, and yellow melted and smeared a rainbow in my grubby hands.

I had to focus on memories like that instead of obsessing over all the horrible stuff that was happening... all the horrible stuff that might happen... that would happen. And I had to stop trying to make myself feel better by making Mom feel like crap.

Chapter 41
Deb

"Deb, honey, go home. Take a shower. Change your clothes." Merritt chuckled. "Brush your teeth."

I breathed into my palm and sniffed then scrunched my nose in disgust. "I can't leave Richard."

"Don't be silly. I'll stay with him." Merritt looked at her phone. "No one expects me home. Wes can forage for his own dinner. Just go home and get some rest. At the rate you're going, you'll never make it through everything that's ahead."

Everything that's ahead. An itchy panic spread from the inside out. I wanted to scratch until I bled.

"Do it for me." Richard's voice was so muted that it took me a second to register that he was talking, but I could still detect the tease in his voice.

"You're awake!" I rushed to his side. "How are you feeling?"

"Doped up." He opened his eyes wider and looked around. "Hey, Merritt."

"Hey, yourself." She gave him an awkward wave. "Glad you could join us."

I squeezed his hand. "Can I get you anything, hon?"

"Water."

I poured ice water from the beige plastic pitcher into the beige plastic cup waiting on the beige nightstand, raised the head of his bed, and held the straw to his lips. He took a few sips, the exertion apparent.

"Enough?"

He nodded weakly, and I set the cup on the nightstand. "Where's Amanda?" he mumbled.

"You just missed her. She went home. She was there earlier, but she had to turn around and come back to bring the supplements."

"Supplements?"

Oh God, he didn't know. How could he? He's been out of it most of the time. I was sorely tempted to backtrack, make up a lie, pretend I'd misspoken.

I sat on the edge of his bed to get closer to him, took his hand in mine, and prayed he would understand. "While you were sleeping, Dr. Armstrong stopped in. He said... well, he said..." I hadn't prepared my confession. "The *good* news is you don't have any disease that could have damaged your liver."

He wasn't smiling. His dilated pupils had overtaken his lime-green eyes, turning them black. "And the bad news?"

My mother had always said, "If wishes were horses, I'd ride like a king." If my wishes were horses, they would gallop me away to anywhere but where I was, confessing my complicity.

I forced myself to look him in the eye. "The bad news is..." I took a breath. "Armstrong says the supplements you've been taking damaged your liver. And he's going to schedule a transplant as soon as a donor becomes available."

It looked like his skin had paled beneath the yellow tint, if that were even possible. He frowned. "How does he even know about the supplements?"

"He asked me if you took any supplements. Amanda brought them from home, and he had them tested for contaminants."

"Contaminants?" He closed his eyes for a few seconds, processing the information, blinked them open. "And?"

Finding it hard to form the words, I squeezed his hand tighter. "A couple of them contained ingredients at toxic levels. He seems certain that's what damaged your liver."

"Shit! So I did this to myself?"

"What? No. Richard, I'm—"

He sat up a little straighter. "Hand me my phone! I need to call Jeff! Tell him to take them off the shelves!"

I squeezed his hand. "Already done."

"Has anyone else gotten sick?"

My focus had been on Richard. I stumbled. "Not, um, no, not that I know of, but you can't worry about that right now."

"Deb, those are my customers, my friends. They trusted me." He slumped back and rubbed his forehead, his IV line swinging in time with his worried motion. "Shit. We could be sued! We could lose everything!"

"Richard, it's fine. We'll be fine. No one has gotten sick, and you didn't stock *all* of the supplements you took at home."

Having depleted his diminishing energy reserve, he collapsed back on his pillow and mumbled something I couldn't understand before he drifted off yet again. I wanted some of what he was taking.

Chapter 42
Amanda

When Graham and his minicar pulled silently into the circular drive of the hospital, he ducked his head to peer at me out the passenger-side window and smiled. His smile was my medicine, my drug of choice. I felt a smile crack open my face. With no patience for the automatic exit doors, I had an overwhelming urge to run, legs flung out like a kid on the playground, and bounce onto his passenger seat.

He reached over and opened the car door, and I climbed in. His kiss held the lingering taste of Urgent Café's unique blend of freshly ground coffee beans and just-out-of-the-oven pastries. The clenched fist in my chest opened up.

"Hey, beautiful."

That was a lie. I looked like death warmed over. And I felt fat—I was stressed, and my appetite had returned with a vengeance. Stress Eating 101. But I loved him for lying.

"So, my dad woke up. Mom told him about the supplements."

"They've already tested them?"

"Yeah, the doctor says he's pretty sure that's what made him sick."

He shifted the car into drive as I fumbled with the seatbelt. "So does that change anything—you know, what they'll do for him?"

I finally heard the seatbelt snap into place. I stared straight ahead as I shook my head, and my unbrushed tangles grazed my cheeks.

A few random strands stuck to my skin, and I swept them away. "Surgery's going to be scheduled as soon as a donor is available."

"Oh, fuck. That sucks. I'm really sorry, Amanda."

Looking down at my ratty fingernails, I sucked in my stomach as I shrugged. "Yeah, me too." We were silent as he pulled out of the hospital parking lot and onto the interstate. When the exit to my house was less than half a mile away, I said, "I don't want to go home."

"No? So where?"

"Maybe your house?"

He gave me his half smile, my favorite. "Sure." Then he frowned. "But your mom..."

"She's got other things on her mind right now."

He glanced at the dashboard clock and sighed. "Anyway, my parents will be home soon, if that helps."

I felt a rush of disappointment mixed with relief—disappointed we wouldn't have a chunk of time alone, relief that I wouldn't have to lie to Mom. Again.

I LOVED THE CHILL VIBE of Graham's house. As soon as we walked in, we collapsed on the sofa. I laid my head on his shoulder, and the urge to sleep swept over me.

The rumbling of Graham's voice broke the drugged feeling. "Amanda, no matter what happens with your dad, I'm here for you, you know. Whatever you need."

"I know." I didn't know much about what was going to happen, but I knew that much.

His mouth was on mine, and I felt a weird transfer of energy, a tingling in my lips that I imagined moving down my chest, my arms, my legs. It was a life-giving kiss. A stupid thought popped into my head. *Am I siphoning off Graham's energy, leaving him weaker?*

I pulled back to look at him just as Navy and Cade opened the front door. I sat up straighter. Navy glided right over and pulled me up from the sofa and into a wordless hug. She took a step back to look me in the eye but held tight to my hands. "I spoke to your mom earlier—"

I stiffened, interrupting her before she could finish. "You talked to my mom? When?" I didn't mean to sound quite so demanding, but I couldn't picture that conversation, especially not now, with everything she was dealing with.

"Not long ago. She just sounds so stressed. I offered to bring her something from the Café."

Deborah Earle and Navy Scott in the same room? I couldn't picture it—not in this universe. "What did she say?"

"Well, she said your dad was holding his own and—"

"I mean about you going to the hospital."

"She was just as gracious as I imagined she would be. I said I would talk to you about when would be a good time to visit."

Cade shoved his hands into his pockets. "How's your family holding up?"

"Not so good. But I think we'll all be okay once the transplant is over and my dad is better." That was a supersized understatement, but what else could I say? *We're fucking fabulous.* Why exactly was I mentally snarking Graham's dad? Even if it was only in my head, I hated myself for it. He and Navy were always so nice to me—and now to my mom.

"Of course," Navy said, biting her lip. "Did they give you any idea of how long it might take to find a donor?" She waved her hand as if to erase the question. "Sorry, that's none of my business."

"It's fine. Could be tonight, could be two weeks from now. We just don't know." I'd been holding strong, but my voice cracked at the tail end of that sentence, and I couldn't stop my tears.

Navy put her arm around my shoulders. "Have you eaten anything? I bet not. Stay for dinner. Please?" She turned to Graham. "Don't let her leave until she's been fed."

"You heard her, Amanda. She's going to force-feed you—like a goose."

Navy frowned at Graham and clicked her tongue. She looked down at me. "Don't pay any attention to him."

My sudden laugh sounded foreign. I wiped tears from my cheeks with the back of my hand. "Can I help?"

"Nope. You go relax, and we'll let you know when dinner is ready. Now, shoo!"

Cade pulled his ponytail tighter as he assumed his position in the kitchen, and together, they began pulling ingredients from the kitchen cabinets, the refrigerator, the freezer—choreographed like they had done this a thousand times, which I was sure they had. I wondered if Mom would create a new rhythm if Daddy... I couldn't let the thought take root.

"Amanda," Graham said, his voice putting the brakes on my racing thoughts. He nodded toward the stairs.

It had barely registered when Cade turned to him and said, "Maybe an hour?" But it sounded like code for "You have an hour undisturbed to do whatever you want." I wasn't sure I would ever get to where I felt comfortable going to Graham's room and shutting the door with his parents just a few stair steps away. They might have been old enough to be my parents' parents, but they treated Graham and me like buds. I half expected Cade to wink at Graham and call him dude.

Chapter 43
Deb

Merritt hung back and waited silently before finally convincing me to take a break, go home, rest. As I walked outside the hospital, it felt like I was exiting one dimension and entering another. I pulled the cigarette pack I'd stuck in my purse and lit up.

I'd taken exactly two puffs when a security guard tapped me on the shoulder and pointed away from the door. "Twenty feet. You need to be twenty feet away from the entrance to smoke."

I hadn't thought anything could make me feel worse than I already did, but the idea that my husband was seriously ill while I was, once again, giving in to a long-forgotten nicotine fetish, did exactly that. I dropped the cigarette, stomped it out, picked it up, and tossed it in the trash. When I turned around, the guard had already gone back inside and was chatting it up with the ER receptionist. I looked out to the highway in front of the hospital and the humming traffic. It was unfathomable that outside the hospital walls, the world carried on as usual as if nothing untoward had happened—as if my life hadn't been shaken to its core and then, just for good measure, given one good stir.

When Ray ran track, he used to joke that his time would have been so much better if he just didn't have to jump those hurdles. He was running in the state finals when he tripped over a hurdle, twisted his knee, and tore a ligament. The other runners kept going—they had their own times to worry about. He dragged himself to the finish line. Never mind that he came in last, had to have surgery, and was given painkillers that kicked off his downward spiral. The point, to him, was that he'd finished.

I just had to jump over the hurdles and finish. And pray that we would all come out the other end, together, whole. Even if we finished last.

I pulled into my driveway, put the car in park, and turned off the key, still gripping the steering wheel, not wanting to enter the darkness of the garage. I sat there, seeing nothing and everything, unable to propel myself forward. *Has it been only three days since we rushed Richard to the hospital? Or is it four…?* Time had folded in on itself, leaving me anchorless, unable to focus on the present.

Rebecca, the busybody next door, peered through the curtains of her bedroom, her eyes bugging out. I calmly lowered the car window, stuck my hand out, and shot her the finger. The curtains swung shut, and she disappeared from sight. I immediately regretted my actions. She'd never liked me, but she *really* liked Richard. She always coordinated her trips to the mailbox with Richard coming home from work. She would linger far longer than necessary to get the mail, smile broadly, and say something inane like "Lovely weather we're having, don't you think?"

Richard would wave and nod before turning his back to her and rolling his eyes. We always shared a good laugh about "Randy Rebecca."

I felt sick. My legs were weighted down with lead, but I forced them to move, and I stepped out of the car just as the clouds parted and the sun shone through. I raised my face to the sky, letting the welcome rays warm my soul, and said a prayer, making the sign of the cross—something I hadn't done in decades. I did it for Richard. For Amanda. For me. Even for Armstrong. Before I could finish, the clouds blocked out the sun. It felt like an ominous sign.

I opened the front door and called out, "Amanda?" No answer. She was with Graham, no doubt. I lacked the mental energy to call and argue again. My phone rang. I fumbled to the bottom of my purse, yanked it out, and answered without looking.

"Deborah?" a voice asked.

I held the phone away from my ear, my finger hovering over the decline button.

"This is Navy Scott. Graham's mom?"

I brought it back to my ear. "Yes?"

"Graham told us about your husband, and we just wanted to see how he was doing and if there was anything we could do—for you."

"Richard is holding his own. And I appreciate the offer, but I'm fine, really."

I'd never met this woman, and I wasn't crazy about her son. I wouldn't be asking for her help, no matter the circumstances.

"He also told me that the coffee at the hospital tastes like dirty socks." She gave a subdued chuckle. "I don't know if Amanda told you, but we own a coffee shop. I'd love to bring you some good coffee and maybe a basket of scones?" When I hesitated, she said, "I find good coffee always helps."

Amanda must have told her about my love affair with coffee. Her voice was so sincere, imbued with so much empathy, that I teared up as I heard myself saying, "Sure, that would be lovely."

After a promise from Navy that she would check with Amanda for a good time to stop by the hospital, I hung up. I needed a drink. I went to the kitchen, dragged the stepladder to the counter, and grabbed a lone bottle of gin from the top shelf. Richard and I were never big drinkers, but the occasional gin and tonic on a hot summer night was just the ticket. It was cold outside, but I needed a gin and tonic more than ever. I poured a tumbler full, more gin than tonic, and downed it in record time. As I felt the gin taking effect, I slogged up the stairs and sat at the foot of our bed. I fell back in exhaustion, my arms above my head, and convinced myself I could close my eyes just for a minute or two as I valiantly fought a losing battle with fatigue.

When I opened them, it was dark outside. I was curled in the fetal position and still wearing my jacket. Sweat had sealed my shirt to my back. I pulled myself upright and wiped the drool from my cheek. Gripping the edge of the mattress, I rocked back and forth, mimicking Richard's middle-of-the-night wake-up call. I caught my dreadful reflection in the mirror over our dresser. Merritt was right. If I was going to be there for Richard, I needed self-care.

I lumbered over to the dresser—avoiding another look in the mirror—pulled clean underwear and a long-sleeved T-shirt from the drawer, and carried them into the bathroom. Resting on the toilet seat, I stared at the floor as I contemplated the effort it would take to turn on the hot water and step in the shower. Richard had laid that black-and-white tile. He had installed those towel racks, the medicine cabinet, and the toothbrush holder, each of them a reminder that he wasn't there with me. And I didn't know when, or if, he would be again.

I turned on the water as hot as I could stand, hoping to loosen my neck muscles stiffened from repeatedly nodding off in the chair next to Richard's bed. I stood under the spray until my back was on fire, my skin red, and my fingertips wrinkled—until I couldn't stand it anymore.

Still, the hospital smells and sounds pinched and poked at me, refusing to allow even a moment of peace, triggering memories that stuck to me like hardened gum under the table—my mother lying motionless in the hospital bed, her organs pickled from alcohol and her brain fried from all the pills. She'd been disappearing before my eyes, and I just wanted it to be over. I spent every minute at her bedside, talking to her, reading to her, praying with her, hoping to finally gain her forgiveness. But if she ever forgave me, she never let on.

My other siblings were far flung and made only the occasional appearance by her hospital bed. Living less than a mile from the hospital, I became the default caregiver. Merritt wanted to help, but she'd just had Josh, baby number five, the most colicky of the bunch, and she was overwhelmed. But one day, Wes stayed home to watch the kids, insisting she spend time with her mother before it was too late. Merritt appeared like a vision from heaven and—just as she was doing for Richard—took over for me, pushing me out the door with love.

I clearly remember listening to the Goo Goo Dolls on the car radio a few decibels too high, grateful for the deafening distraction and the chance to get away from my mother's deathwatch, take a few deep breaths, and reset. While I was singing off-key with the windows rolled down, breathing the fresh autumn air, my mother took her last breath.

The memory felt like the snap of a rubber band on my heart. I stepped out of the shower and took a towel from the rack—the navy-blue one with His embroidered in white block letters. A Christmas present. Richard always neatly folded his bath towel over the rack so he could use it again. It now seemed like an incredibly optimistic ritual. As I stood, water dripping off of me and pooling onto the tile, I pressed the towel to my nose and slowly inhaled. I'd heard of people putting their beloveds' belongings in vacuum-sealed bags to save the scent long after they were gone.

I opened the lid of the dirty clothes hamper, threw the towel in, and grabbed another one. *What the hell is wrong with me?* Richard was sleeping soundly at St. Joseph's Memorial, Merritt was watching over him, and according to Armstrong, the odds of a successful transplant were good. Yet there I was, already rehearsing the role of Widow Earle.

The bed beckoned me, seducing me once again. I pulled the covers back and, still damp from my shower, climbed in naked, relaxing into the soothing feel of the sheets. I was ready to give myself over to the blank slate of sleep when my cell rang. It was the hospital.

"Hello?"

"Deborah, this is Bethany at the hospital."

The sound of Bethany's voice triggered a five-alarm panic. I sprang up.

My silence left space for her to speak. "Deborah, it's good news. A liver is on its way by airlift from Houston. ETA nine p.m."

I gasped, trying to reset my panic to relief. But instead, ugly sobs escaped, taking me by surprise. Richard was being tested and prepped. If I wanted to talk to him before he was wheeled into surgery, I needed to get there right away. *If?* I wanted to beam myself into his hospital room, the room I had selfishly left so I could recharge.

My husband needed me, and I wasn't there. *What made me think it was okay to leave?* I hung up, grabbed my jeans from the floor, pulled a T-shirt over my head, and absentmindedly slipped my feet into the pink Crocs on the floor by the bed. Normally, I refused to wear them even to get the mail, but I didn't have the patience even to tie the laces on my sneakers. I snatched my jacket from the bed. My purse and keys were downstairs in the entryway.

What else? I had the absolute certainty I must be forgetting something. As I rushed down the stairs, my clunky Crocs caught in the carpet, and I stumbled but saved myself from shattered bones when I grabbed the wood railing with both hands. My phone flew out of my hand, landing face down on the tile below. I collapsed on the bottom step, my jacket still draped at the top, my phone on the floor, my heart pounding in my chest, and I sobbed, wailed, keened, but there was no one around to share my panic.

Amanda! I needed to let Amanda know.

I picked up my phone, the screen freshly cracked, and called her, slicing my fingers on the shredded glass. No answer. I called back. Again. And again. She answered on my fourth attempt.

"Mom?" she asked, breathless. "What happened?"

I had to keep my cool for her sake. I took a breath, and the words spilled out in a carefully measured cadence. "Sweetie, the hospital called—"

She was already crying mournful sobs.

"No, no, Mandy. It's *good* news. They've got a liver for Daddy. Surgery should be in the next couple of hours or so."

She gasped. "What? Now? Tonight?"

"Yes, it's on its way. Where are you? We need to go *now* if we're going to get to see him before surgery. They're not going to wait for us."

Her voice trembled. "What? No! I have to see Daddy! Graham'll bring me. You go on. I'll meet you there." The phone disconnected. I could only imagine the frantic scene as she scrambled to get to the hospital in time. I worried about them rushing, running red lights, ignoring stop signs. But Graham wasn't Hadley. For the first time, I was glad she was with him.

I pulled into the parking lot, shoved the car into park, and sprinted to the sliding doors. At the last minute, I turned around to aim the remote at the car. Richard was always a stickler about locking the car doors, even if it was only to run into the Stop and Shop to pay for gas. I pressed the remote. Nothing. I stiff-armed the remote and pressed again. Still no sound. I sprinted back to the middle of the parking lot and frantically held out the remote and pressed the button with both thumbs. The beep rang out, and insane with worry that I wouldn't make it in time, I ran back to the entrance.

Visiting hours were over, and the hospital was quiet, at least compared to the frantic pace I'd witnessed during the day. There was only the hiss of automatic doors, the squeak of tennis shoes on tile, and the scraping sound of the elevator I'd just missed. *Shit!* I stood in front of the doors, peering at my frazzled reflection in the stainless steel, and pressed the up button more times than I could count. I wanted to take a sledgehammer to it. When the doors finally opened, I stepped in and stared up at the digitized numbers, thankful when the elevator went straight to Richard's floor.

As I exited, Bethany came out from behind the nurses' station and walked straight to me. "Deborah, could I speak to you for a minute?"

The apologetic tilt of her head was an air brake on my forward movement.

Chapter 44
Amanda

Mom's bloodless face greeted me as I stepped off the elevator, signaling that my world was about to blow up, leaving me fatherless. Just minutes before, I'd been brimming with optimism after the good-news call from Mom. But when I heard her say to the nurse, "Oh God. What? Is it Richard?" my optimism bubble exploded, and I was sinking in rapidly rising quicksand. If this was what grief felt like, I wouldn't survive.

"Richard is fine," the nurse said softly. "He's resting comfortably."

I slapped my palm to my chest, my breath coming in gasps. Relief washed over Mom's face.

"Deborah, the liver arrived, but I'm afraid it's not viable."

Mom blinked twice. "But what... why not? I thought..."

"You should speak with Dr. Armstrong, but the liver is not in good enough shape for the transplant. The surgery won't be happening tonight. I'm so sorry." It was like someone had dangled a winning lottery ticket in our faces then took a match to it and made us watch it burn.

"It's okay, sweetie," Mom said, trembling as she put her arm around me. She looked as wrung out as I felt. "Daddy's okay. Surgery's just been postponed."

My brain froze, my thoughts moving at the speed of a slowly melting Arctic glacier. I'd propped up my slumping sadness with hope that he would always be there for me—for graduation, to drop me off at college, to give me away at my wedding. A new thought triggered my tears as if it were the biggest tragedy of all—we never got our Daddy's Day together.

I wiped snot from my nose with my sleeve and slapped my forehead, sure that I had broken out in a raging fever. I turned to the nurse. "Does my father know?"

It was important to me that he was in the loop and not at the mercy of doctors and nurses who didn't really give a shit about him. Mom turned expectantly to the nurse, who was hovering just outside our tight huddle of two.

"Yes, he's been told. He's awake, and I'm sure he'd like to see you both right now."

I wanted to pull out my snarkiest voice and say, "Jeez, ya think?" But Mom stepped in front of me, blocking my tactless remark before it could form.

"Thank you," she said, sounding genuinely grateful and irritating me in the process. As we turned to speed walk toward Daddy's room, I suddenly remembered. *Graham!* He was awkwardly hanging by the elevator, clearly confused as to what his role should be in this family drama.

"Go ahead, Mom. I'll be there in a sec."

She gave a quick noncommittal glance in his direction.

To my horror, instead of him retreating, he was walking toward Mom. Before I could process the scene, he was face-to-face with her. "I heard most of it," he whispered to her. "I'm really sorry, Ms. Earle."

Mom stared at him, unblinking. I wanted to shed my skin and slither away.

He swallowed hard and shifted his weight. "So, that's it. I just wanted to let you know."

"I appreciate that," she said begrudgingly before heading toward Daddy's room.

"Well, that went well. I guess I should go, huh?" Graham whispered.

An unexpected geyser of anger bubbled up. "What, now that things have gotten worse, you just take off?"

His face went slack. He was stunned, hurt. "You want me to stay, I'll stay. I just thought—" My tears erupted, and he pulled me into a warm hug. "It's okay, Amanda. It's okay."

"I'm sorry. I'm just so freakin' stressed."

"I know," he whispered. "I know." His understanding turned up the dial on my tears.

If he stayed, there wouldn't be anything he could do, and he'd have to deal with Mom's sideways glances. When I finally pulled away, I said, "Actually, you're right. You should probably go. We'll stay as long as they'll let us, and I'll go home with Mom."

"You sure?"

I shrugged. "I need to go see my dad. I'll call you in the morning."

He brushed my lips with a kiss and stepped into the elevator. We stared into each other's eyes until the doors slid closed, leaving me to deal with whatever waited in room 504.

I tiptoed in. "Daddy," I whispered.

If it were possible, he looked even less like himself than he had earlier in the day. His eyes were open, if barely. I wanted to scream to release my built-up angst, my fear for him—for us—but I forced down the lump in my throat and smiled at him instead.

"So, I guess you heard my spare part has been recalled," he said, his voice hoarse.

I nodded. He motioned with his hand, bruised from needle sticks, for me to come closer. Mom walked back to make room, and I half lay on the bed, resting my head on his chest, listening to his familiar heartbeat and the deep rumble of his voice. When I was little, it would lull me to sleep as he read *101 Dalmatians* to me for the thousandth time. I breathed in, expecting a familiar blend of hair products, laundry detergent, and shaving cream. He smelled musty.

"It'll be okay, baby girl." He took a raspy breath and patted my arm. "There'll be another one, and this time it'll be the right one. You'll see. I've probably got better odds for getting a liver match than I would finding a love match on Match.com." He looked at Mom and gave her a wink, and I watched it turn into a grimace.

I should have been comforting him instead of the other way around. But then, parents were supposed to make their children feel better. It was their job.

Dr. Armstrong burst in unannounced. "Well, Mr. Earle, Mrs. Earle." He didn't bother to look at me. "Sorry for the false alarm, folks. I know it's disappointing, but this is not at all unusual. It happens more often than we'd like." He heaved a sigh and lowered himself into the chair by the window, stretching his long legs out as if the room were his. "I had a patient recently who had two..." He looked off in the distance as if his next words would be out there somewhere. "No, *three* false alarms before a viable organ was delivered. But it all worked out in the end. And that's all that matters. Right?"

Why is he telling us this shit? Is that supposed to make us feel better? No wonder Mom was not a fan.

He raked his long double-jointed fingers through his thinning sandy hair. If he was having second thoughts about his pep talk, it didn't stop him from continuing. "I examined the organ myself, and unfortunately, the hepatic artery of the donor liver was obstructed by a thrombus that had impaired hepatic function, making the organ unviable."

I wanted to scream at him, "English, you fuckwad!"

Mom squeezed my hand—another signal to keep my mouth shut. "I see. Thank you, Dr. Armstrong."

"Just stay by the phone, and keep your bags packed," he said, smiling, as if we were planning a trip to Aruba.

It must have all been too much for Daddy, because he had drifted off again. I left his bedside and whispered to Mom, "Should Aunt Merritt know?"

She shook her head slowly, the exhaustion on her face even more clear than before. "It's late. I'll call her in the morning."

"Mom, it's only ten o'clock."

She looked at her phone, sighed, and without another word, went into the bathroom and closed the door. I hung by the bathroom door, but all I could make out were a few mumbled words and muffled sobs until I heard her say, "Okay, I'll call you in the morning."

I scrambled to the other side of the room just before she opened the door. Her eyes were a shade redder than when she'd gone in.

"I left a message. I'll talk to her tomorrow and tell her what happened." She took a tired breath. "I think I'm going to stay the night. Can Graham take you home?"

"He left," I said and quickly added in his defense, "I told him to."

"Take the car. Go home and get some rest. Between you, me, and Aunt Merritt, maybe we can take shifts. It doesn't do Daddy any good if we're all exhausted."

"I can stay. You didn't even get to rest when you went home."

"Actually, I did get a shower and a change of clothes, so I'm fine. Really. And I want to be here if he wakes up."

I leaned over the bed and kissed Daddy's forehead. Mom looked at me and nodded, a reassuring gesture. She dug the car keys from her purse and handed them to me—the silver beaded keychain I'd helped Daddy pick out on Etsy for her last birthday. As our fingers touched, we both looked down at the inscribed words: *Drive safe. I need you here with me.* The corners of her mouth almost lifted into a smile, but her chin quivered.

"I love you so, so much, Mandy." Her voice cracked. "More than you know."

I hugged her as hard as I could, the keys in my hand jangling against her back. "I love you too, Mom."

More than you know.

Chapter 45
Deb

One lesson learned over the last two weeks—hospitals were essentially walk-in freezers. Curled up in the chair by Richard's bed, I pulled the loosely woven blanket over my doggy-cold nose, ready to attempt the impossible feat of sleep. I would have gone down to the nurses' station to ask for a second blanket, but last time I checked, Sarah—"Nurse Ratched"—was on duty. She would probably just lecture me on how the cold temperatures were needed to discourage the spread of germs, telling me it was for the well-being of the patients and I should deal with it. I made a mental note to warn Merritt and Amanda to wear heavy jackets and maybe bring a blanket or two from home.

I'd curled myself into as tight a ball as possible and had just closed my eyes when the door opened. *Shit.* I unfurled, reminding myself to be nice to Nurse Ratched. In the middle of the night, she alone was responsible for Richard's care. I flipped myself over to face her.

The light from the corridor backlit her outline, obscuring her face in the dark. "How are you doing?" Bethany's warm voice offered a welcome measure of relief from the cold.

"Oh, you know. Not so good."

"Has Dr. Armstrong been by?"

"Yes, he said..." I stopped myself. Bethany probably knew Armstrong's *false alarm* speech by heart. "Yeah, he was here."

"Deborah, I don't know if you're a religious person..." She hesitated. "But I'm praying for you and your family. I lit a candle for you."

Prayers, candle lighting, incense. As a kid, I'd gone to Mass every Sunday and every holy day with my mother. I stood when I was supposed to stand, knelt when I was supposed to kneel, said the prayers, and made the sign of the cross. I lit candles, certain that the striking of a match and the melting of candle wax somehow solidified my prayers. I was once a believer—*was* being the operative word. Now prayer, to me, was no different from making a wish on a falling star, throwing coins in a fountain, or knocking on wood.

"That's very kind of you. Thank you," I said.

"Can I bring you another blanket?"

My chattering teeth must have triggered her offer. "That would be much appreciated. Thank you."

With the aid of a second blanket, I was able to doze off, but the constant traffic in and out of the room prevented any real rest. It brought me back to when Amanda was a baby and I would drag my exhausted postbaby body out of bed to feed her, not knowing whether it was midnight or dawn. Now it was Richard's needs that had to be met, regardless of how exhausted I was.

Nurses came and went, as if through a revolving door that never came to a complete stop, taking his blood pressure and his temperature, checking his urine output, waking him from a deep sleep for him to rate his pain on a scale of one to ten. Just as I would doze off again, someone else would come in, making no effort at a stealth entrance, and perform their checklist of patient care. When I'd fallen into my deepest sleep yet, someone came in with a breakfast tray.

Stretching and moaning as I sat up, I asked, "What time is it?"

"Seven thirty."

"Wow." I slowly stood up, my ankles cracking, and stumbled to the window to open the blinds. "Richard, hon, your breakfast is here."

It felt strange seeing him like that, the incredible shrinking man diminishing right before my eyes. His appetite had followed suit and had all but disappeared. His "breakfast" consisted of two cans of supplemental drinks—a sad attempt to get some nutrition in him while we waited for a viable organ and the surgery that I hoped would keep him with me for a very, very long time. If he couldn't get these drinks down, Armstrong would order a tube feeding, pushing him further into physical decline. I was determined to do everything in my power not to let that happen.

"Richard? Wake up. You have to drink these." I opened the first one and shoved a straw in.

He opened his eyes just a slit, enough that I could see the green of his irises. "I'm not hungry," he slurred.

I pressed the bed's remote control and watched the head rise in slow motion. His always perfectly coifed hair was wild, matted down in spots and spiked in others.

"Deb! Let me be. I just want to sleep."

"Listen to me. If you don't drink these, they're going to shove a tube up your nose and down your throat to feed you." I took no pleasure in bullying my sick husband.

His eyes opened wider, showing the yellowing whites. "Who told you that?" he croaked.

"Armstrong."

"Ah, the caped crusader." His weak attempt at humor comforted me, a much-needed reminder that my husband was still there with me. He sat up straighter, and the sheets slipped down, exposing his increasingly swollen abdomen beneath the cheerily patterned hospital robe.

I wanted to cry, to turn away, but I simply held the drink and steadied the straw for him as he took baby sips. "That's not so bad, is it?" *Oh God, I'm channeling Nurse Ratched.*

After he managed to down one of the drinks and had fallen back asleep, I lowered the bed, tucked him in, and pulled my phone from my purse. I had five missed calls from Merritt. I went into the bathroom, gently closed the door, and pressed her number.

"Merritt?"

"I've been trying to call you!" she said, her voice infused with panic.

"Sorry. It was late last night when—"

"What happened? Is Richard okay?"

I took a halting breath. "The hospital called last night and told us they had a donor liver and—"

She interrupted me with such gratitude that things were going our way. I jumped in and gave her the update before she could go on. Her heavy sigh said far more than her words. "Shit. How are you holding up?"

"Everyone keeps asking me that. I guess the answer is, I'm not. Not really."

"And Richard? How did he take it?"

I gave a half-hearted chuckle. "You know Richard. He was joking with Amanda."

"I'm getting dressed now. I'll be there in... half an hour, and you can go home. Okay? You just hold tight."

"Merritt, one more thing."

"Yeah?"

"It's freezing in here. Better bring a jacket and a blanket—or two."

Chapter 46
Amanda

I was vegging out on Netflix, trying to distract myself from anything remotely related to real life, when I heard the key in the front door. Mom's presence warmed the house and comforted me. But after a brief update on Daddy's condition—no changes—we retreated to our own private spaces, doors closed, coming together only to order Chinese takeout, a rare occurrence in the Earle household. Even then, we barely spoke. There was no sound but plastic forks scraping against takeout containers. The kitchen had always been the place where most of our family conversations—and arguments—happened. But the unexpected late-night call with good news, followed by the shocking disappointment, left us numb and nonverbal as we tried to deal with the jolting transition.

I shoved my leftover kung pao chicken into the fridge and returned to my room. I needed a major distraction, so I called Hadley. She was offering to do the most selfless thing I'd ever seen her do—maybe the *only* completely selfless thing, come to think of it.

"I'm the only one who can do this. I mean, Karin's whacko parents know you, and Rocket's mom knows Graham and his parents. Who better than *moi* to make it happen? And sooner rather than later, right?" She took a breath. "So, my mom's always got money shoved in a ton of purses she never uses that are stuck in the back of the closet. It's like my personal bank account, and I make regular withdrawals. Anyway, I've set aside some cash for Karin, and when

Mom sends me to the grocery store, I've been buying a few prepaid Visa cards. She never checks."

She was really going to do it—help Karin and Rocket escape their nightmarish lives.

"You're a sneaky shit, Hadley. Remind me never to leave money lying around."

She laughed. "Ever since my dad sold his company... well, let's just say, they won't miss it."

I lay in the bed that night, thinking about Hadley's selflessness, her generosity—even if the money wasn't really hers to share—and what it would take for me to stick my neck out to help someone I cared about, no matter the risk. I tossed and turned, obsessively thinking about the possibilities. I gave up on sleep at around two thirty in the morning and opened my laptop.

I was so deep down the Google rabbit hole that the sun startled me when it bled through the curtains. I snapped my laptop shut, brushed my teeth, shoved my legs into my jeans, pulled a T-shirt from my dresser without looking, and tiptoed down the stairs, careful not to wake Mom. I grabbed the keys and headed to the hospital.

At the digital directory near the elevators, an ancient man with a thick head of unruly gray hair stood in front of me, leaning on a well-worn wooden cane, haltingly touching the digital directory screen with his free hand and tilting his head back, slack-jawed, to read. After a few minutes, he turned around. "Hon, can you help me? My eyesight isn't what it used to be."

The gray hairs sprouting from his ears were a shade or two darker than the hair on his head, which was surprisingly thick. He carried a faint scent of cigars and spicy aftershave.

"Sure. Who are you looking for?"

"Her name is Comrey." He cleared his throat. "Um, Marsha Comrey. I think."

I typed in her name. It was actually Millicent Comrey, one of the ER docs who had taken care of Daddy. “Suite 106,” I said.

He turned and looked down the hall, seeming unsure of where to go from there.

“I think the doctors’ offices are at the end of the hall and off to the right.”

He smiled at me and nodded. “A word of advice, hon. Don’t ever get old.”

I watched as he shuffled his way to the end of the hall and leaned on the corner wall for support before he turned right. I couldn’t imagine my parents ever being that old, but then, I couldn’t imagine the alternative either. And it hit me—there was a real chance Daddy might be following the old guy’s advice and would not even be around to get gray. A wave of nausea washed over me again. I inhaled and exhaled slowly until the feeling passed.

I found the room number I was looking for in the directory of the office and followed the path of the old man. I hurried to the end of the long hallway to a simple wooden door with a plaque that said Suite 115. My heart sped up. I grabbed the doorknob, hesitated, and steeled myself before walking in.

When the receptionist with a blue streak in her hair, who didn’t look much older than me, said, “Can I help you?” I stood up straighter.

“I want to talk to someone about being a living liver donor.”

Chapter 47
Deb

Clueless as to the time of day, I opened my eyes. Sunshine blasted through the panes of the east-facing windows in my bedroom. It was still morning. But I couldn't for the life of me conjure up the day—it was the same disconcerting feeling as when you wake up in a hotel room and, in the first few moments of consciousness, think, *Where the hell am I, and how did I get here?* A vaguely familiar sadness washed over me, and for a nanosecond, I couldn't remember why.

But as the clock on my grace period of ignorant bliss ran out, my brain screamed, *Richard!* I sat bolt upright, swung my legs over the edge of the bed, and grabbed my phone. Ten thirty. No missed calls. I heaved a sigh of relief. *No news is good news.* At least that was what I'd been telling Amanda.

I stumbled out of the bedroom and knocked on her door. No answer. I knocked again. "Amanda?" As I opened the door, the beaded curtain clinked a jaunty tune. Her rumpled bed was empty. I dressed, slipped on my Crocs, and hurried downstairs to the kitchen. No crumbs on the counter, no cup in the sink. She hadn't even made coffee. I peeked in the garage. My car was gone.

I texted Merritt: *Is Amanda with you?*

Merritt *No. Thought she was coming later today.*

Me: *Ok.*

As I stood in front of the microwave, my reflection assaulted me—wild, unbrushed hair and puffy bags under my eyes, with an added schmear of mascara for maximum effect. I raised my arm, sniffed, and recoiled.

"I'll get the paper." I said it out loud, as if I needed to give myself explicit instructions on the way forward. Hopefully, the paperboy had hit his mark, and the paper was waiting for me right in front of the door. Open door, snatch paper, close door. No need to venture out into the front yard and alarm the neighborhood children with my disheveled appearance.

I opened the door, and there it was. I smiled, recalling Mandy's comment that I was old-school for reading an honest-to-God real newspaper. To her mind, I was ancient, primed for Social Security and a walker. I remember thinking the same thing about my mother, but life circumstances had accelerated her aging process.

Maybe that was what was happening to me.

I leaned over and was about to pick up the paper when the rumble of a car pulling into the driveway stopped me. Still bent, I looked up.

"Debby!"

Looking daisy fresh in a baby-blue shirt and jeans, he stepped out of his red Toyota, and I stood, instinctively patting my hair in place, wishing I'd showered and was wearing something other than faded yoga pants, a torn T-shirt of Richard's, and—the coup de grâce—my pink Crocs. And a bra would have been nice. With both hands, I pressed the newspaper to my chest as if it were a tightly held secret.

"Tim, what are you doing here?" I wanted to convey a casual, fancy-meeting-you-here tone, but it wasn't working.

"I heard about your husband." He took a few steps in my direction. "I'm really sorry." He waited a beat. "I thought I'd bring some of Amanda's work by." He waved a folder of papers in my direction. "You know, so she doesn't get too far behind."

"That's very thoughtful." I reached out, and he came closer. As I accepted the folder, I couldn't help but wonder if he did this for all his students. He shoved his hands into the pockets of his well-worn jeans, looking more and more like the boy I'd once loved.

"How are *you* holding up, Debby?"

"Oh, you know..."

"It's tough. My niece was in the hospital recently because of a kidney condition. Joey and his wife were exhausted, alternating shifts, but she's home now and doing really well."

"Joey? Joey has a daughter?"

"Yep, she's fourteen."

All I could picture was Tim's annoying little brother, whose sole purpose in life had been to aggravate him. Tim and I would be in Tim's room, and Joey would burst in making kissing sounds and chanting, "Timmy's in lo-ove. Timmy's in lo-ove."

And Tim would throw the nearest object at the door. "You're an asshole, Joseph Arnold!" Joey hated his full name. "Get the fuck out of my room!"

"Joseph Arnold," I said under my breath, remembering his behavior with a fondness I wouldn't have thought possible back then. That shared memory overshadowed my self-consciousness, and without any forethought, I heard myself say, "Would you like to come in for coffee? I just made a pot."

"You sure you're up for company?"

"I have some time before going back to the hospital. And yes, I would love some company."

Tim followed me into the kitchen, sat down at the table, and began bouncing his knee, a habit that apparently hadn't faded with time. I could still hear his mother's plea. "Timothy, stop that! You're rattling the silverware and driving me crazy!"

"How are your parents?" I asked, genuinely interested. They were always incredibly nice to me, making my mother's dislike of Tim that much more upsetting.

"Good, actually. They still live in the same house in South Austin. They travel when they can. How about yours? I remember your mother was not my number-one fan."

"They've both been gone for several years."

"Oh, I'm sorry."

I seriously doubted that. My mother had treated him horribly. "You still play guitar?"

He chuckled. "God, that band was awful."

"No, you weren't. Okay... maybe you were." We both laughed, and I felt lighter. I couldn't believe I was allowing myself to feel better. I set his coffee mug in front of him on the table. "So, how long were you married?"

He took a sip and raised the mug in my direction. "It's good."

"The marriage or the coffee?"

He chuckled, but I could see him debating just how much to divulge.

"Sorry, that was rude," I said. "It's none of my business."

"No, it's okay. Really. Jillian was a force to be reckoned with. I guess all that energy is what I found so attractive, at least in the beginning. We were horribly mismatched. I should have known better. Anyway, she left me for some Brazilian artist. I think they live there now. And so I moved back to Austin," he said, shrugging, palms raised in surrender. "And that's my sad story."

"Is he any good?"

His eyebrows shot up. "What?"

"The Brazilian artist. His work."

He laughed. "His stuff seriously sucks, actually."

"Good." I nodded with conviction and smiled in his direction.

My phone rang.

"It's Merritt," I said. "Sorry, I need to get this."

"Of course." He picked up his coffee mug and took another sip.

"Deb? Is everything okay? Have you heard from Amanda?" Merritt asked.

"No, but not answering my texts has become her MO of late. How's Richard?"

"Richard's fine, I'm fine, Nurse Ratched is a bitch, but I guess she's fine too. I'll call you if there's any news. Have you had a chance to rest?"

"Yeah, I have." I didn't want to tell her that my body was experiencing major jetlag even though I'd never left the ground.

Tim coughed in the background.

"Where are you?"

I gestured to Tim with one finger and mouthed, "One minute." Stepping out of the kitchen, I put the phone to my ear. "I'm at home."

"Who was that?"

I sighed. "It's Tim. He just stopped by to drop off some schoolwork for Amanda, and I invited him in for coffee. He's leaving as soon as we hang up." Merritt had teased me unmercifully when I met Tim for a parent-teacher conference. Now I worried she might be judging me, imagining I'd invited him in for coffee and a quickie. "I'll leave for the hospital as soon as I shower and get dressed. Tell him I'll be there soon."

I closed the call and took a breath. The sound of Tim's chair scraping across the kitchen floor triggered an unexpected twinge of—regret? I stood at the doorway and watched him put his mug in the sink. His brief presence had allowed me to feel lighter than I had since the night I rushed Richard to the ER. Was it terrible of me to want him to stay just a little while longer?

"You leaving?" I wondered if he could hear the note of disappointment in my voice.

"Thanks for the coffee, but I really should get going." He took two steps closer. "Debby." That single word was infused with such caring, such empathy. I looked up at him, and before I had time to register what was happening, he wrapped his arms around me and whispered, "If you need anything, anything at all, please let me help. And you know me. I mean it."

I did know him, at least a past version of him. His embrace was warmly familiar and comforting, as if two decades hadn't passed since we'd been together. I desperately wanted him to stay, to never let go, but I simply nodded into his shoulder, my tears leaving a dark blot on his light-blue shirt as I pulled away.

"Thank you, Tim. That means a lot."

Chapter 48
Amanda

As I sat in the waiting room, reconsidering my decision but ultimately coming back to my original conclusion, a short, heavy woman with soft lines on her face opened the door. She smiled and greeted me cheerfully. “Amanda Earle?”

I dropped the *Sports Illustrated* I wasn’t reading onto the table and stood up.

“I’m Lucy Devane, the organ-donation coordinator here at St. Joseph’s.”

She ushered me into her small office. “Please, have a seat.” The place was bare except for a small stack of files on her desk along with a mug of coffee, a half-eaten blueberry muffin, and a family photo of three little kids and a not-hot husband. She shoved the muffin aside. “I’m sorry for the wait. Now, what can I do for you, Ms. Earle?”

“My dad is here in the hospital, and he’s in liver failure. I want to see if I can be a living donor.”

I thought I detected a slight kink in her right eyebrow before she said, “You’ll need to get parental consent before we can even discuss it.”

“I’m eighteen.”

“I’ll need to see a photo ID.”

I reached into my purse, dug out my driver’s license, and handed it to her. If she’d asked me to do a cartwheel on her desk, I would have done that too. She quickly scanned the license.

"Okay." She smiled and slid it back across the desk. "What is your father's name, so I can look up his records?"

"Richard Earle. Richard Anthony Earle. He's in room 504."

She gave a sympathetic nod. "I know his case. I'm so sorry about the false alarm last night. It does happen, unfortunately, but I know how incredibly disappointing it is." Unlike Armstrong, she was offering genuine sympathy.

She began asking questions about my expectations and my state of mind and gave some pretty graphic—read *gory*—descriptions of what I could expect. Then she gave me written orders for a chest X-ray, a psychological evaluation, blood work, a urine analysis, an EKG, a CT scan, and a pregnancy test. I would meet with the living-donor nurse coordinator, who would give all my results to the Living Donor Committee. They would make the final decision about whether or not I could be a donor for Daddy. It was way more complicated than I'd expected, even more so than my late-night online research had suggested.

"How long does all this take?" I heard the warble in my voice as the hope I'd nurtured overnight shriveled.

"It all depends on your availability and the availability of the appointments for all the exams. Then—"

"I'm always available!" *Do I sound too anxious? Will that be a mark against me in my file?*

"May I call you Amanda?"

She could call me Bitch Face if she wanted, as long as it would get Daddy a liver. "Sure."

"Amanda, normally, we don't use a living donor for someone who's in acute liver failure, like your father. Living donors are more commonly used for people with chronic liver disease—when the need is not quite so urgent. For your father, it would likely be faster to find another donor."

I slumped back in my chair and stared at my fisted hands in my lap.

"And," she said.

I jerked my head up.

"Because he's already had one false alarm, and I believe..." She stopped to tap on the keyboard and leaned into the monitor. "Yes, he's been prioritized on the waiting list to receive a liver."

I was about to embarrass myself by ugly crying.

She took a breath. "But I don't see any reason why we can't move forward—as a backup plan. You can cancel the testing at any time should a donor liver become available."

My tears retreated. "So, if I'm a match, and another donor doesn't come available before I'm approved, then it would be a go? I mean, you know, my dad is really, really sick, and I just want to check out every possibility."

"I understand, Amanda. I do. But I want to make sure *you* understand that a committee decision is not made overnight. It can sometimes take weeks for the process to be completed and for a decision to be made. You should use that time to think this over."

I sat up straighter and crossed my arms. "I don't need to think it over. I just need my dad to be okay."

WITH ALL MY PAPERWORK and medical orders in hand, I stood in the hallway outside the office and texted Graham. He would understand my decision better than Lucy Devane, who had given off the distinct vibe that she thought it was a bad idea. Graham was going to help me get through it all. But his support would add another item to my mother's running list of "Reasons Why I Hate Graham Scott" that she seemed to be working on so diligently. I wouldn't have been surprised to get home and find the list stuck on the refrigerator next to one of Daddy's sticky notes.

I needed to mentally prepare for the emotional showdown I would inevitably have with her. I never doubted she loved Daddy and wanted what was best for him, but she would not be on Team Amanda for this. She would pull the mommy card and call foul. I had to have a solid argument in place.

Karin had been on the debate team, and she always talked about making a list of pros and cons to prepare for every possible argument thrown her way. But when I opened the note function on my phone to make a list, the pros so far outweighed the cons that it wasn't even worth the time it would take to type them in.

As if Graham could sense what was on my mind, a text came through: *Everything okay*?

Me: *Yeah, just need to talk to you.*

Graham: *Meet me at Urgent?*

Me: *Be there in 20.*

I pulled into the parking lot, watching through the glass panes of Urgent as Graham, Cade, Navy, and Adaolisa rushed around serving customers, bussing tables, making espresso. Their lives made sense. They had purpose. Everything was going according to plan. Karin and Rocket now had a way forward. Hadley had just gotten word that she'd been accepted to the University of Texas School of Business. She had a clear path. My path was covered in muck, and there I was without a shovel.

The cowbell hanging at the top of the door clanked as I walked in. Navy locked eyes with me, wiped her hands on her apron, and rushed over. She wrapped me in a Navy-scented hug. "Amanda, honey, how are you?"

"Okay."

"Graham told me what happened with the false alarm. I'm so, so sorry."

"Thanks." There was really nothing else to add.

"Sit, sit. Would you like a cold brew? What about an espresso? A pastry?"

I sat at a table in the corner. "An espresso would be great."

She gave a reassuring squeeze of my shoulder before disappearing behind the counter.

Graham left the counter, came to my side, leaned over, and kissed me. The chair scraped across the floor as he pulled it close, set a recyclable coffee cup on the table, and took my hand. "Man, last night was..."

"Yeah, I know. It was." I rested my head on his shoulder.

"I know it's lame, but I wish there was something I could do to help."

He'd just made it easier. "Actually, there is." I lifted my head to look at him.

He cocked a single bushy blond eyebrow. "Name it."

"I need you to back my decision."

"What decision?"

I looked over at Navy, still busy behind the counter, and lowered my voice. "To be a living organ donor for my dad."

"A what?" He let go of my hand.

"Shhh." I gestured for him to lower his voice. "A living donor. I can donate a part of my healthy liver to my dad, and it will actually grow, and if everything goes well, he would be fine. We'd both be fine."

He frowned and slumped back in his chair. "Don't you have to be an exact match or something?"

I excitedly reached into my purse, pulled out a pamphlet I had gotten at the office, and opened it on the table. "It's not like with a heart transplant or a kidney transplant. It says here the main thing is that our blood types match. And there's a better chance of a successful transplant if it comes from a living donor. I met with the organ-transplant coordinator, and she told me everything. I have to make a bunch of appointments to be tested and evaluated, but this could be it! If all the tests come out okay, I can be the one." Excitement built up in my throat, my lungs, my heart. "Then if I get the green light from the Living Donor Committee, they would schedule surgery." Talking about it with Graham made it real. I could be the one to save Daddy's life.

Graham took the brochure from the table and flipped through the pages. "Isn't it dangerous? For you, I mean." He stared at it. "It says it's... it's, like, a six-hour operation and can take three months for the donor to recover."

I snatched the brochure from his hands. "What would you do if it was your dad? Just hang back and watch him die if you thought you could do something?" My stomach wrenched. The one person I thought would back me up was about to let me down.

He looked over at his dad, who was smiling, schmoozing with customers. "Yeah, I would do it. One hundred percent." He raised his head and looked me in the eye. "You're right. I'm just freaking out over you going through all that."

He took a sip of his coffee and pushed it aside just as Navy brought me my espresso. "Can I get you anything else, sweetheart?"

"No, I'm good. But thank you."

"If it's okay, I thought I'd drop by the hospital today. It's a small thing, but..."

I hoped Mom would be nice to her—nicer than she'd been to Graham. "That's so thoughtful. She should be there soon."

"I'll leave in just a minute. I won't stay long."

As she walked away, Graham leaned in and whispered, "What does your mom say?"

He'd asked the question I was afraid to ask myself. "I haven't told her yet. But I'm eighteen. I don't need her permission."

"Okay..." He hesitated. "But... but, I mean, it's not like you can go through this in secret."

"Obviously. But I want to at least wait until I find out if it's a definite go. She's stressed out to the max. I don't want to open a conversation with 'Oh, by the way, I'm going to have a six-hour operation and give Daddy part of my liver.' Not until it's, you know, a sure thing."

He reached for my hand again.

My phone dinged with a message from Mom: *Going to the hospital. Taking Daddy's car.*

She hated driving Daddy's standard-shift Passat. *Strange. And she didn't even ask where I was.* "I gotta go," I said to Graham. "We'll talk later."

"Okay, but don't forget, Rocket and me are going to that skate competition at House Park tonight—his last one before he and Karin leave. I may be unreachable for a while, but I'll check in after. Okay?"

He leaned in and kissed me softly. "I love you," he whispered. "No matter what."

"No matter what," I echoed back.

My phone rang as I was walking to the car. I didn't recognize the number. "How's your dad?" a voice said.

"Karin?"

"I can't talk long."

"Your parents gave you your phone back?"

"No, it's a burner phone. Rocket got it for me. This is my number, at least for now. So, how's your dad?"

"Not good. I guess Hadley and Rocket filled you in. We're just in waiting mode right now." She had enough shit going on. I didn't want to weigh her down with my plans. So I sat in the car, listening to Karin spill about everything. I was relieved to focus on someone else's problems for a change.

She said she'd been taking a few of her things from home, one item at a time, leaving them at Hadley's, and packing them in a suitcase Hadley had given her. She had a cover story ready to go. Her parents would drop her off at her Tuesday night Bible study group, like always, but instead of attending, she would meet Hadley in the back of the building. And then poof—she would disappear. Her parents were going to freak. And if they caught her, they would come down hard. Like, brutally hard. Like, notify-Child-Protective-Services hard. But she would be eighteen in four short months, and then they wouldn't have a say, at least not legally. The risk of those four months before her birthday freaked me out more than the escape itself.

"Are you sure you want to do this, Karin? Why not wait for your birthday?"

"I overheard my parents, and they're gearing up to ship me off to that religious school I told you about, to finish my senior year. I told you, they've wanted to send me there forever, but couldn't afford it. I have no idea where the money is coming from now. I'd be a prisoner with no chance of parole. And Rocket is an indentured servant. We—Rocket and I—know what we're doing, and we understand the risks. But neither of us can continue living like this. Our parents have put us both in untenable situations. We plan to get jobs, attend community college. We have a plan. And... I love him. This is it for me. For us."

That was not the life I'd imagined for scary-smart Karin, but I guessed even she had a limit to what she could endure. Her rogue plan was better than a future in which being good, being selfless offered her nothing but pain and sadness from the two people who should have loved her the most.

As for me, I was in some kind of limbo—not Karin's hell but a long way from heaven. And then there was the New York University application I'd mailed on the sly to bypass Mom's constant checking in—"Have you heard? Have you heard? Have you heard?" But if I got in, I wasn't sure how I could seriously think about leaving Daddy lying in a hospital bed with me not knowing anything.

And if I got to be his donor, I might not even be in good enough shape to take off for New York. And what about Graham? How could I leave him? All I could do was wait for the future to play out and hope it would all make sense in the end.

My emotions were duking it out *Fight Club* style, and it was wearing me down. The coffee soured in my stomach. As I put what was left of it in the cup holder, I was seized with cramps. I gasped and clenched my stomach, certain I was going to faint right there in the parking lot. Beads of sweat formed on my upper lip, and I wiped them away with the sleeve of my T-shirt. I pulled down the visor to look at myself in the mirror. My lips were whiter than my skin. *Breathe in, breathe out. Breathe in, breathe out.* I laid my head on the steering wheel, trying to talk myself out of fainting, while I waited for the sickening cramps to pass. As the waves of pain gradually receded, I took a deep breath and exhaled as I felt the blood returning to my lips, and it was as if it hadn't happened at all.

Chapter 49
Deb

I was stuck in an exhausting time loop with no jumping-off point—entering the hospital, greeting Bethany or receiving disgruntled looks from Nurse Ratched, steeling myself to enter Richard's room, and listening to the beeping machines that reassured me that he'd made it through another minute, and another, and another. I wasn't even sure what day it was. Every day simply folded into the next and the one after that and the one after that.

When I entered the room this time, Merritt was curled in the chair by Richard's bed. She was wrapped in a patchwork quilt. I recognized it from our parents' bed. She looked up and snapped her book shut. She'd been reading aloud to a sleeping Richard from *The Boys of Summer* by Roger Kahn. It was a favorite of his, all about the triumphant Brooklyn Dodgers in the 1950s. Merritt wasn't a sports fan, which made her gesture that much sweeter.

"Hey, feeling better?" she asked. "You look more rested."

Merritt looked good, as always. Spending the night in that godawful Naugahyde chair hadn't wreaked havoc with her skin tone like it did mine. Every hair was miraculously in place. But I had to cut myself some slack. This was her first all-nighter.

"I'm okay." I glanced at Richard's sleeping form. "How is he?"

"No change. Armstrong stuck his big, fat head in. Said for you to call. Said you have his number."

"Shit! I missed him."

"Not by much. He left like five minutes ago."

I checked my phone. Armstrong had called while I was on my way to the hospital. I wouldn't have missed him if I hadn't spent that time chatting it up about the "good old days" with my high-school boyfriend. "Did it sound urgent?"

"Hard to know. He wouldn't tell me anything. He just said for you to call." Merritt folded the blanket and gathered her things. "Let me know what he says, okay?" She kissed my forehead, just like I always kissed Amanda when I wanted to assure her everything was going to be okay. She was about to leave when she turned back to me. "So, how's Tim?"

Merritt had a knack for lightening up heavy conversations without being dismissive.

"It was thoughtful of him to bring Amanda's schoolwork."

"Thoughtful Tim." She sounded wistful. "I guess he really hasn't changed. One of the good ones." She looked at me, eyebrows arched. I was certain she was about to dig deeper, but she asked, "Did you ever find Amanda?"

"I texted her, but I assume she's with Graham. I'll try her again in a minute. First, I want to call Armstrong."

"Want me to wait?"

"No, that's okay. Your shift is done."

"Okay, hon. I'm gonna take off, but you let me know the minute there's any news, even if it's the middle of the night. Promise?"

"Promise," I said.

Before the door had even closed, I dialed Armstrong's number, but it went to voicemail. Once again, I was left alone with Richard, waiting. Always waiting. No one ever told me that keeping vigil would be the hardest part. But I didn't have to wait long before there was a knock on the door and a soft voice I didn't recognize said, "Deborah?"

I got up from the chair, set my book down, and pulled open the door. "Yes?"

"Deborah, I'm Navy Scott, Graham's mother?"

If I was going to meet the mother of Amanda's boyfriend, this wasn't the scenario I'd envisioned. "So nice to meet you, but, um, are you looking for Graham? Neither he or Amanda are here right now."

She struck me as a gently aging earth mother extracted from old photos of Woodstock, complete with a braided basket brimming with an assortment of muffins and scones. From what I remembered of her husband that night at the police station—a night I would rather have forgotten—they were perfectly matched bookends.

"Actually, I came to see you. I know there isn't a good time, but Amanda said you would likely be here, and I just wanted to drop these off and ask if there was anything I could possibly do to help."

She held out a basket of still-warm goodies with a thermos of coffee nestled inside. I had no choice but to accept. "That's so thoughtful. They look delicious." I paused, unsure where our stilted exchange was supposed to go from there. "I'd ask you in, but Richard—that's my husband—is sleeping."

"Of course." She looked down at her empty hands. "Graham told me what happened with the donor. I'm so sorry, truly."

"Thank you. We're hoping another organ will come available soon."

She reached for my free hand and, with a tilt of her head, said, "I can only imagine how difficult the wait must be." She'd read my mind, and her words, infused with such sincerity and genuine caring, brought unwelcome tears to my eyes. "Is it okay if I give you a hug?"

I was taken aback, but considering my initial impression of her, I would have been more surprised if she hadn't offered. She pulled me in, and I awkwardly held the basket off to the side and gave her a one-handed hug. The subtle scent of incense permeated the air around her.

She said softly, "Amanda is a lovely girl. I know you must be proud. We've so enjoyed getting to know her these last few months."

Her words triggered a burst of pride, and I decided right then and there that I liked this woman, and maybe, just maybe, I should ease up and give her son the benefit of the doubt. I thanked her again, more genuinely this time, and we said our polite goodbyes. I stared at the basket. My mouth watered. I couldn't remember when I'd last eaten. I grabbed the coffee, took a sip, and was about to bite into a luscious-looking cranberry scone when there was a knock on the door, and Armstrong burst into the room. I tossed the scone back into the basket as if I had been caught cheating on a diet.

"Dr. Armstrong, I, uh, I tried to call, but—"

"Ms. Earle." His voice was tentative, less sure than it had been. I tensed. The beeping of Richard's monitors amplified.

"Yes?"

"Your husband has taken a sudden turn for the worse, and—" His delivery was interrupted when Bethany and a scrub-clad man I hadn't seen before appeared out of nowhere. "We need to move him to the ICU."

"Now?" I jerked my head in Richard's direction. He was sleeping peacefully. But the scrub-clad duo was already prepping Richard for the move, unplugging monitors, sliding him over to a gurney, and laying his half-full Foley bag next to him. My heart thundered in my chest.

"A bed has just freed up, so we're moving him up now."

"But what happened?"

"His liver enzymes have spiked, and his vitals are declining."

"Is... is he dying?" I whimpered, the words leaden on my tongue.

He took a heavy breath. "As I said, I believe in being frank, Ms. Earle."

As if he'd ever been anything else. I braced myself.

"He needs a donor within the next few days."

My mind leapt from the hospital room and this life-altering conversation to our sunlit kitchen, Richard sipping his coffee to make sure it was sweet enough, me dutifully lining up his supplements, and Richard washing them down one by one... while I simply stood by and watched.

Chapter 50
Amanda

I groaned as I drove home, the cramps coming in waves, intensifying. My period. Or stress. Whatever it was drained me, and as soon as I walked in the door, I beelined to my bed, curled my knees to my chest, and collapsed into a dreamless sleep within seconds.

I wasn't sure how much time had passed when a stabbing pain yanked me from sleep. That and the disgusting feeling of damp sheets. Definitely my period. It was dark outside. I reached for the lamp on my nightstand, the movement magnifying the gross stickiness between my legs and on the sheets. *Disgusting.* It was going to be a bitch to clean, but it wasn't the first time I'd woken up to a surprise period. I sat up and threw back the covers, horrified. It looked like the aftermath of a crime scene. Red streaks smeared my thighs. The sheets were glistening, soaked through.

"Mom!" I yelled. No answer. "Mom, something's wrong!"

Shit. She was at the hospital with Daddy. With trembling hands, I picked up my phone. Before I could dial, another cramp seized me, the worst one yet. I panicked. I was alone. Hyperventilating. I was going to die right there, in my bed, lying in a pool of my own blood.

I looked at my phone. My brain went blank. *My password. What's my fucking password? Fuck! Focus, Amanda. Focus!*

When I finally pulled the password from the back of my brain, I scrolled down to *Mom* and hit Call. It rang. And rang. And rang. *Crap!* With each unanswered ring, my panic ballooned. *Who else can*

I call? Graham? Hadley? Will I wake them? On the fifth ring, she answered, her voice echoing.

"Mom! You have to come home. Right now! Something's really wrong. I'm bleeding like crazy!"

"What?" She sounded groggy.

I was crying hysterically, talking in between convulsive sobs. "I'm bleeding all over the bed! It's not my period. Mom, you have to come home!"

"Are you still in the bed?"

I nodded.

"Amanda?"

"Yeah, yeah, I'm still in the bed."

"Stay right there. I'll call 911. Don't move. I'm leaving now." She hung up.

I couldn't just lie there in my own bloody mess. I sat up and swung my legs over the edge of the bed, but as I pushed myself upright, a wave of nausea grabbed me and wouldn't let go. *Am I going to have to clean up puke along with the blood?* I tried to think of something else, but the pain hit with all the intensity of a lightning strike, and I screamed out. But there was no one to hear. More blood. And tears. And terror. I'd never been this scared.

My teeth chattered. I watched the blood drip, drip, drip onto the beige carpet just before everything went black.

Chapter 51
Deb

My head snapped forward as I screeched into the driveway and braked hard, instinctively grabbing my purse before it slid onto the floor. I expected frantic activity—the flashing lights of an ambulance, dogs barking, neighbors standing curiously in open doorways. But the street was quiet, dark. *Did they already take her to the hospital? Which one?*

I jumped out of the car, fumbling with my keys to the front door. They slipped from my fingers, hitting the porch with a resounding clank. "Fuck!" I bent over, picked them up, and took a deep breath to steady myself. This time, the key slid into place, and I swung the door open, slamming it against the wall, deepening the puncture left by Richard a lifetime ago.

"Amanda!" I called as I hurled myself up the stairs. The sound of a siren rushed through the open door. "Amanda!" When I reached her doorway, I stood staring through the beaded curtain into the abyss of her room. Her bed was no longer girlish in pink and white but dark, awash in red. Blood. Everywhere. And my baby girl lying in it. I choked out her name. "Amanda! Amanda!"

The beads frantically swung back and forth like a Newton's cradle as I rushed to her bedside. I grabbed her by the shoulders and shook. Her eyes were closed, her head rolled to the side, listless.

"Mandy, wake up! No, no, no, no!" The flickering red lights of the ambulance pierced the curtains, and I ran to the window, opened it, leaned out, and shouted, "Hurry! Hurry! Upstairs!"

I sank to my knees at the side of the bed, counted her shallow breaths, and held her hand as I brushed strands of hair away from her face covered in a sheen of sweat. She was cold to the touch. I breathed deeply and steadied my voice, hoping she could hear me. I needed her to know I was beside her and for her to believe that I was stronger than I actually was.

"Amanda, sweetie, the ambulance is here. You're going to be fine. Everything's going to be okay."

I heard heavy footsteps and the creak of the stairs. "What the fuck took you so long?"

One of the EMTs calmly began his assessment of Amanda's condition—heart rate, blood pressure, pupil dilation. He pulled the stethoscope from around his neck and lifted her bloody shirt to listen to her chest and her abdomen for bowel sounds.

The other EMT turned to me. "Any existing conditions?"

"No, no. She's always been healthy."

"How far along is she?"

"Wha—what?"

"The pregnancy. When is her due date?"

My confusion, fertilized by dread, sprouted faster than I could weed it out. "She's not pregnant!"

They looked at each other. "Yes, ma'am, she is. There's a heartbeat."

The feeling was akin to shoving my finger in an electrical outlet. My ugly sobs startled me. One of the EMTs took my arm and lowered me into the chair by Amanda's bed.

"We're taking her to St. Joseph's. We need to leave now. Do you want to come or follow?"

The same hospital as Richard. "What? Of course I'm coming!"

I stood and looked down at my blood-soaked knees. Amanda's blood. I had to remind myself to breathe. I absentmindedly grabbed her princess pillow—it would offer her some measure of familiar comfort—and stumbled down the stairs behind them. Amanda was strapped to the gurney. Her head lolled back as they made their way down the stairs, their expressions urgent but focused. Her arm slipped out and hung limp. I heard myself gasp. My mother used to tell me that God never handed you more than you could handle. But that was before I got pregnant.

My thoughts were everywhere they shouldn't be and nowhere I wanted them to be. I climbed into the back of the ambulance, taking up as little space as possible, and touched Amanda's shoulder with the tips of my fingers to maintain physical contact. I called, "Amanda, Amanda, can you hear me?"

But she didn't respond. Not even the jarring sound of the siren could wake her. My heart jackhammered in my chest. My fingers turned icy cold, my breathing shallow. A stream of blood pooled on the floor of the ambulance. I squeezed my eyes shut to insulate myself in the comfort of darkness.

Unable to reject the piercing reality of the moment, I opened my eyes to the sound of one of the EMTs speaking urgently over the radio. "Pregnant female..." He turned to me. "Age?"

"Eighteen."

"Pregnant female, eighteen years, unknown gestational stage, hemorrhaging, fetal heartbeat steady, no preexisting conditions, BP eighty over sixty, pulse one twenty, tachypnea, respiration twenty-five." The words "pregnant female" reverberated. I glanced at the name tag pinned to his crisp white shirt splattered with Amanda's blood. Aiden Strauss. The bald one with the five-o'clock shadow on his head inserted a needle into Amanda's arm for an IV. I felt it. With a steady hand, he connected a bag and thumped the line to make sure the clear liquid was flowing. He seemed to be on autopilot, not hesitating, working from muscle memory.

My body quivered as I sucked in air. My teeth chattered uncontrollably, and a black mist seeped into my brain. I fought it.

Aiden's voice cut through the black mist and jerked me back to reality. "This should help," he said, his expression flat, serious.

I nodded and thought, *He's trying to assure himself as much as to assure me that Amanda is going to be okay*. But nothing was going to ease my panic.

He checked her blood pressure again and announced over the radio, "Seventy over fifty."

I wanted to tell him that couldn't be right, it was too low, but my tongue was stuck to the roof of my mouth, and I couldn't generate enough saliva to swallow. The bald one stood. Too tall for this claustrophobic box careening down the street, he lurched forward as the ambulance made a sharp left turn. The shelf contents shifted and slid together. I grabbed the seatbelt hanging behind me.

"Ma'am, buckle your seatbelt," he instructed, still stooped, his voice infused with concern and a growing impatience. He righted himself, pulled out a zippered bag, and quickly opened it. I expected him to retrieve an ampule of something—a needle, a miracle potion, anything to stop the bleeding—but he held clean gauze sponges in his latex-gloved hands that turned crimson as they soaked up the blood that was oozing out from Amanda, dripping onto the floor. She was so pale.

The air was filled with the scent of alcohol and terror. I wanted to barter with God on the off chance he might be listening, but I had nothing to promise in return.

"Tell me what you're doing." I'd found my voice. The two EMTs exchanged a look that made my throat constrict, and my silent tears turned into gasping sobs. "Please."

Aiden opened the Plexiglas partition and shouted to the driver, "ETA?"

"Five or less," she said, her voice hard and clear. I hadn't even thought of the person behind the wheel. Until we pulled up to the hospital, Amanda's fate was in her hands.

Aiden looked at the blood pressure gauge. "Sixty-five over forty-five." He took one look at me and placed his hand on mine, leaving behind a trace of blood. "We'll be there soon. She'll be well taken care of."

The wail of the siren wound down, and the doors of the ambulance swung open, frigid air surrounding me. I was blinded by the canopy lights of the ER. As the EMTs lowered the gurney onto the concrete in synchronized rhythm, the wheels frantically spun before they aligned, and the glass doors to the hospital whooshed open. The EMTs bolted through the ER entrance with the gurney, and I told myself to be strong, that I *had* to be strong, but I was drowning in a tsunami of fear. Lightning had struck my family twice. Dread and hope competed for space in my heart as I tried to breathe a normal rhythm.

I couldn't stop the self-recriminations, the nagging guilt. *How did I miss the signs? How could I not have known?*

Chapter 52
Amanda

Bodies of blue and green hovered. Coughing, bells dinging, machines beeping, heavy footsteps, a phone ringing, and faraway voices slipped into the background when I heard Mom's voice in a high-pitched panic. "Oh, sweetie, you're awake." I turned to look at her. She was blurry around the edges. I tried to sit up but was strapped in, the sting of an IV in my arm.

One of the hovering bodies leaned in, speaking in a soothing tone. "You're at St. Joseph's Medical Center. I'm Dr. Stewart. We're going to take good care of you. Can you tell me your name?"

"Amanda."

"When's your birthday?"

"What?"

"Amanda, I know it seems strange, but I need to ask."

"October thirty-first."

He looked at Mom, who confirmed my answer with a quick nod.

"It's going to be okay." It was Mom. "You're going to be okay." She took a breath. "Oh, Amanda, I wish you had told me."

"What? I called you!"

"No." She looked off into space before looking back at me. "Why didn't you tell me you were pregnant?"

"Jesus, Mom, I'm not pregnant."

Before I could counter her bizarre accusation, another pain grabbed me and wouldn't let go. Shocked by the piercing scream that echoed off the walls—a scream that was coming from me—I had to get away from the pain. I tried to sit up again, but hands on my shoulders gently pushed me back down.

Sobbing, I looked at Mom. "It hurts so bad!"

The nurse cut through my blood-soaked shirt with shears in one swift motion and squirted gel on my stomach. She quickly ran the sonogram wand across my abdomen and turned the screen toward the doctor.

"What? What is it?" I demanded.

He frowned and stared at the screen for a few wordless seconds and nodded to the nurse. A woman stood next to me and gently put her gloved hand on my arm. "Amanda, we're about to take you into labor and delivery."

I slapped my free hand to my stomach. "But I'm not... I'm not pregnant."

"Yes, dear, you are. Based on the sonogram, you're about five or six months."

"Fuck no! That's impossible."

"I just don't understand." Mom was shaking her head. She had my hand sandwiched in between her sweaty palms. "How is that even possible? She doesn't look... when I was pregnant..."

"I know, it's shocking, but it happens—more than you'd think," one of the scrub-clad bodies said, not pausing from whatever she was doing and not looking at me or Mom. Her back was turned. "We've had women come in with full-term pregnancies who didn't know they were pregnant."

"But... but... it makes no sense."

Another pain hit me. My sobs were replaced with wails of pain. I jerked my hand from Mom's grasp and held my stomach. "I think I'm dying!"

My IV bag moved. "We're giving her something to calm her." He wasn't talking to me. "The sonogram shows the placenta has separated from the uterus. That's what's causing the bleeding. It—"

He was interrupted by a disembodied voice. "Dr. Stewart, the surgical suite is ready."

"Surgery? For what?" It was Mom.

"C-section. It's okay, Mom. We'll take good care of her."

She stood, panicked. Everyone around me began moving urgently, hustling. And then, still flat on my back, still strapped in, I was floating down the hall under dizzying ceiling lights. It was all happening so fast. I couldn't process the news that I was having surgery. *And a baby?*

"Mom!"

She broke into a jog to keep up with the fast-moving gurney. I was flanked on both sides by blue and green. The colors parted to let Mom in. She took my hand. "Sweetie, I'm here. I'm right here."

"Call Graham!"

"It's okay, Mandy, I'll take care of everything."

"Promise me you'll call Graham."

"I promise."

"And don't tell Daddy."

"I'll be right here when you come out. Everything's going to be okay. I promise. I love you so, so much." She kissed my forehead, her red hair a blur. I didn't want her to let go, but her hand slipped from mine as the gurney picked up speed.

Another pain punched me, knocking the air out of my lungs. I tilted my head back in vain to see her and screamed, "Mommy, help me!" As her sobbing faded into the background, they hurried me through the double doors, the Arctic chill of the room intensifying the pain.

A woman wearing a surgical mask patted me on the arm. “It’s okay, sweetheart. I’m going to give you something now to make the pain go away. When you wake up, it’ll all be over.”

As the cold hit my vein, I mumbled, “Thank you,” and drifted off into the sweetest sleep.

Chapter 53
Deb

I waited. And cried. And waited. And paced. And waited. I drank the hospital coffee that tasted like toxic sludge and waited some more along with at least a dozen other people, who radiated misery yet were somehow just as full of tenacious hope as I was. At regular intervals, someone in scrubs would enter the waiting room, their blue shoe covers shuffling across the tile floor. There would be a collective intake of breath as we all straightened expectantly, worried meerkats popping up to see if it was safe. One lucky family would be called, pulled aside, there would be a few whispered words, and with hands on hearts, their faces would lift, and the tension would melt away. And each time, the knot in my chest tightened another notch.

I was just as worried about Richard. He was in the ICU. I couldn't even tell him what was happening to our daughter. *And our grandchild?* The thought took my breath away. Would I be helping to raise Amanda's child alone while she went to college? Would she and Graham be stupid enough to say they wanted to marry? Amanda was still a child herself.

Graham, that little shit! My instincts had been right all along. He was bad news. Amanda's future would be forever altered because of him. But I'd promised her I would call, so I did. It went to voicemail. I tried again. I wanted to wring his neck, rip those stupid earrings out of his head, make him bleed, make him suffer the way Amanda was suffering, the way I was suffering. Still holding the phone, my arms went limp, and I collapsed in the chair. I began to question myself. She was pregnant long before Richard was admitted to the hospital. Had my preoccupation with wanting another child—my self-absorption—left nothing for Amanda?

Dr. Stewart emerged. His eyes darted around the waiting room. "Ms. Earle?"

I popped up, squeezing Amanda's princess pillow close to my chest, my heart pounding. The worst was over. Richard would get a transplant, he would get healthy again, and we would figure it all out.

Together.

Chapter 54
Deb
Three Years Later

It's misting rain, unseasonably cold for October in Austin, and I'm without an umbrella. I pull my coat tighter as I hike up the hill and down the third row, avoiding the muddy puddles as best I can, and stop at the same grassy spot I've visited more times than I could possibly count over the last three years.

The first time I stood here was after everyone had expressed condolences and left behind casseroles that would never be eaten, flower arrangements that would wilt and brown, sympathy cards that would have gone unanswered were it not for Merritt. After I'd closed the door behind the last well-meaning straggler, I rushed back, expecting to feel a presence. But when I said, "I miss you so, so much," my voice drifted off without resonance, and the realization slapped me that I was simply talking to a block of granite stuck in the freshly turned dirt.

Mandy was gone, and she was never coming back.

From the moment Amanda was born, I promised myself I would never emotionally disappear the way my mother had. It never occurred to me that Amanda might be the one to disappear. Still, today of all days, I have to tell her, "Happy birthday, baby girl." My throat constricts as I lean over to rest sunflowers on her headstone engraved with the words, *To live in the hearts of those you leave behind is not to die.*

Richard chose those words, but they ring hollow to me now. My heart separated three years ago. I have gingerly stitched it back together, but thick scars remain that I obsessively run my fingers over, bringing back her last words to me, "Mommy, help me!" on continuous replay in my mind. It's like the opposite of amnesia.

When the surgeon finally appeared in the waiting room that night, but before he said a word, Schrodinger's cat stupidly popped into my head. Amanda was either okay or she wasn't—both possibilities existed. I wouldn't know how she was doing until he opened his mouth.

And then he did.

The wall kept me from crashing to the floor. I stared at him, my vision constricting to a narrow tunnel. The tightness in my chest threatened to suffocate me. He offered a hand to steady me, and I furiously swatted him away as his words ricocheted in my brain, refusing to settle in any kind of logical order.

"We did everything we could."

For the first time in my life, I understood with a piercing clarity that each one of us is just one declarative sentence away from the end of everything.

When I'd watched her being wheeled away, I naively felt relief. She was in good hands. The thought never entered my mind that that was the last time I would see her alive—that my baby girl would be gone forever.

I don't remember making my way to the hospital's meditation room. I don't remember collapsing onto the floor, reciting Hail Marys imprinted in my brain from childhood. I reluctantly remember someone else's muffled cries echoing in the silence. The organ-transplant coordinator walked in, sat on the floor next to me, and held my hand as I convulsed in sobs. She calmly informed me that Amanda was a match and could be Richard's donor. Richard was unconscious. The life-or-death decision for him was mine to make.

Amanda should be turning twenty-one today. Instead, she'll be forever eighteen. Forever on the cusp of adulthood. Forever my baby girl. It feels like five lifetimes ago that Merritt asked me if I would choose to have a child if I knew they were going to die young, like Ray. I thought I knew the answer to her question then. Now, I couldn't possibly wish Amanda had never been born—not to nurse her, see her crawl, watch her take her first steps, hear her say her first words, teach her to read, see her grow, and love her with a ferocity I never knew possible.

But I wouldn't have chosen this—to have eighteen short years and be forced to go to bed each night praying she'll visit me in my dreams. Her death delivered a stunning, paralyzing pain that, for a time, left me rambling, incoherent, and dumb with disbelief. Grief is a flesh-eating monster—savage, frightening, unrelenting, and incapacitating. And there is no cure, only palliative care. If I've learned anything, it's that death is relentless.

When I heard that Karin and Rocket had eloped, my only thought was that I would have given anything to be wringing my hands with worry but knowing Amanda was out there—somewhere. And when the acceptance letter from NYU arrived just a few weeks after we buried her, I imploded with sorrow and grief. Merritt rushed over and talked me down from the ledge, where the view seemed so much clearer than looking ahead to the next day and the next and the one after that—without Amanda. And we cried together.

My thoughts are interrupted by the sound of footsteps. "You want me to get the umbrella from the car?"

"No, I think I'm ready to leave."

Graham shifts Ruby to his other hip, and she leans on his shoulder. "Daddy, I cold."

"It's okay, baby girl." He plants a kiss on her forehead, she lays her head on his shoulder, and her blond curls blend with his. "We're leaving soon."

After Amanda died, I wanted him dead. I screamed, "You'll get married, have other children!" I stopped to catch my jagged breath, insane with fresh grief. "But I can never replace my Mandy!"

If I'd had a sharp object in my hand, he wouldn't be standing here with me now, holding Ruby. Forgiveness was not even close to being an option.

But miracles do happen, and seeing him here beside me, holding Ruby, it's hard to resurrect my anger. With time, the acid in my throat receded, the ugly knot in my heart unfolded, and I could see how desperately he wanted to be a part of Ruby's life, how much he loved his baby girl. And how much he'd loved Amanda. And how Amanda had loved him in a frantic, irrational, cross-your-heart-and-hope-to-die kind of way. And they'd made a baby. As odd as it might seem, we have shared custody, Graham and I. Navy and Cade help out so he can continue his studies—prelaw, like his dad.

Richard is doing well physically—the liver transplant was a success—but his emotional recovery is a work in progress. There came a point when my very presence was excruciating for him—I was a constant reminder that while I had carried Amanda in life, he was left to carry her in death. He had lost control of everything.

So he left. His last words hollowed me. "I still love you, Deb, but I have to get some peace of mind. And I just can't. Not here. Not with you." He lowered his head, and his voice cracked. "Not with Ruby."

I thought Richard and I were unbreakable. I was wrong.

I miss him, miss what we had. But I buried that version of myself in the cold, dark earth beside Amanda.

Tim's quiet presence during the unbearable worst of it helped me climb over my impenetrable wall of darkness, and over time, my gratitude morphed into love—a very different love from what we had when we were teenagers. It's deeper, stronger. And it's a very different love from what I had with Richard before death and disease cracked our world wide open.

I've come to accept that I'll never have the untainted happiness I had with my precious family for what I now realize was an incredibly brief period of time. There's a part of me that will be forever raw, forever tender to the touch. I've heard it said that pain is the price you pay for love. Well, I've paid in spades. But even with everything that's happened, everything I've lost, all the grief and sorrow I carry, I can't deny that I'm incredibly lucky.

I have Ruby.

She reaches for me, opening and closing her little fists. Graham hands her to me. "Look, Grammy, look!" Ruby bucks and points her stubby finger toward the sky at two orange-breasted robins in flight. One separates and soars above us, only to softly land atop Amanda's headstone. "A robber!"

Her words knock the wind out of me. I almost choke on my sudden sob but clear my throat as I pull myself together and kiss her soft cheek. "Yes, sweetie girl, it's a robber."

Acknowledgments

I've said it before, but it's worth repeating—it takes a village to create a book. Writing may seem like a solitary venture, but it actually takes a team for a story to make it out into the world. First and foremost, I have to thank my dear friend and long-time critique partner, Wila Phillips. This story wouldn't exist without her. She reviewed every word, every page, every chapter many times over during the drafting and rewriting. Her input was invaluable, and I can't thank her enough. An additional thank-you to Kristyne Bollier, who made the time when she had none to spare to read my draft pages. And to my decades-long friend and coconspirator, Dana Walker, who was with me when "I got the call" and was every bit as over-the-top excited as I was. I would be remiss without expressing gratitude to the members of the Women's Fiction Writers Association and to the TGIF Writers Zoom gang, whose sharing, support, and camaraderie keep me going. A special thank-you to Dr. Joseph S. Gelati from the Houston-based Liver Specialists of Texas for his time and medical expertise. I just hope I got it right. Thank you to Zachariah Claypole White for his input on an almost-final draft. I would also like to thank Angie Gallion at Red Adept Publishing for her wonderfully thoughtful and thorough insight into my story. You made it better. A shout-out to Sarah Carleton at Red Adept, who forced me to really think about each comma, each word, each sentence—whether I wanted to or not. I also want to express my appreciation to Streetlight Graphics and Erica Lucke Dean at Red Adept for my absolutely gorgeous cover. It far exceeded my expectations.

And last, but certainly not least, I would like to thank Red Adept publisher, Lynn McNamee, for enthusiastically embracing my story and carefully tending it all the way to publication and beyond.

About the Author

Densie (not Denise) Webb has spent a long career as a freelance nonfiction writer and editor, specializing in health and nutrition, and has published several books on the topic. She grew up in Louisiana, spent 13 years in New York City, and settled in Austin, TX, where it's summer nine months out of the year.

Densie is an avid walker (not of the dead variety, though she adores zombies, vampires, and apocalyptic stories). She drinks too much coffee and has a small "devil dog" that keeps her on her toes. She has arrested development in musical tastes, and her two grown children provide her with musical recommendations on a regular basis.

Read more at https://wordpress.com/view/densiewebb.com.

About the Publisher

Dear Reader,

We hope you enjoyed this book. Please consider leaving a review on your favorite book site.

Visit https://RedAdeptPublishing.com to see our entire catalogue.

Don't forget to subscribe to our monthly newsletter to be notified of future releases and special sales.

Made in United States
North Haven, CT
07 July 2022

21050312R00176